THE LOST DIARY OF CÉCILE DUBONNET

FORGETTING THE YESTERDAYS OF WORLD WAR II

A.P. HARPER

A.P. HARPER

Contents

To everyone who needs to be forgiven

PREFACE

Charon is the ferryman in Greek mythology who, for a fee, carries newly deceased souls across the river Styx that divides the world of the living from the world of the dead. One must wander the shores as a wraith for eternity if one cannot pay the fee, which for some is not the obol placed on the dead's eyes but absolution from their sins.

CHAPTER 1

DISCOVERY

Tuesday, 19 October 1999

They say that your life flashes before your eyes the moment you die. Ironically, the same cannot be said for someone who has been waning for the past fifty-four years. The white-walled room did its best to confine her in its dull environment. The bed in the middle of the small room was neatly made with crisp white sheets carefully tucked in.

The room lacked shelves with pictures of family members or fresh flowers on the nightstand. To the room's inhabitant, there seemed to be no present and no future—just the lapsing pain of the past.

There was no use in keeping the door to the room locked from the outside anymore. The patient, Cécile, has not responded to anyone who was not Élizabeth, as she spent her days wheelchair-bound in the corner of her assigned room.

The old, frail woman stared out the window, her faded blue eyes sunken in her wrinkle-covered face. A haunted hope surrounding her made the staff highly uncomfortable at their first interaction. The nurses of *Centre Hospitalier Sainte-Anne* were not afraid of residents who threw tantrums. They loved the challenge of working in the psychiatric ward and always prepared for the worst whenever they stepped into a room. They paid the most attention to schizophrenic and psychotic patients. There was slight, unnoticeable angst around them, mainly because they were utterly unstable, even when their medication worked as it was supposed to. Each day, they worked wholly prepared to encounter wild commotions, but patients who came in and out of stupor needed vigilance. They snapped when a strong current of unpredictability came and swept them out to the sea of the unknown.

"*Mademoiselle* Cécile, please calm down!" The nurse said, calmy in a soft voice as she wrapped her strong arms around the fragile body and helped her back into the wheelchair. Cécile usually did not resist the nurses. Not anymore. She was too tired and weak to put up any fight. She obeyed quietly most of the time. However, something had triggered Cécile as she slowly transformed from a catatonic patient into a frantic madwoman.

"Please, no!" She begged out of nowhere as the nurse lightly touched her wiry, fading gray hair.

Cécile moved her arms back and forth before burying her tired face into her hands. She saw and heard something nobody else could either see or hear.

"I will not do it. I cannot, oh dear God, make it stop! Stop it!" Cécile wailed, clutching her hair.

She continued mumbling tearfully, but she did not particularly speak to the nurse or anyone in the room. She begged for someone else in the distance, far away, perhaps someone in her memory. No one knew. The nurse did not mind her outburst as it was rare and mild compared to the other patients. Cécile continued sobbing and wailing as if her entire being were on fire. The nurse felt bad for the old woman who had spent most of her life in this institute in Paris, but she did not know her story and wondered what type of life she had led before she wound up here.

She gently tried to soothe the distraught Cécile.

"Élizabeth will come to visit you tomorrow, *Mademoiselle* Cécile!" The nurse said ecstatically, trying to distract the old woman. It was obviously a lie, but it was a lie that always calmed her down, no matter how often told.

She slowly gained composure before she faintly whispered Élizabeth's name. Most nurses heard Cécile often muttering this name like one would whisper a prayer. "Élizabeth, Élizabeth, Élizabeth."

The chanting soothed her as she rocked back and forth, like a mother rocking her crying child, until she nodded with a small smile. Her tantrum was long forgotten, and hearing the nurse saying Élizabeth's name pulled her out of whatever nightmare she was plunged into.

The nurse sighed in relief.

"I will come back and brush your hair. Élizabeth cannot see you with your hair looking like a bird nested there. She might think that we aren't taking proper care of you," said the nurse as she chuckled at her joke, but Cécile did not acknowledge her.

She had spent most of her years waiting for Élizabeth's visit, but sadly, Élizabeth never came. She was humming her name under her breath with hopes of Élizabeth hearing it in some way, but occasionally, this mantra brought the pain along with the hope.

Nurse Élizabeth was the only staff member whom Cécile showed any signs of life many years ago. Not only did Élizabeth care about her, but she also gained Cécile's confidence. She let Élizabeth comb her hair, change her gown, and put her to bed without resistance. They would walk in the garden while she could, often sitting on the bench, watching the flowers come and go with the seasons. She was a chatty and lively nurse who brought a small drop of happiness to the residents' lives, and Cécile was a good listener.

Élizabeth often wondered how much her patients grasped their surroundings. From time to time, Cécile would give a small sign that affirmed that her stories were being heard. Her face would light up, and she would smile at her now and then as Élizabeth told her about her boyfriend, who, over the years, became her husband. She would tell Cécile about his romantic side, which she loved, and some quirks she did not, then spoke about her children, year after year. Since Cécile's movement became restricted to the wheelchair and Élizabeth retired,

Cécile no longer went on walks in the hospital park. She simply sat by the window consumed in her madness and memories.

Élizabeth was no longer there to make her happy. She screamed as she threw herself onto the floor from her chair whenever they crossed the hallway heading to the elevator. The staff tried to take her outside, but she refused and often threw quite a stir. None of the nurses tried after a while, so she just sat by the window, waiting for Élizabeth. It was a different Élizabeth she was so desperately hoping for, unlike everyone in the hospital thought.

The truth behind Élizabeth's lack of visit was quite sinister and dark. Élizabeth had died, but Cécile could not remember from one day to the next, so she held onto her hopes or false memories. Nobody knew. She lived every day believing that Élizabeth would come to visit her one day.

Cécile had turned eighty-one years old a few weeks ago, but her mind faded long before her thirtieth birthday. The nurses often left Cécile by the barred window of her room that had seen curtains at some point but was utterly bare now. These bars caged the patients at society's will, and they were constantly reminded that freedom is only a word in a crossword puzzle.

Cécile sat in her chair motionless and watched the seasons change while her fellow patients played games, watched television, or did crafts in the dayroom next to her. To most people, it would look like she was looking out of the window from her second-floor room, admiring the garden beneath her, but the truth was that she kept staring into the oblivion of her mind.

Cécile had been severely sedated at the beginning. She was violent to the male staff and even stabbed one of the nurses with a pair of scissors a week after she was admitted. She could not handle her locked doors and was preparing to die every night when staff put her to bed. As she grew older and nurse Élizabeth tended to her, the outbursts became less frequent and nonviolent. Now she was the bride of her delirious mind.

Cécile Eisner was transferred from another hospital, the *Hôtel-Dieu*, fifty-four years ago, in 1945. The doctors and nurses only knew that Cécile was found extremely thin and barely alive when she was first seen in Auschwitz on 27 January 1945. Soviet soldiers discovered her lying atop a pile of bodies, starved and tortured.

The number 23871 tattooed on her left arm permanently labeled her a victim of the Holocaust. No amount of scratching helped erase that number and the nightmare carved into the root of her memory by the Nazi tyranny. Since then, she has spent her days waiting for the arrival of someone. No one knew whether the person she had waited for was still alive or if she waited for the end to come and take the pain away.

★★★

One part of Paris held such despair, recalling the time of the Nazis overtaking Paris, while the other held the promise of hopes and new dreams. Where one waited to meet their end, the other could not wait for their new beginning.

Hénri was a photographer, a young man in his early thirties. He was finally making his dreams come true, as he had become able to own his dream studio. He now owned all three neighboring apartments the city was selling, with windows facing the street on the fourth, the top floor of 7 *Rue de Tlemcen*, in the twentieth district, just a minute's walk from the famous *Père Lachaise*.

Hénri was excited to be next to Paris's largest and most visited cemetery, which possessed a great collection of deceased talents. Moliere, Chopin, Jim Morrison, Oscar Wilde, Edith Piaf and hundreds more. The graveyard was peaceful, timeless, and offered serenity to anyone who wished to escape the everyday chaos or just needed some quiet from the constant thrum of the city.

Some visitors admired the masonry work of headstones and chapels honoring the dead as they sat on many of the cemetery's benches. Some wandered aimlessly among them like a soul who could not pay Charon for the trip across the river Styx.

Hénri often walked the cobblestone alleys for hours, taking photos of the sculptures. He believed he gave them personalities through his lens. The sculptures had different expressions and feelings depending on the day or the season. They told the life of the person they were watching over. Their youth on an early summer morning, their sorrows on a rainy afternoon, and their death on an eerie foggy night in late November. But he did not only come here to find subjects for his next photography book. No, Hénri found solace in the cemetery. He was looking for wisdom from the deceased to give meaning to his life.

Hénri felt like he had died when his fiancée of nearly six years left him.

"You must have seen this coming, Hénri," his friends told him, almost sounding accusatory, but he did not see his relationship ending. The woman he loved leaving and exiting his life hit him like a train. There were no sobbing break-up talks—no desperate late-night phone calls and no letters were waiting for him in the flat they shared. It was silence and emptiness on that cold winter night Natalie left about a year ago.

Hénri lost his way and gradually became a recluse. He has not taken any photographs since that night, but either sat in the dark flat pondering or walked the cemetery aimlessly for hours. The police even detained him for trespassing after he jumped the fence of the *Père Lachaise* at night, listening to love ballads by his favorite singers' tombs and waiting for the sun to rise and bring light to his broken heart. But the light never came.

His mother, Frances, could not see her only son waste away, so she threw a lifeline by purchasing these apartments. Refocusing on his work helped for the time being, but Hénri still felt that Natalie took his purpose in life—the very fabric of his being—with her in her suitcase.

Hénri found the neighborhood perfect for his new studio and was grateful for his mother, although he still very much was in denial about needing help. As much as he was very tempted, he did not want to move to *Montmartre*, where some of his friends had studios, for two reasons: he liked being close to this cemetery and could afford his current area.

Hénri had friends who shared rooms in Montmartre, a vibrant and famous part of the 18th district, but they paid hefty rents: quite the opposite from the time when Renoir, Monet, or Van Gogh called it home. Then, the rent was low, and creativity ran high on absinthe, producing masterpieces and green-fairy delirium. A few months ago, he may have made a different choice. He related more to the great masters of the past than he did to anyone living. *Montmartre* would have seemed perfect.

While Natalie was still in his life, Hénri had a good and steady income from selling his photography books and doing wedding photos on the weekends. But settling down in *Montmartre* was neither financially feasible when the love birds were looking for a place together nor something that he wants to do now despite his friends' nagging.

The city district once owned the apartments he is now renovating, and because these spaces needed a lot of upgrades, the city sold them well under market price. They kept them on their books but always had more pressing issues they spent their budget on other than fixing them. Finally, after being empty for a decade, the city decided to sell them and get rid of the liabilities, which is the only reason Hénri could afford them, with financial help from his widowed mother. It was a solution where everyone benefitted.

Now, with weeks into construction, his dreams were in motion. The crew knocked out the main walls separating the three apartments, and they looked like a truck drove through them. There were huge holes in the middle of each one, and piles of bricks were scattered around the floor. Before the crew could continue, the architect needed to inspect the remaining structure's stability to ensure the walls would hold.

The vision was to open all three apartments into one big room and create two smaller bedrooms. It was an open concept, a rather unconventional layout, but spacious. Converting the flats into a studio was not a small task, and Hénri learned about this relatively late in the construction process. It was running late and over budget. Everything had to be stripped down to bricks and rebuilt from bare-bones—challenging work. The apartment dwellers may have stayed in these units for years but never treated them as their own homes. They were only a temporary roof over their heads while they completed their assignment for the municipality; then, they moved on.

"*Monsieur* Hénri. Come, come. Look what we found," the crew supervisor waved him over as he pulled out a small package from a hole in the floor. It was a dirty and mold-covered cloth that seemed to have been hidden.

"What is it?" Hénri asked, with a frown on his forehead and his jet-black eyes staring at the foreign object. Most people in Paris always turned their heads to stare at the handsome, tall man who styled his black hair back into a ponytail. His Mediterranean features made him look intoxicating, which he inherited from his Greek mother, who met Hénri's father while she was studying at *Sorbonne* as a foreign exchange student. He was a "sight for sore eyes," as his mother often joked to her friends.

"Why are you bringing this to me?" Hénri asked after he looked at the dirty cloth, "Just throw it away."

"We found it under the floorboard. You should at least see what it is, and it might be worth money," the bald crew supervisor, Jakov, said with a comical look and heavy Croatian accent.

Hénri hesitated to take it from him, but the supervisor nudged him, and Hénri took the rag. He held his breath and slowly untied the twine that secured the cloth. It was an old and battered journal.

"Hmm, it has surely seen better days," murmured Hénri, slightly disappointed. Maybe he was expecting something valuable after Jakov insisted. He ran his thumb through the yellow-stained pages, dust flying everywhere around it. Some pages were torn out, and some were ripped in half, but most were readable.

The journal had a dark leather cover, worn and shiny, but the original color was unidentifiable. Hénri put the journal back into the rag and slid it into his shoulder bag, thinking he would look at it later after he got home. He had more important things to do at that moment.

After his work was done, Hénri rode his bicycle from his soon-to-be new studio to his current rental flat. His temporary home was in the 18th district at 21 *Rue Cave*, one block away from the Roman Catholic Church, *Saint-Bernard-de-la-Chapelle*.

Hénri cruised along the boulevard on this sunny but cool late autumn afternoon. He was smiling, pondering when he would be able to move in, probably within a couple of months, despite the delays. Construction was the only thing on his mind on his way back home. He was impatient and wanted the work finished, but he also wanted it done right. He was aware that making the crew hurry would be a bad idea.

Hénri did not even think about the journal until he came to his apartment block and looked for his gate keys in his bag. His hand brushed against the cold, damp rag as he dug into his pocket and ruffled through papers, but he did not heed it. He hung his bicycle on a prominent hook on the wall between his neighbor's and his door. Hénri's apartment was the closest to the staircase, so it was a good compromise—much better than blocking the hallway with his ride.

Hénri opened his apartment door and tossed his bag on the kitchen counter. He took off his hat, scarf, and jacket and hung them on the back of the front door.

Hénri's current rental was small but habitable. While he shared it with Natalie, it was vibrant and alive, but now it was more of a shelter than a home. Frances begged his son to move and leave the memories behind, but for Hénri, that is all he had, and he was unwilling to let go of those memories.

The flat was livable, maybe a little chaotic, with scattered lenses, shades, and tripods covering the floor. Hénri's black and white images covered the living room walls. He used to work exclusively with portraits, massive pictures of Natalie were on prime display all over the tiny flat. But after she left, capturing old cemeteries and architecture eased his pain. He did not want to see life through his lens. That is how Hénri experienced time. Life before and after Natalie.

A red couch dominated the living room, and its size demanded attention. Not much else fit into the room except a small computer table. Hénri piled his books and photo magazines on the floor so they reached different heights like organ pipes.

"Alice, I'm home!" Hénri said in a sing-song voice as he always did. Alice came to greet him and swirled around his ankles, meowing for some dinner. Alice, a Russian blue cat with green eyes, was his only companion now. After Natalie left, his mother gave her to him after she failed to convince him to move.

"It's good to have someone waiting for you when you come home," she had said caringly.

"What am I going to do with a cat?" Hénri asked, slightly annoyed at the seemingly random gift, but Frances knew that she needed to divert her son's attention from dwelling on his misery.

"Take her," she said with a sigh, "she needs you." And as it happened, he grew quite fond of this dominating feline.

Hénri's mother was an opinionated and strong woman, like most females in his life, even Alice, and raised Hénri to accept that women are far from weak and helpless creatures.

Frances adored Natalie. She had the brain, the heart, and the soul and followed her dreams of helping women as an obstetrician/gynecologist in Congo, working for *Médecins Sans Frontière*, Doctors Without Borders, an NGO, while she finished her residency. Hénri was not ready to go to Africa, and Natalie was not willing to stay in Paris. Still, Hénri stuck his head in the sand, and he did not see her slowly drifting away until the day she packed and left without a note.

Frances saw her young self in her, and, as much as it broke her motherly heart, she could not blame Natalie for following her passion—something she would never tell Hénri, ever.

Hénri fed Alice, who was continuously bugging him for dinner and some well-overdue attention, then poured himself a glass of wine. He preferred red over white and liked Pinot Noir best of the variety of excellent French wines. It was plain yet delicate, rarely blended with others, and a great type.

Hénri grabbed his bag, sat on the couch, and reached for the phone to call his mother. As the phone rang, he opened his satchel and took out the journal wrapped in the old, smelly rag.

"Hi, Mom," Hénri greeted his mother.

"Hénri, how's construction?" she asked immediately.

Hénri and his mom had grown closer since his dad died from a massive heart attack a few years back. Hénri begged his mother to move to Paris, but she liked living in Lyon in her apartment facing the *Rhône* River. Besides, the TVG train could take her to Paris in two hours. She quickly nipped Hénri's nagging in the bud each time the topic came up. He could never argue with it, and now he avoided bringing it up altogether.

Frances stepped back after Natalie left to give her son some space to grieve but had to reinsert herself as Hénri did not seem to slow down on his way down the rabbit hole of self-destruction and pity.

"It's going well, Mom. The crew knocked out the main partition walls between the apartments, and the engineer will come out next week to ensure everything is stable. If all else fails, we can put up some beams to strengthen the ceiling," Hénri summarized the progress with one breath.

"That's marvelous, Hénri. I am still planning to see you next weekend, and we can walk through together. I have some great ideas," she said. Frances was a commercial interior designer for a local architectural firm in Lyon. Hers was a prestige position she grew into after she and Jean-Baptiste married days after they graduated from the university. Her current position was another reason Frances did not want to move to Paris. However, she could have easily found a job there if she had wanted to.

"Great, Mom. It'll be amazing. Thank you," said Hénri as he took a sip of his wine. "Oh, I almost forgot; the crew ripped up the floor and found a journal stashed away underneath the boards in the corner of one of the rooms."

"Really? Has the floor not been changed since the 1900s?" She asked, ignoring the journal altogether. Frances was like that; she took construction and design seriously and did not hear anything unrelated. Her main concern was that the city had not disclosed the state of the floorboards.

"They did change it in the fifties. Jakov said that the floorboard was decent but probably will need to be replaced in the next few years. I'm having them do it now. I never liked that yellowish floor."

"What did you pick?"

"Solid gray wood to complement the color scheme we chose," Hénri said, then he continued, "Did you hear what I said about the journal? Jakov found it under the floor, crammed deep into the wall as if someone had purposely carved a hole into the mortar to hide it. Whoever this belonged to wanted to keep its content a secret. If it were not for the crew checking the pipes while the board was out, they wouldn't have found it."

"Oh, yes, the diary," Frances said as if she needed to remind herself what Hénri wanted to talk about. "Whose is it?"

"I don't know; I haven't read it yet, but it is a woman's diary and relatively old."

"Interesting. How do you know it's a woman's?"

"I can tell from the graceful handwriting, almost calligraphy-like, and nobody writes like that anymore."

They talked a little more about the studio and Frances's visit the following week. After they hung up, Hénri topped his glass with more wine, grabbed the journal, and flopped back onto the couch with his feet on the table. Alice jumped beside him and curled up next to him, like a child waiting for their bedtime story.

He unfolded the rag very carefully. The mildew hit his nose and made him grimace. The smell slowly filled his apartment and lingered, floating ghostlike. Hénri looked at the journal more closely. A severely deteriorating black ribbon ran across the leather spine. Despite its state, it still fused the front and back.

Underneath, Hénri could see some signs of the original color, but he could not identify it. Hénri guessed it could have been either maroon or dark red. Otherwise, the entire diary was shiny, blackish brown. It might not have weathered the elements if it were not for the leather cover.

"Who knows how old this is," Hénri said aloud, as he usually did when focused on something. Judging by the smell and its condition, it had to have been there for decades. Hénri ran his fingers through the embossed cover in a Braille-type attempt, and he could not make out the design. Although he briefly flipped through the journal earlier, he felt uneasy opening it.

"At least I can find out to whom it belonged, and I cannot find that out if I don't read it. Isn't that right Alice?" Hénri asked his cat for confirmation, and she obligingly meowed in response.

"That's what I thought," he chuckled. "Let's see what's hidden inside this journal. If I find out to whom it belongs, perhaps I can return it to its rightful owner," he nodded as he agreed with his conscience.

Hénri was unsure what awaited him on the other side, but it was too late to turn back. He flipped the cover open and began to read.

Chapter 2

Dear Diary

Dear Diary,

Today, on the 20th of October 1938, on my twentieth birthday, Mama gifted me with you. She said that sharing my thoughts with someone would ease my mind.

"Write about whatever you want, Cécile," she said as if it were that easy! I have so many things going through my head that I can barely sort them out. I have never kept a diary, and writing my thoughts sounds exciting, but I do not know how I would feel reading them back. It is like looking into a mirror but not wanting to accept the girl looking back at me. But still, I will try and tell you all about myself. I will fill you with my plans, hopes, dreams, and inspirations through the last page. I will not let you go to waste but allow me to introduce myself first.

Bon Soir, my name is Cécile Dubonnet, and I live in Paris, the city of love with Mama and Papa. I wish I could say that the weather is constantly beautiful and the air is always filled with romance, but that is not always the case. It has rained for the past few days, and the streets are wet. The autumn leaves stick to the ground or float around in the puddles like sailboats.

Although I have not been to many other cities besides Cherbourg, Paris is the most spectacular. Papa's sister lives in Cherbourg, and I like, or used to like, visiting her because I am very fond of the ocean, but it has been a while since I saw her. Aunt Elodie lost her only son, my cousin, and her husband in a horrible fire five years ago, and she has not invited anyone after the accident. It is so sad. Poor Aunt Elodie. I do not think Papa saw her either, not counting the funerals. He writes her often, and occasionally she writes back, but Papa says she has sunk into deep sadness and hardly ever leaves her house.

What can I tell about myself, Dear Diary? Well, let me start at the beginning. I was born on the 20th of October 1918. I am the only child of my parents. I did have a sister when I was one year old, Camille, but she died of the flu before her first birthday. I do not have memories of her or our lives as a family of four.

I felt lonely growing up, but the older I grew, the less I thought about it. I imagined from time-to-time what life would have been if Camille had been with us. We would have played with dolls, ran around in the park, and had silly quarrels. I often felt jealous that my friends had siblings. They spent a lot of time complaining about them, but they always had each other after the lights went out.

The feeling of loneliness slowly faded, and I grew up used to having my own space. Thinking about sharing it with someone seems impossible now. Besides, I had Mama and Papa's attention to myself, and they fussed over me.

I have two great friends who make me forget about my solitude instantly. One of them is dearest to my heart, Esther. She is older by two years and works as a nurse in the general hospital in the 10th *Arrondissement*, the neighboring district from where we all live. Esther is unmarried, just like me, and writing this makes me blush a little because I am constantly being reminded of my marital status by my family.

Esther's father, *Monsieur* Klotz, is a lawyer, and Mama works for him as a secretary. They often discuss their desire for courtship for us, their daughters. Esther's grandmother, Mami, has even arranged for her granddaughter to meet highly acculturated bourgeois Jews from Eastern Europe who live in Paris. Thankfully, Mama does no such thing other than share her opinion about it with *Monsieur* Klotz. We giggle at their attempts because we only want love, not social status.

My parents made my birthday incredibly special. They had their fair share of struggles with losing Camille and me being a constant reminder of a missing child, but they never showed it. We do not talk about Camille unless Mama and I visit the cemetery on her birthday. We take flowers and sit by the grave as she reminiscences about her as a baby before she fell ill, then we go on with our day, and the memory fades until the next year.

The food's aroma hit my nose as I walked up the stairs, and I am sure every passerby on the street thought Christmas came early. I took a big breath, trying to guess what Mama had prepared, but the flavorful combination made it difficult. My stomach growled in response as I walked through the door, and my mind finally connected the smell with the sight of dinner already set on the table. Mama was busy going back and forth from the kitchen, ensuring everything was perfect. She was putting the finishing touches on this beautiful evening. I offered to help, but she hushed me away and made me sit down.

"It's your day, Cécile. Enjoy it," Mama said, guiding me to the dining room. I sat at the table and greeted Papa, who was lost in reading his newspaper, the *Paris-Soir*. He kept mumbling under his trimmed mustache that I used to play with as a child. I could not exactly understand what he was saying, but he said something about a Munich Agreement, which he calls the Munich Betrayal. I do not know why, but he is exceptionally passionate about disliking it. Unlike me, he loves reading the paper and discussing political affairs with his friends.

On the other hand, I flip through the pages to look at the advertisements and not read any articles, but I hear Papa conversing, so I am practically up to date with the current events. Papa and his friends always get upset over this Munich Agreement. He argues that Nazi Germany is annexing a part of 'Czehcosolvakia,' and there is not much anyone agreeing with other than the Germans, of course—this might be incorrect. This country is too hard to spell. The truth is that I do not understand any part of it, and I do not want to bore you with politics, Dear Diary! Where was I? Oh yes, the birthday dinner (because, as I said, politics is my least-favorite topic.)

The heavenly smell that guided me up the stairs was a nice roast! As you see, being a single child has many benefits. A small but lovely piece of meat was sizzling in the pan as Mama put the last dish on the table. We would mostly have vegetables, potatoes, and soups for dinners, and while, just like for most families, meat was a treat, at least we would go to bed with our bellies full every night and still have the means to have fun in our life from time to time. It was 'Depression,' as Papa called it. My parents had outdone themselves, splurging on a roast, but in my opinion, cakes are the best part of a birthday, and I think everyone would agree.

Mama's cooking is the most amazing, so her cakes are always perfect. This year she surprised me with a chocolate cake with hazelnut meringue and layers of whipped cream. I often tell her that she wastes her talent typing up legal documents for Monsieur Klotz and that she should become a chef!

"*C'est complètement absurde*, Cécile!" She found it to be utter nonsense, but I do not think finding your dream is a drivel.

Papa and Mama work respectable jobs, but we are neither rich nor poor. We are in the middle of the economic ladder and could enjoy the best of both worlds, as they say, although I am still determining what the benefits of being poor are. I would rather be on the top end, so I can afford glamorous clothes and visit Hollywood!

I would never need to worry, unlike Papa, who is always careful where he spends his hard-earned living. He is a cautious man where the matters of money are concerned. He counts the content of his wallet every night before going to bed; then, he neatly tucks it in the middle drawer of the cherry-wood dining room credenza. Like you would tuck a child in for the night.

"You have to save for rainy days, Cécile," he often lectures me when I spend my earnings on clothes and cinema tickets. Papa knows how many francs are in his wallet at any time of the day. If I were to take any, he would immediately suspect me since Mama would never do such a thing. I did get into trouble once when I was around eleven years old and before I knew about his money-counting ritual. I had not seen him so angry, which taught me a valuable lesson. Never touch his money.

Papa works as a store manager in a prestigious tailor shop on *Avenue des Champs-Élysées* called the *Triomphe*. The owner did not have much imagination when he named it after the triumphal arch, but it was nearby, so I suppose he thought it was clever. Maybe it was the same person who called the tobacco shop *Tabac Odéon*, where I work. People around here are not creative in choosing a name for their establishments. I dream of seeing a play from a box at the *Odéon*, the theatre, and sipping champagne during intermission. Still, I am afraid living in the middle of the economic ladder does not come with such benefits.

The tailor shop is exquisite and very expensive! Papa is a much-respected man there, a renowned store manager and sought after for excellently matching his customers' personalities to suits and accessories.

Papa often says that knowing his customers' likes and dislikes is good business. I think it is a form of art, but he would rather have his skills identified as a part of his job. It is not easy to know what people want; yet, somehow, he understands it without knowing them personally, and it gives him a reputation that reaches far. Men coming to see him from as far as New York! I do not think I could recommend cigarettes based on my clients' characters.

After devouring a magnificent dinner, Mama brought in the cake that transformed me into a little girl. To inspect just how thick the layers were, I dug through the cream with my finger until Mama slapped my hand. We chatted for a while and enjoyed each other's company before I received my presents.

Mama held up her gift wrapped in red paper with white oval dots. It had a pale green ribbon and was neatly tied in a bow. Mama became a little emotional, but tears never ran down her face. She fought to hold them back. Maybe the past flashed in front of her eyes like a film, and she was sad about the time we would never have again.

From the shape and feel of the gift, I thought Mama was handing me a book. Seeing how special this was for her, I opened it very carefully.

I took my time to untie the bow and unfold the paper ... and there, in the middle, lay a beautiful notebook with a red leather cover and a tree embossed on the front. My heart jumped with joy at seeing it as I cuddled the diary to my chest. Mama knew me better than anyone else. I always wanted a journal! I gave her the biggest kiss I could and hugged her tightly.

"Mind the hair," she warned and patted her head to ensure it was intact.

Her chestnut-colored brown hair is set in Marcell waves and suits her fair skin and fragile frame. She only has her hair done a couple of times a year. I constantly remind her that her hairdo is outdated, but she loves the waves. She always says, 'old is gold,' and carries on having the same hairstyle for years.

She looks beautiful, and I may be jealous because my hair is the opposite of hers. It is wiry, rugged, and does not respond to reason or my brush, and I cannot possibly put enough brilliantine on it to style it to hold a form. We even tried cold wave once, but we failed miserably. My short hair curled up so close to my scalp I looked like a brush thrown in the fire.

I was incredibly grateful that I did not have a job then because I did not want to leave the apartment after that catastrophe unless it was an absolute must. Still, even then, I wore the most oversized hat I could find. I cried when I first saw the result. Oh, how hideous I looked! Not only did I worry about my hair falling out, but I also looked like a clown. Thank God you did not see it, Diary! Otherwise, you, too, would have ridiculed me!

Esther laughed uncontrollably when she saw it for the first time. She said I looked like an extraordinarily wealthy old woman's lap poodle. Not sure why the woman had to be rich, but there you have it. Mama did her best to tame my unruly hair, but it often resulted in foolish looks I discarded after a week, so she left it alone after many failed attempts. That means that this very day, at this very moment, my hair is like a wild goose that never laid a tame egg!

See, Diary, I have a million things going through my head, and I can barely keep myself in a straight line. My mind is like a forest. Once you venture far into it, you get completely lost with no way out. I keep going wayward from what I am supposed to write. Mama knew I had always been such a thinker. She sometimes tells me that I inherited this trait from her.

Writing about Mama makes me wonder why she was almost close to tears when she gave me this journal. Oh, now you mention it, I may know the answer. She and I used to be close when I was growing up. We would play silly games and cards, go to the shops, and have the best time in the world.

But alas, adulthood caught up to me, and we started spending less and less time together. Once I had the means of spending my money, I felt more independent. I feel guilty about it sometimes, but Mama tells me not to worry. She says that she understands how I am a 'fine young lady' now and that it is normal for any girl my age to venture into the world.

Once I started working, it was natural that we would slowly drift apart. We could not find the time, and it is not only me who is growing old as the years pass. Mama would be too tired after coming home from work and tending to the household, so we would chat briefly after dinner before retiring to our bedrooms. Gifting me a diary was her way of saying that she would, one day, love to read all about my days. Or my secrets, although I am sure one is not supposed to read someone else's diary.

As they say, Mama is like an open book because she does not, or perhaps cannot, hide her feelings, which is the opposite of Papa, who is very upfront and straightforward about all life matters. It is a trait I did not inherit, for better or worse. He wants to avoid making as many complications as possible, albeit he rarely shows his softer side. The way he gave me my present was very different from how my mother did. He cleared his throat, pulled out cinema tickets from his suit pocket, and handed them to me.

"Go with your friends," he said plainly.

Papa does not know what to do with his emotions, so he tucks them away like his handkerchief in his suit pocket and wallet in the credenza, but he embraced me warmly in his arms, which reminded me of the old days when he took me to the park to play and chase pigeons.

"You need to sprinkle salt on their tail feather," Papa instructed me every time the birds flew away before I could catch them. Not until a few years ago did I realize what he meant. It had nothing to do with salt, although I thought it made them unable to fly. The hidden meaning was that if I could sprinkle salt on their feather, I would be silent enough and close enough to catch the bird without salt anyway. Children believe the silliest things!

As a small child, I spent a lot of time clinging to him, but I realize now he only tolerated my closeness. When I was four or five, such things did not cross my mind. Love was unconditional and never-ending. He still smells of cigarettes mixed with cologne, a slight scent of unused fabric, and a touch of sewing machine oil. This fragrance will forever remind me of my childhood.

My other dear friend, Agnes, is just as sweet as Esther, but they could not be any more different in how they look and the dreams they chase. Agnes is a clerk at the local municipality office, processing building permit applications, and dreams of becoming the city's architect one day. She is overly ambitious and does not want to get married, although she could have plenty of suitors if she wished to.

Esther is a nurse, and she finds fulfillment in this profession. Unlike Agnes, she does want to get married and have children, but she does not think she would give up her job to stay at home. "Times are different now," she says, but I would happily stay at home and care for my husband and children. I am old-fashioned in that sense, I suppose.

There are three cinema tickets for Agnes, Esther, and me to watch *Algiers* on Saturday, and it was lovely of Papa to think about my friends. I saw the poster advertising the film, and oh my, Charles Boyer is such a handsome gentleman! I appreciate his good looks and acting skills, and I would marry him if he insisted, but my first choice would be that

American fellow from New York—Humphrey Bogart. Oh, did I say his name aloud? Such a charming man! I cannot stop squeaking as I think about him. Americans do have swoon-worthy accents.

It is no secret that I am a fan of the silver screen. Being in a cinema makes me feel like a different person, much like reading books; watching the story come alive is mesmerizing. I am transported from reality into a fantasy I do not wish to end. I become Her in the darkness as the rhythmical noise of the film projector fades and whisks me away with it ... ah, but look! It is nearing midnight, yet I have so much to say. I wonder if I will become the heroine of my own story one day, or maybe I already am.

Chapter 3

The Stranger

F riday, 21 October 1938

Dear Diary,

It indeed was an awful *faux pas* I committed today. Even thinking about it is making me blush. I cannot believe I did something so daft in front of the most handsome man I have ever laid eyes on. Is it even sensible to feel ashamed over something so minor? I fret over it because the buyer was not only good-looking but was sophisticated and had no ring on his finger. He was very well dressed, which meant he was from an excellent financial background. Mama always said judging someone based on their appearance is not right, but how can you not? Yes, even you must be thinking how shallow I am for thinking in that manner, but if you had eyes, Dear Diary, you would see the tall, dark, captivating stranger I was blessed to meet today, but allow me to start at the beginning.

It is hard to believe that I am twenty years old, facing the world alone. Most girls my age are married, but I cannot even claim I have any prospects. I am not as concerned as Papa because neither do Agnes or Esther, but I am keen on finding true love. I will surely be at least engaged by my next birthday. And maybe more responsible. That is a promise! Yet the first thing I am responsible for is taking care of You, but I need to continue about my day and my embarrassing encounter.

I quickly freshened up in the morning and wore a short-sleeved sweater with my favorite striped skirt, not thinking what the day would bring later, but it was perfect for a sunny and dry autumn day. It was not warm by any means. It is October, after all. My coat is not the latest fashion, but it is well-kept and in good condition. Most importantly, I have a matching hat to compliment my attire. My shoes all have heels to make me look a little taller. I want to think I have an average height, but the reality is more disappointing.

I wish I were as tall as Esther, but I would be equally happy if I reached higher than her shoulders. Only in my dreams, or if I wore three-heeled shoes at once, could I reach her height. That would be a terrific sight. Esther is not only tall but also has a figure for which I would kill. Both of my friends could easily be fashion models.

Mama was already preparing breakfast while Papa was busy making coffee, which was the only thing she allowed him to do in the kitchen, or maybe it was the only thing he would do. He carefully fills the percolator with ground coffee the night before and places it on the stove. It is faithfully waiting all night, so after Papa gets dressed, he turns the gas on and brews the most fragrant coffee.

Making coffee is another ritual Papa carries out slowly and thoroughly. He is forming a bond with the day ahead that starts the night before, involving his beloved coffee cup he never lets Mama wash. It has stains from heavy use, but cleaning it would be a sin.

"It preserves the coffee's character that otherwise would be lost if it was washed," Papa says, but I do not believe that to be true.

He takes his espresso with just one small spoonful of sugar; that is all that goes into the hot black brew of life. I prefer *Café au Lait* because coffee is bitter without sugar and milk. Much like life without love. It is often sharp, even sour *sans l'amour*.

Papa was methodically stirring his coffee, trying to get the sugar to dissolve. Luckily, he drinks it fast, which leaves most of it at the bottom that I can spoon out. That is a ritual I adopted as a small child, and I carry it out to this day. We all like our little habits.

I feel nostalgic for the days when Mama and I made breakfast together before I went to school. Papa would eat the morning meal without complaints, even if I served him burnt toast.

Being a child is living worry-free about the future. As we get older, we change the roles in which we vest our attention. Marriage gives me mixed feelings because Papa pesters me frequently, and I, too, want to find my knight in shining armor, but talking about it does not ease my worry.

"You do need to get married soon," Papa says firmly a few times a month as he and I are having a conversation in his head, and he needs to verbalize it to affirm his ideas.

I am sure I will hear more now that I have turned twenty and will soon be considered an old maid, which sounds awful. Maybe a wealthy gentleman will marry me soon, and I will have to turn down Charles Boyer, Humphrey Bogart, or Johnny Weissmuller with great sadness. I will not be Jane to my Tarzan.

I hoped Papa would not bring marriage up on our way to work. That would have been very embarrassing. I did not want the prying eyes of passengers on me on the *Métro*, but to my great relief, I was spared the life lessons today. Since more men than ladies come into the *Tabac* for cigarettes, I have plenty of opportunities to see eligible bachelors.

Still, I think I would have a better chance to meet prospects in Papa's tailor shop. I do not understand why the owner, *Monsieur* Morel, did not let me work there or why Papa has not pressed him, considering he is the one wanting me in front of the altar. Papa thought I would be much happier if I worked in the *Tabac*, but I think the real reason is that *Monsieur* Morel did not consider me pretty enough. He did not say it to me, and I am sure he dared not mention that to Papa, but I think that was the real reason. I do not look anything like Ginger Rogers like Agnes does, that is certain, but I am pretty enough, although my wiry hair and short stature do not support this statement very much. I suppose it all worked out because I am glad to be in the *Tabac*. I do not know if I am happier there, but I am undoubtedly pleased.

Papa brought more coffee and placed it on the table. His smile vanished when he sat down and picked up the newspaper. It was always the same routine every morning. He would read the paper grudgingly, murmuring under his nose. I do not understand why he reads something that would put him in a bad mood. Who would want to start their day grumpy?

I once asked Mama why she did not care for the news as much as Papa. She said that the war taught her never to touch the paper again. I remember asking her about it when I was younger. I had never seen her so sad, and I swore never to ask her again. To this very day, I am too scared to know the reason. She had cried hard that day, and as a thirteen-year-old, I did not know what to do. Papa had warned me never to mention it again.

"A lot of dreadful things happened, Cécile. Your mother suffered through too many losses because of it. Do not bring it up again," he said so harshly, even I cried a little. I did not like it when Papa got strict with me. His tone was not angry, but his stony expression only conveyed how severe the topic was and that I was never to ask Mama about it again.

All I knew about the war was that it took place four years before I was born and ended a month later. People sometimes called it the Great War. I always wondered what was so great about it, or was it called the Great War because it was so widespread? As I mentioned, politics is not a topic I am versed in. Nor do I care about it, really. Mama never touched the newspaper after the war ended, and I had to ask Esther's mother because Mama's silence further fueled my curiosity.

Her mother, Ada, said that there were too many atrocities. People witnessed carnage and destruction throughout the continent. Millions of people died, the living suffered because everything was scarce, and most of Europe was destroyed from its roots—the worst of humankind the world has ever seen.

She could not speak for Mama, but I can imagine how terrified she must have been being pregnant during it all. She made me realize why everyone avoids talk of war. It was as if they were either still traumatized or wanted to leave it behind. But memories live on even if no one talks about them.

Papa had a sour expression as he flipped to the next page, his coffee long forgotten. I do not know whether he was thinking about the articles he had just read or about the topic of marriage, and I was hoping it was not the latter, no matter how selfish that sounds. He let out a long sigh before closing the newspaper and putting it aside with a concerned look I was too busy to recognize.

I work in the tobacco shop between the *Sorbonne Université* and the *Cinéma Le Champo*. It is not too far from where we live, but far enough to walk, so I take the *Métro*. The closest station, the *Père Lachaise*, is a short walk from our apartment. The subway takes me to *Cluny* in just a little under twenty minutes. As we approached the station, I kissed Papa.

"*Adieu*, Papa! See you tonight," I said and leaned toward him.

"Have a wonderful day *Le Chérie*," said Papa as he held his left cheek for my kiss. I would not say I liked when he called me 'sweet' because I was no longer five years old. I was a grown-up lady, but today I did not fight it; he was not himself this morning.

The *Tabac* is managed by a middle-aged woman, *Mademoiselle* Renée, *Monsieur* Morel's niece. The shop looks inviting, with orange-lit space and rows of glass displaying cigar pipes and a variety of tobacco. It is well-known around Paris for its classy atmosphere and because a lady who is not married runs it. Most people believe it is something a woman should not do, run a business, but Renée does not listen to naysayers. She built the establishment after her uncle bought the real estate and is very good at trading. Running a shop must be a family trait because *Monsieur* Morel owns several around Paris, and they are all managed by someone in the family. Remarkably successful man indeed.

Renée is nice, but she can be unbending when needed. She likes everything to be done in a particular way, so I do my best to work diligently. Anyway, today was not my best day, however.

A customer was already waiting for the shop to open when I arrived. He wore a dark gray suit and a hat tilted on his head. He must have come by car or a taxi because the weather was not warm enough to be outside without a coat. He leaned against the wall, legs crossed, puffing on a cigarette, and reading a newspaper.

"The sign clearly shows opening hours," I murmured, displeased.

He looked up from his paper but did not acknowledge me. I hoped he did not hear my comment.

He was smoking *Gitanes*. I could tell from the distinctive smell. Although burning cigarettes somewhat smelled identical to the untrained, I could pinpoint the brand—most times. Maybe Papa is right about knowing customers and being able to match products to their personalities.

The gentleman folded his paper and stashed it under his arm as he stepped inside the store. I took off my coat and hat and went behind the register. There is a lot to do when I open the *Tabac*, so having a customer immediately upon my arrival is somewhat bothersome. I need to open the register, make an opening statement on how much money we start the day with, and ensure the shelves are stacked. If any products run low, I need to fill them in from the storage room.

We sell many tobaccos and related articles. Cigarettes, cigars, tobacco, whole pipes, papers, bowls, and stems—a wide variety of any of these goods. There were many unfamiliar words I had to learn the first week on the job. Like 'bowls.' In my mind, a bowl is found in a kitchen, but it is also the front part of the pipe where you stuff tobacco. I learned words I did not know existed, and I had to learn more about tobacco and several types of wood used to make pipe bowls.

To make matters worse for such a young lady, they all have different names. I cannot tell you those because, luckily, no one ever asks, but I have it written down on a piece of paper that I keep in the drawer under the register. The most precious pipes are made from briarwood, which I know because those are the most expensive ones. More interestingly, there are distinct types of tobacco leaves, too. I only remember the 'oriental tobacco' and the *Perique*. I do not know why I remember these two, but I do. The others have skipped my mind, which is a lot of information for such a young head. On the other hand, cigarettes are easy because they are a package, their names are on the box, and everyone knows them. No one asks for a fancy history; they just come in, get the pack, and leave.

Tabac is not a large shop but spacious enough to fit two tables and a few comfortable armchairs in the left corner by the window beside the wall-to-wall counter. The chairs are deep, dark green leather and amazingly comfortable. Sometimes I feel like they were built for a giant because they swallow me whole when I sit in them.

The gentlemen spend hours trying some tobacco before buying it or simply enjoy the smokes they have just bought. They discuss politics, as they all do, read the newspaper, or watch life pass by on the streets. Some customers can not even get themselves to leave. Men, that is.

The ladies who come in do not tend to stay. They are always so well dressed, so stylish, and they all look like they have just got out of a *Vogue* photoshoot, wearing fancy hats, fur coats, and leather gloves. I cannot tell the difference between furs, but if you have one, you are wealthy because I cannot afford one. I often dream about standing on the other side of the counter in my magazine-worthy clothes, buying the shop's most luxurious cigarettes. One day!

The gentleman waiting outside when I arrived stood patiently by the glass and did not say a word as I prepared for the day. After I opened the register, I finally turned to him.

"Bonjour, Monsieur, how can I help you?" I was a little annoyed that he made me feel rushed, but I forced a smile and tilted my head. I had a chance to look at him, and I admit the man was very posh and incredibly handsome. For a minute, I lost myself staring at him. He had dark brown wavy hair styled back, a clean, shaved face, and slender lips. Gorgeously handsome! Although he did not exactly look like him, he resembled that American actor ... hmm.... What is his name? I saw him in 'A Yank at Oxford' earlier this year. He reminded me of that star, and it felt like I was staring at him for hours.

"Mademoiselle?" He asked in a wondering tone. I quickly snapped out of my trance and started fiddling with the cash register—how

embarrassing. That has never happened to me before. He must have answered my questions, which I do not believe I heard or remember asking.

"Two packs of *Gitanes, S'il Vous plait*," he repeated. He leaned on the cherry wood counter as he took the paper from his armpit to get his wallet. I was so embarrassed he caught me that I had not noticed that a couple of other customers had entered the shop. I needed to get my head back together. However, as I turned around and reached for the *Gitanes*, I knocked several packets of cigarettes off the shelves. This *malheur* made me so nervous that I hit the boxes on the counter with my elbow, and they all fell to the ground with a loud thud.

My face turned RED. I mean, RED, just like you, my Dear Diary. Luckily, my back faced him, so he did not see me, but I felt his eyes burning holes in my back, and I swore I heard him laugh. As I turned, I tried masking my embarrassment with more or less luck. I brushed my hair with my hands and smoothed out my dress. I put the cigarettes by the cashier and looked at him, trying to smile, but I think it turned out to be a half-grin. He gave me a sympathetic look and the most gorgeous smile I have ever seen.

"First day?" he asked with an accent I could not identify.

"Yes, *Monsieur*," I lied quicker than my mind could comprehend. Why did I say that? Good riddance.

"It is quite all right, *Mademoiselle*; you are doing wonderfully."

"Oh, thank you, *Monsieur*, and I am terribly sorry for my clumsiness," I said with even more embarrassment.

"Nothing to apologize for. You will be dancing around in this store like a feather in the wind in no time. I will be in Paris for a few months, and I will be sure to come by to witness it first-hand," he said in his baritone voice that made me blush before he continued, "Pardon me, but I could not catch your name *Mademoiselle*."

I do not remember introducing myself, but there was so much charm in how he said *Mademoiselle* I did not question it. I felt my heart flutter at his smile and became giddy at seeing a dimple.

"Cécile. My name is Cécile," I said while avoiding eye contact, but he grabbed my hand from the countertop and lifted it to those lips.

"Married?"

"No."

"Widow?"

"No!" I said, annoyed that he thought I was old enough to be one.

"Why not?" he joked. "*Küss Die Hand, Fräulein* Cécile," he said as he kissed the top of my hand.

He paid for his cigarettes, nodded with a smile, and left the store, and just like that, I was smitten. I nearly fainted. I think I came around when the next customer was in front of me, trying to get my attention. I was still holding the francs in my hand, staring at what may have appeared to be a ghost going through the front door. I forgot to ask his name. Oh no, what a loony I am.

I spent the rest of the day in a dreamy haze. I kept thinking about you, my Dear Diary, and all the stories I would share. I tried soaking up every moment of my interaction with the mysterious gentleman. I replayed it in my head repeatedly, but the more I thought about it, the more I realized how much of a mess I was. It nearly made me forget to telephone Esther and Agnes about the film.

When I told Esther over the wire what had happened, she laughed and told me I was a fool for running after a man or any man, in her opinion, but she confirmed what I felt. The gentleman liked me. Esther and I agreed to meet in the park after work if the weather held up and discuss our plan to go to the cinema this weekend.

Time slowed and crawled painfully until four o'clock, when I closed the shop and hurried to meet Esther. Agnes could not come to the park today, but she promised to meet us at the cinema on Saturday. I did not mind—not today. Her always calm manner would have agitated me. I needed to have a *tête-à-tête* with Esther, and I could not wait.

The weather was just like I had hoped. The sun sprinkled gold dust all over the city, which now has a beautiful new carpet of red, yellow, and brown leaves. Children were collecting them into bouquets to take home, kicking them up into the air with their tiny feet. Their laughter echoed through the park. It was a beautiful warm autumn day.

Esther was already sitting on our bench under the willow tree when I arrived at our favorite park, *Parc Des Buttes Chaumont*. She saw me walking toward her, jumped up excitedly, and waved. I like Esther's style. Not only was she beautiful, but she also knew how to dress. The Klotz's had more money than we did because her Papa was a lawyer, but she has never made me feel poor or not worthy of her friendship.

Esther wore a long wide-belted tweed coat that extended under her knees with high pockets that fell below her tiny waistline. The coat had cuffs, a large collar, and was burgundy and brown plaid. Her hat just sat slightly tilted on her head, waiting to fall off, but it was secured with confidence. Esther is always so put together that fashion *faux pas* does not happen to her. I envied her sometimes. All the time, actually, but she was still my best friend. I was the complete opposite of her. With my short, wiry hair, petite frame, and less-than-stylish wardrobe, I should not be surprised I ended up in the *Tabac*, but today I fell in love with a stranger.

★★★

Hénri chuckled. He poured another glass of wine and reached for his headphones. Alice hopped off, annoyed that her cat nap was disrupted, and headed to the kitchen for her leftover food. The wine made Hénri tipsy, and the diary made him travel back in time. He found an old Louis Armstrong CD in the stack of discs towering over his stereo. He popped it into his Discman and pressed play. He liked jazz over the loudness of swing, but he wanted to connect what he was reading to the music—for authenticity.

"It'll do," he thought and wondered if this woman, Cécile, listened to the American trumpeter's music. The tunes, mixed with the wine, were perfect for this late-night visit to 1938.

CHAPTER 4

MADEMOISELLE BOSSARD

Sunday, Sunday, 23 October 1938

Dear Diary,

It is Sunday, and it is only eight o'clock. The night has barely begun, but I can hardly keep my eyes open. I am sorry I skipped an entire day of writing. I was too caught up in life on Saturday. Oh, and what a day it was.

A lot has happened after meeting Esther in the park on Friday. We talked about the mysterious stranger who resembled Robert Taylor, the actor whose name I could not remember at the time. He looks so charming on the silver screen, especially when he smiles. Now that I think about it, I cannot believe I met someone who looks like him. I must pinch myself to ensure I am not in a dream.

In hindsight, I wish Agnes had been with us, but we did not know we had a few surprises waiting for us on Saturday. But let me tell you about Agnes first.

Agnes works as a clerk at the local municipal office, but I said that before. She could not join us because she stayed late to finish typing up a permit paper for some 'wave transmitter.' I had no idea what it was, but Agnes said this tower would revolutionize the world.

Typing up building permits sounds boring, but Agnes says it pays well, and she is grateful even to have the opportunity. Her grandmother was not allowed to have a job, and Agnes was not about to let a man tell her what she could not do. She was working hard toward her dream of being the chief architect. Agnes is a true feminist.

I suppose being in an office can be exciting. Agnes works with many people, ladies, and gentlemen alike, so she says it is becoming her second family. They form a different bond than I do with my customers, as they eat lunch, have coffee breaks, and see each other daily. My customers, on the other hand, just come and go. I call them one-minute acquaintances. Some come more regularly, and I get to know their names after a while, but some just step into the shop unexpectedly, and I never see them again. I have small talks with them sometimes, but our encounter is so brief that they remain strangers, even if I see them often. I can never befriend someone that easily, so working in the office may not suit me.

Agnes is breathtakingly beautiful, but she does not care about her looks. She is slender and tall, well, even taller than Esther. Everyone is taller than me, even a donkey. I despise how short I am.

While Esther and I have dark hair, Agnes is blonde, much like Ginger Rogers, although I do not understand why she chose Ginger. She is not a redhead at all. I know a lot about films and that stars pick different stage names when they become famous, but she should have picked something more fitting. If I were her, I would be Gaby Dale.

I always tell Agnes she should become a model for *Vogue* magazine, but she says she does not like the lifestyle of modeling. She believes a woman can do more than sell her looks to hungry men. She wants to make something of herself other than being a pretty face. She wants to be acknowledged for her intellect and not for her beauty. But it is hard for her not to capture everyone's attention with those azure blue eyes, tall frame, and blinding blonde hair. She is a magnet for marriage proposals, but thus far, she has turned down all of them, declaring herself 'running late for being ready for love.' It is a pity, and I wish she could give me some of that glamour. I would happily sift through those suitors and say *Oui Je le veux*, I do, at the altar.

Times are slowly changing, and more women are coming forward to hold jobs. I understand why Agnes wants to have a career. It is an exciting time to be a woman. M. *Girard*, Agnes's father, is the Deputy to the Director-General of the *Gendarmerie*, the police. He is well respected within the municipality. Agnes could easily live a lavish life and afford it without working. Despite having many connections in high society, Agnes still opts for a life filled with arduous work. So, my Dear Diary, some days I want to be like Agnes and have a remarkable career, but other days, all I want is a husband and a family to care for. But look here, my thoughts keep straying off again.

Esther and I stayed in the park until sunset and spoke about the mysterious stranger at the *Tabac*. Then we talked about her day at work and watched the sun slowly disappear below the horizon as families headed home for dinner. We fed the geese with leftover bread and walked around the lake at least a million times, non-stop, like a needle on a phonograph record.

After I arrived home, I had supper with Mama and Papa. It was another meal where Papa discussed the government's decision while Mama and I dutifully listened to him. Then, I retired to the living room, reading my new favorite book while Mama listened to the radio. She did not listen to the news but always tuned into her dear radio dramas. We often listened to them together, but I was captivated by my crime novel to join her.

Papa was sitting in his armchair, forever lost in the newspaper and his favorite cigarettes. He was smoking *Gitanes*, and I was immediately reminded of the stranger who had smoked the same brand. I shook my head and continued reading my book about a Belgian detective, Hercule Poirot. Did I ever mention how much I love all of Agatha Christie's books? I read *Murder on the Orient Express* earlier this year, and now I am fully immersed in *Death on the Nile*. I am at the part where the murder occurred, and Poirot started interviewing all the passengers.

I love reading just as much as I love watching films. One of the things I treasure about Agatha Christie's stories is that I get to travel to many places in my mind. Her mysterious murders take me to unimaginable places. Many of them are set in England, which I have never visited, but I feel I know everything about the country from what I read. Her other adventures are set in exotic places like Istanbul or Egypt. They are all quite different from Cherbourg and Paris! I wish I could travel there in person, not just in my mind, but I would be happy to visit England for now or Aunt Elodie. Reading about the world makes me want to see these places with my own eyes. Imagination can only take me as far as I allow it to go.

Mama always tells me how dangerous it is to get lost in the stories, but I never heed her warnings. What can be so harmful about dreaming of other places? I find myself completely lost in the books I read, and I cannot put them down until I finish them. I imagine being in the story—sometimes as the protagonist, but more often, I am the strong female character who is beautiful and rich—very posh.

I am in Egypt on the boat, sipping my cocktail in my white tea dress, feeling the warm desert breeze on my arms. I lean over the railing and watch the setting sun painting the Nile orange and red. As women gather around an impromptu fireplace, local farmers get water in their palm-leaf woven pitchers, and camels graze in the background. The words on the paper become the world in my mind that is alive, and I am at its center. I am the story.

Papa also thinks I live in a fantasy world and should focus on life as an adult, but I quite like escaping to exciting places, even if there is a murderer or a thief to love. I picture a better me, which is why closing a book always feels like I am parting from another world. After returning to reality, a wave of sleepiness hit me, and I decided to retire for the night, hoping for romantic dreams.

I telephoned Esther and Agnes on Saturday morning and agreed to meet up for pastries and to plan our night out. I was yearning for something sweet and did not want to go alone. My favorite dessert was the *mille-feuille*, a layered puff pastry with vanilla custard. Heavenly. Mama makes it sometimes, but she says it is very laborious, so I do not pester her. I am delighted with the one they serve at the coffee shop, which is nearly as good as hers, but only nearly.

We met by *Café de Luna in Parc des Buttes Chaumont*, by Belvedere Island, a beautiful pavilion in the heart of the park. The owner puts chairs and tables outside when the weather is nice, but it is also pleasant to be inside and watch the rain. We can sit there for hours.

Agnes, Esther, and I basked in the sun and enjoyed our Saturday morning. We made plans for the night as we drank coffee and smoked cigarettes. Annoyingly, I skipped the pastry because no one else had eaten, and I did not want to feel awkward being the only one. Esther was someplace else in her mind. Her attention wandered off occasionally, but not often or long enough for us to notice at the time. Agnes, on the other hand, was on fire.

"I propose after *Algiers*, we go and dance," Agnes recommended, as she took a sip of her coffee before continuing, "We can celebrate Cécile's birthday and my promotion."

"What promotion?" I asked.

"Oh, I didn't tell you, did I? I am now working as the assistant to *Monsieur* Prost. He has a special project for urban development here in Paris."

"Prost? I don't know who that is, Agnes."

"You know why this is exciting, Cécile? Agnes asked, ignoring the part where she should explain more about this gentleman. "He was helping with the planning of *Casablanca*!"

"Oh, That's in *Algiers*!" I yelled with excitement but quickly realized I was wrong.

"Casablanca is in Morocco, silly! You may think of Casbah; that's in Algiers."

Agnes continued filling the air with constant chitchats about her office. She was extremely excited about this opportunity.

Algiers did not disappoint. How could it have? We all were awed by Charles Boyer, the actor who played Pepe, and we could not help but think how charming he was, even as a thief. I could not believe Gaby would marry that big man for his money and not Pepe, who she clearly loved, but, of course, to complicate this story, there was Ines, Pepe's mistress, who was really jealous of Gaby.

What a love triangle! It was a pity that Gaby chose to marry that unattractive older man. Charles Boyer's song, *C'est la Vie*, played over and over in my head as we exited the cinema, and its words rang true. '*...you don't need money if you got a little honey...*', and I swore I would never marry for money. It is hard to find true love as it is, and money loses its meaning when the person you marry is not someone you love.

The cinema rarely puts on multiple shows in one day, but *Algiers* is so popular that the world wants to see it. Thankfully, our tickets were for an early show, so we had plenty of time to go home for dinner and still be ready to meet later. We had agreed to go to our favorite bar later in the evening, the *Le Gaston.*

Mama tried to do something with my hair like she does every time I go out with the girls, but we could not talk much sense to it again either. Over the years, I came to terms with how unruly my hair was, but it still managed to get to me now and then.

Esther was wearing a beautiful but simple black dress. I thought she would be more attentive, but her mood had not changed much since we saw her in the morning.

The *La Gaston* is a mid-size bar decorated in art deco style, but everything is art deco nowadays. Mama thinks it is too progressive, but I love it. The bar is oval-shaped but thinner and longer, reminding me of a stretched-out rubber band. It has four copper pillars holding up another oval top with square lights hanging low. High chairs are lined up right along the front. Four booths are in the back, which are spacious, and each easily accommodates six-to-eight people. These booths are available on a first-come-first-serve basis, or how attentive the accompanying gentleman is to the waiter with tips. We hardly ever sit there, of course.

Smaller tables are scattered around, occupying about half of the floor giving enough room to dance. There is also a small stage and a piano where live bands perform now and then.

While waiting for Agnes to arrive, I asked Esther what was bothering her. She was slightly off from earlier in the morning, and I am surprised

I even sensed it. Usually, I am more oblivious than being able to pick up cues, and Esther gave me a bewildered look as soon as I asked.

"Are you not reading the news, Cécile?" She snapped at me, and her tone shocked me for a moment.

"Yes, somewhat," I lied hesitantly. I tried to remember anything Papa may have said in the last couple of weeks or any headlines I saw in the paper as I flipped through the pages, but I failed to recall and could not form the faintest of lies.

"Oh, Cécile, *C'est Bon*, it's okay. I'm sorry," Esther quickly apologized when she noticed the guilty look on my face. I just sat there in utter disbelief as she softly and quietly explained that her family and other Jewish friends were anxious about news coming from Germany.

Esther's family came to Paris from Budapest when she was still a baby, and her little sister Ruth was not even born yet. Esther neither remembers much about Hungary nor speaks the language. *Monsieur* Klotz made sure his family had fully integrated and spoke French fluently without an accent. Despite running a small practice, he was very particular about his customers. He only took on a handful of patrons, Jewish families, and *Monsieur* Klotz wanted to keep it this way. Small, tight, and very private. I do not think their neighbors even knew them.

Esther said Germany had introduced a new law that made Jewish people add either "Israel" or "Sara" to their names. That would make Esther, Sara Klotz, which does not sound right. Why Sara? I wondered. She explained that her name would not change, but she would need a "J" stamped onto her passport if she lived in Germany.

"Good thing you live here in Paris. I don't think you would have to be afraid of having someone scribble into your passport or have to change your name," I declared with confidence.

"Cécile, I like how naïve you are. It is not about changing my name or my passport. The Germans do not like Jews and do everything possible to drive us out of the country or strip us of our rights. It's troubling, but I don't know how troubling it is," she said and paused for a minute.

This law shook Esther to her core despite not living in Germany, and I do not understand why. As quickly as she snapped at me, Esther became her usual old self. Or maybe she pretended to be.

She had nothing to worry about. France would never allow such a law to be passed, and I do not believe having my own opinion would make me naïve. Papa often calls me naïve, and now my friends do, too. That is unfair.

We were quickly distracted from our thoughts by Agnes checking her coat in the cloakroom. She wore a very stylish red dress and looked stunning. She turned heads as she walked by the patrons. Men glared at her with desire and women with utter jealousy. She is extraordinary in a most ordinary way.

"*Bonsoiiiiiir*," she greeted us as she had just stepped off the silver screen. "I am sorry for being late, but the taxi driver did not know where the *La Gaston* was! Imagine. The best bar in Paris," Agnes said as she sat down and screened the table, "What are you drinking?"

"Champagne," I said.

"Oh, too light for such a cold evening," she signaled the waiter. I hoped she referenced the night and not our apparent mood. "*Un Soixante-Quinze, s'il vous plaît*," Agnes ordered the 75, champagne, with gin and lemon juice with a bit of sugar to make it sweet. She held a cigarette between her fingers and waited patiently like a Hollywood starlet for a light. As the waiter embarrassingly looked for his matches, she slipped a small package over to Esther under the table. It was wrapped in her handkerchiefs and about the size of my palm. I caught it only from the corner of my eye, but I forgot about it instantly because I spotted the "stranger." He was sitting across the bar in one of the booths, enough for six people but all by himself, and for a split second, I locked eyes with him.

I jolted unexpectedly, which resulted in me missing my mouth. I wanted to sip my aperitif, but it all landed on my lap. DISASTER! This was the second time the stranger witnessed how clumsy I was. The waiter lit Agnes's cigarette finally and immediately handed me his handkerchief. I tried to clean up as much as possible while feeling my face flare up. I could not believe I had done something so embarrassing in front of this man again. Agnes and Esther were still whispering but burst into laughter when they realized what I had done.

The waiter quickly disappeared to attend to other tables. After cleaning my skirt, the waiter returned with three glasses of champagne.

"*Mesdemoiselles*, that gentleman in the corner is sending you these drinks," the waiter stated as he gently signaled toward the booth with his head, "He would also like to invite you to join him."

Esther and Agnes glanced toward the booth with curiosity while I looked the other way, trying to avoid making eye contact, and they immediately noticed my nonchalance.

"Who is that, Cécile?" Esther and Agnes asked almost at the same time in interrogative voices. Rightfully so, because I have never had a committed relationship since we have been friends, and we go back a long time. We were starting elementary school and ended up in the same class, and we became friends almost instantly. We were so close that we felt we had acquired two new sisters. We had no secrets then; now, they wanted to know why a stranger was sending us drinks and why I acted so avoidant.

"Why is he sending you drinks and inviting us over?" The interrogation continued. Both looked confused before Esther's face lightened up as she snapped her finger.

"Oh, I know. That is the stranger you mentioned yesterday, isn't he? The stranger who came to the *Tabac* to buy cigarettes, didn't he, Cécile?"

I hushed them down as I passed a look at the handsome man I swooned over on Friday. He seemed to be staring at us with curiosity swimming in his eyes.

I lowered my voice and nodded, "Yes, he is the one. How embarrassing! I spilled my drink when I noticed him, and he saw that!"

"It's not embarrassing. Your clumsiness makes you so endearing, Cécile," Agnes laughed and stood up with her champagne in her hand.

"So, are we going or not? This gentleman went through the trouble of buying us drinks. Let's thank him," Agnes said with the utmost confidence of a femme fatale. How does she not want to get married? I wondered.

Although Agnes declares how independent and career-oriented she is and that men should judge her based on her intellect, she sure knows how to get what she wants. Esther stood up and joined Agnes, and I prayed that the floor would open underneath my feet to bury me alive. I reluctantly followed them to the booth like the brood's littlest and most ponderous duckling.

"*Mesdemoiselles*," he greeted us as he stood up and offered seats as we approached his table. He looked much taller than I remembered, towering over us like a giant, or maybe I was tiny, like *Alice in Wonderland* when she drank the 'Drink Me Potion' and shrank.

Once I stood solidly on my feet, I could not help but think how handsome he looked in that black tuxedo. On the other hand, I was nowhere near as lovely a sight, which embarrassed me the most. I felt beet red from head to toe, especially with a large wet patch on my skirt.

"It is my pleasure to introduce myself. My name is Ludwig König, and I'm honored to have such lovely ladies accompanying me this wonderful evening," he said in his charming voice.

Esther nearly fainted and grabbed the table for support as we sat down but did it so elegantly that no one noticed. I was still very embarrassed, so I nudged Esther to sit by him on his left while Agnes occupied his right side.

"Pardon me," Esther said as she pushed me out of the booth, "I need to powder my nose," she rushed off toward the ladies' room. At first, I did not know why Esther left so hastily. Then, I realized how cunning she was. She wanted me to sit closer to him because she knew I was in awe of him, and I was star-struck, so to speak. See, Diary, what good friends I have!

Her plan worked as Ludwig turned his attention toward me. "*Mademoiselle* Cécile," he said as I moved in to take Esther's seat. "It is my pleasure seeing you again, and I wouldn't have dreamt of seeing you so soon. You are a sight for sore eyes this beautiful evening."

"*Monsieur* König, it is my pleasure as well." I swallowed my embarrassment with a big gulp of champagne and smiled.

"Please, call me Ludwig," he said as he grabbed my hand again and kissed it.

Agnes was looking at me with her eyes wide open, and I could not help but notice that Ludwig paid no attention to her. He ignored Agnes completely, even though she was in her dazzling dress and behaved in a manner fit for a diva. She acted surprised because she had never seen any man flirting with me.

Ludwig smiled, and I tried making sense of why a man as handsome as a Hollywood star would rather have small talk with me instead of Agnes or anyone else in the bar. There sure were plenty of gorgeous ladies he could have chosen, and Agnes was not used to not being in the center of attention, so if Ludwig did not give her what she thought she deserved, she was there to take it.

As Ludwig turned to Agnes, I drank my champagne and put the empty glass on the table when Esther returned from the bathroom. It started to feel hot, or maybe the drink was getting to my head. Whatever it was, I felt lightheaded, but drinking the champagne helped douse my embarrassment, so I did not mind. Before I knew it, the waiter was there with another glass of this bubbly goodness. I grabbed it and held onto it like a life preserver, and I soon joined in the conversation with Agnes and Ludwig. Agnes was ready to introduce everyone formally.

"This is *Mademoiselle* Cécile Dubonnet," she pointed to me, "but you have already met her," she said with a teasing tone. I am unsure if I smiled or grinned, but I was too hypnotized by Ludwig's mesmerizing eyes to notice the difference.

"And this is *Mademoiselle* Élizabeth Bossard," she said as she introduced Esther, placing a hand on her shoulder and giving me a subtle kick under the table. My face must have given away my confusion. I was ready to open my mouth and say something when Agnes quickly kicked my leg again, but much harder this time, and shook her head ever so slightly, indicating that I should stay quiet.

"*Bonsoir Mademoiselle!*" Ludwig said and kissed Esther's trembling hand. Luckily, no one noticed my actions.

We had a few more glasses of champagne and had a really fun time. All four of us danced. Ludwig took turns with whom he took to the dancefloor, but he showered me with his attention the most. I felt pretty that night! The champagne calmed my nerves and made me feel special. I did not mind my hair, the now-dried spot on my skirt, or recall any embarrassing moments. I was a new me, a *femme fatale* like Agnes.

Sadly, our night had to end since our curfew was eleven o'clock. We said our goodbyes to Ludwig as we headed home.

"*Mademoiselle* Cécile, I had a wonderful time with you this evening, and if you allow me to, I would love to see you again," he said and kissed my hand again. I could feel butterflies in my stomach as he smiled, but I quickly recovered with a smile of my own.

"*Merci, Monsieur.* Thank you, I would like that," I answered as he helped me with my coat; then, he attended to Agnes's and Esther's. I mean Élizabeth's. I was still confused about the name change, but I forgot about it as we headed out the door.

Esther and Agnes reminisced about the night on our way home. They giggled and laughed about me spilling my drink and how much fun they had. Agnes teased me about Ludwig liking me too much, but I did not mind. My head was light and spinning like I was in a merry-go-round. I am unsure if it was the champagne, Ludwig's attention, or this perfect mixture of both, but I was floating, humming the last song playing when we left. I was drunk off my happiness, and I welcomed the way Agnes teased me. What a great night we had.

Agnes and Esther sat me down on a bench just outside the *Métro* stop and quickly dragged me back to reality from my romantic thoughts. I did not want to come down from the clouds, but I had no choice, and Agnes gave me no choice.

"Cécile," Agnes started firmly, and I did not like how serious she looked suddenly.

"I want to explain what happened in the *La Gaston* tonight. Germany is signing restrictive laws against the Jews, and before this happens in France, we must ensure that Esther and her family are safe."

"What do you mean safe?" I asked with total confusion, "They are safe."

Agnes patted my arm with a strange look on her face. I could not decipher what she was thinking.

"Papa got new identification cards for Esther's whole family. Listen to me, Cécile," Agnes shook me gently because I was trailing off, "It is important that you stay strong and committed."

She looked deeply into my eyes with a warning look and continued, "Do not call her Esther again. Ever. She is now Élizabeth Bossard, and you should address her as such."

"I feel less confused why you introduced Esther as Élizabeth, but France will never follow Germany's antisemitic views, would it?" I asked as I turned to Esther, "Would it?"

"I don't know, Cécile. I don't know," Esther said as she shook her head in disbelief. She seemed lost but not the way a vagabond traveler would be lost. Esther found nothing wander-worthy in this wilderness she headed toward. "The only thing I know is that the change will not be easy for us," she said in a dreamy voice but not speaking to any of us, particularly. "I need to get a new job, and we need to move to a different district where no one knows us." She gazed at a leaf in a puddle, hunched over by the unknown problems that would face her.

"You're moving away? And this new identity. Does that mean that we can't be friends anymore?" I asked them in shock and disbelief, breaking the momentary silence.

Esther gave a small smile as she sat up and came back from staring oblivion in the face.

"We can still be friends, of course, and even your mother can continue to work for my father," Esther stated, "But all of us will have to remember who we are now and never mention the Klotz name again."

My mind was running with a thousand questions, and I did my best to get all the answers.

"You told me nothing about this on Friday or this morning." I wanted to sound accusatory because I did not want to show them how hurt I was for their ruining my mood.

"Cécile, I couldn't at the time, but I am telling you now."

"Do you already know what your family now will do for a living?" I asked, terrified that I was losing her right there and then on that bench.

"I have a new job in the *Centre Hospitalier Sainte Anne Hospital de Paris Psychiatrie Neurologie Neurochirurgie*. Papa will set up a new practice in the fifteenth district, and we will move to district seventeen," she replied, detailing the plan.

"That seems very scattered… and a loony bin? Out of all places, you will work at the loony bin?" I sighed, but she assured me it was far less messy than the general hospital. "I don't know, Esther. Are you sure Paris is large enough for you to hide under a new name?" I asked her hesitantly. I still could not believe this was happening. I could not have had that much champagne. It was unimaginable how I had had so much fun just a few minutes ago, but suddenly the ground felt like quicksand, swallowing us all.

"It is not just a new name, but a whole new character we must play now. Just like in the films. Paris is now our stage, and it's a risk we have to take," she replied wistfully and then continued with a determined look, "If we have to leave France, we will, but at the moment, we are just taking precautionary measures."

I kept firing my questions while Agnes remained the quiet observer because she knew about this change. She knew all of it, planned it, and perfectly executed it without anyone noticing.

"*Tres Bien*, very well," I replied sadly with defeat.

"I know I can trust you, Cécile, but promise you won't let anyone know me as Esther anymore."

She gave me a confident look, and I could see the trust shining brightly in her eyes. I clasped Esther's hand in my own and gave her a nod.

"You have my word Esther, I will support you, and I pledge my life that I have never known an Esther Klotz."

"Let us swear that we will never disclose this to anyone, no matter the circumstances. We have to keep this locked away forever," Agnes finally said and placed her hand on top of ours. We hugged each other tightly, and that hug sealed our secret.

On my way back home, the only thought I had was not how lucky I was for having been showered with attention by a gentleman. Oh no. All I could think about was hiding you, Dear Diary, so no one could find you. I have to find a spot better than my dresser drawer.

I searched for the perfect place and soon found a loose floorboard under the radiator that had leaked at some point. The water had bent the board, and the nail came right out without even pulling on it too hard. Underneath was an endless system of pipes, just like the subway, which was a good start. I pushed some furniture around to cover this area, but this was still not good enough. I swore to my best friends that I would keep their secret safe and needed a place no one could even think of looking.

Chapter 5

Wound Up in a Journal

Tuesday, 19 October 1999

Hénri set the diary down in his lap as Louis Armstrong started his greatest hits all over again.

"What a crazy story," he thought and wondered if Cécile were alive. He knew that many teenage girls wrote diaries, but he did not realize that adults did too. Perhaps they wanted to capture a part of their life to reflect on later and reminisce, like a photo album without the pictures. Or maybe a part of them was lonely, and they were using the diary to keep company, or perhaps it was therapy.

Whatever motivated Cécile, Hénri could sense some loneliness in her words. The need for love and affection came through those stained pages. She had kind friends, a loving family, and lived a relatively good life, but a part of her craved attention from a man who had merely smiled at her. It took one smile, one dance, and a few glasses of champagne to thoroughly sweep her off her feet.

Reading a love story was one thing, but Hénri acutely picked up on the replacement of identities—so bluntly done but perfectly executed.

"Cécile Dubonnet. What did you see?" Hénri wondered.

Hénri thought he might be witnessing the budding of the *La Résistance*, but he knew that the movement did not start until Germany invaded France in 1940. This was still 1938. Although a crisis was looming, there was no war in sight. Yet, it did not make sense to him why Agnes's father would arrange new identities for Jewish families, and suddenly he found himself just as confused as Cécile.

Hénri knew Cécile's full name now and where she lived. He intended to return the journal to its rightful owner, but he could just as easily toss it aside, but if he did, no one would ever know, but his conscience would make him miserable for the rest of his life. He knew that, but he also knew that although there was no need to continue reading such a private journal, something, an invisible force, was pulling him in.

Hénri felt many emotions: Why did he want to know more? Why did the woman's story entice him in the first place? Where would he start if he wanted to find her?

He knew he needed to do research but had to start in the library since he did not bother to have internet service installed in his temporary home. He would get it in the studio once he moved in, but until then, Hénri needed the library's computer to access the web.

There was something about an old, musty, and dim library—a portal into the past, but with internet access, it was also a gateway into the future. Hénri did not mind going because he loved visiting old libraries just as much as wandering about in old cemeteries. He knew that if he wanted to succeed, he needed to go to the more extensive libraries of Paris. The larger ones kept massive archives of historical documents, unlike the local branches; only old ladies visited for their weekly dose of mystery.

Hénri placed his headphones on the coffee table and got up from the sofa to fill his empty wineglass. He contemplated what he would do, but only for a moment before grabbing the bottle off the kitchen counter and returning to the couch.

Hénri sat down and basked in the silence. Reading the journal made him feel like an intruder, venturing into territories that did not invite him. He was peeking into a woman's life and uncovering what went through her mind and maybe even more. Does it have a happy ending, or will it reveal something sinister? What would Natalie do if she were here, he pondered, but Natalie was not here to break the silence.

Reading fictional novels is a pleasure, not only for Cécile but also for Hénri, but reading someone else's private journal without their knowledge was another. Still, Hénri felt compelled to continue, especially since he loved learning about her arcane or hidden thoughts. He finally gave in to his temptation after glancing at the diary on the couch. His entire body burned with curiosity and hunger to learn more about the woman who won him over, but, unlike Natalie, he felt as if he would betray Cécile's trust and break a promise he had never made.

Hénri dialed the first name that popped into his mind, and he waited patiently as the phone rang on the other side. He became so immersed in the journal and did not realize the passage of time. His eyes fell on the clock hanging on the wall, and he groaned in response. It was too late to cut the call, even at half-past twelve. He rubbed his tired eyes and blinked a few times as the phone rang.

As soon as he heard a clicking noise, Hénri gushed out.

"Mom, I'm so sorry for calling you so late … I can't believe you answered, but you won't believe what I found out!"

"You don't call twice a night, Hénri. Is everything all right, dear?" Frances asked in a concerned tone.

"Of course, Mom, I just wanted to tell you what I came across in the journal."

"Oh, yes," Frances remembered, "Did you read it?"

"Yes, well, not entirely, but I started it." He tried to tell her more, but she cut him off with a gasp.

"Did you find out the name of the owner?" She asked in her eccentric manner.

"Mom," Hénri sighed and asked every existent and non-existent God why he had to be given such a fiery woman as a mother.

"Okay, okay, dear, go on. I won't interrupt, I promise." Frances became quiet, and Hénri picked up the diary.

"As I thought from the handwriting, the diary belongs to a woman named Cécile Dubonnet, dating back to 1938. Isn't that crazy? This diary is over sixty years old." Hénri could not hold back his excitement.

"Oh, that's very interesting," his mother commented, and Hénri knew he had her full attention now, and she wanted to hear more.

"I know, and it gets better," Hénri talked fast with excitement in his voice, almost too rapidly for Frances to understand. "The apartment I'm working on was where she lived her whole life. She hid the diary under the floor, meaning she did not lose it but left it there on purpose. I think I know the reason, but I have only read a few days of entries. She had two best friends, and they became rather giddy from time to time. Some of her entries are truly funny.

"Funny, how?"

"She loves movies, and I think she was in love with every actor on the silver screen. She wanted to marry all of them. I don't recognize most names, like Charles Boyer, but I do Johnny Weissmuller, the swimmer turned Tarzan."

Frances laughed at the other end of the receiver, "Times are not much different now, I suppose."

"Then, the story takes an odd turn because one of her friends was a Jewish girl, and she and her family had received a new identity. Isn't that insane? I didn't know that changing identities through unofficial channels was attainable back in the day."

"Unofficially? Do you mean illegally? Frances asked in a clarifying manner.

"I am not sure, actually," Hénri shrugged and caught his breath, "It seems her other friend got them through her father. He was the Deputy to the Director-General of the *Gendarmerie,* so he could have pulled some strings."

"Well, it was probably difficult, but getting them was not impossible by the sound of it. It's insane and fascinating at the same time," she declared.

Hénri nodded in agreement, though, of course, Frances could not see his actions. "That's what I thought. Good to know I'm not the only one who finds this bizarre. But I also thought maybe this was the beginning of the Resistance, which was why she hid the diary and concealed their secret."

She ignored his remark, but Hénri did not press.

"I wonder if she's still alive," she said instead. Hénri noted that the discussion at least had piqued her curiosity.

"I thought the same thing," Hénri said and continued outlining his plan, "I'll do some research after l read the diary further and see if I can find more details. It won't take me long. Some pages are missing, and some of them have burnt a little. I'm unsure whether someone or Cécile deliberately set it ablaze or the building caught on fire at some point."

Hénri caught himself. He called her Cécile for the first time, and it felt like he had given life to her by saying her name aloud. Frances was concerned about the fire, and she instantly changed the subject.

"Did you notice any evidence of fire in the building?"

"Not yet, no, and Jakov didn't say anything either. That's why I think Cécile tried destroying it. But the building itself is also old, so who knows? It may have been rebuilt completely at some point, and the damage wouldn't be distinguishable."

"She may have tried to destroy it. It would make perfect sense why she would not want this to be found," she said, and Hénri could picture her gesturing while saying that, as if waving her hands would make her voice louder. "What else did you find out?" Frances continued.

"Well, the diary was a birthday gift from her mother, who belonged to a middle-class family; Cécile was an only child. She sounds like a naïve young girl who, as I said, is in love with Hollywood. It's almost as if I know her now," Hénri said as he looked down at the diary resting in his lap.

"Well, you're reading her thoughts. How does it feel to be inside the head of a twenty-year-old woman?" she asked him curiously but immediately regretted it. Hénri was too focused or tipsy for his wounds to be torn by his mother's question, and he did not even notice.

"It feels. . . eerie, to be honest," Hénri admitted. His mother laughed, and Hénri chuckled along with her. "Oh, Mom, I miss you and your antics," Hénri said.

"I miss you too, darling. But tell me more about this woman; she sounds fascinating," Frances said.

Typical mother… switching the topic when she knows it will make her face her emotions, Hénri thought. Quite frankly, she reminded him of Cécile's father.

"Well, when she wasn't in the cinema with her friends, she read mystery novels and ate sweets," Hénri snickered at the simplicity of her life before continuing, "I might visit the shop by the *Odéon*, just to see if it is still there."

"You know where she worked?" she asked him in surprise.

"Indeed. This woman wrote everything down, from where she worked to where her friends worked. It's almost as if I'm reading a fictional story. I know her friends' names, where they lived, and what their parents did for a living. I know everything about Cécile now. All of it is written here," Hénri continued and lifted the diary as if his mother could see him through the phone.

"It seems like it should be effortless to track her down if she's still alive. But remember, this diary dates just before World War II, so who knows where she is," Frances reminded him.

"I want to know if she's alive. I want to find her and give the journal back to her. I know the *Cinéma Le Champo* is still there, and it's functional to this day. That was the cinema she went to most frequently. The shop where she worked was in the area, too. I'll go by there tomorrow and see if it's still there, and if it is, someone might know something about her," Hénri said and instantly realized that he was now living in a parallel universe with Cécile. At least, that is what it felt like.

"Oh, how exciting, Hénri! I wonder if we can call a museum or someone. This person could be as important as Anne Frank. Who knows! Or we can call the police," Frances exclaimed excitedly.

"What? Why would we call the police?" he asked in bewilderment.

"Okay, okay, not the police, then. I do not know. I've never come across something like this in my life, and I've lived long enough to have my fair share of oddities, being as old as fifty-four."

"So, you admit you're old, then?" Hénri joked, knowing that age was a delicate subject with his mother.

"Only as a number, dear. Only as a number," Frances said, and Hénri could hear the smile in her voice. He could tell that she was smiling. "The museum, son. The museum isn't a bad idea!"

"That isn't a bad idea, but I think I'll keep the museum as a last resort if I hit a dead end with my research," Hénri told her as he closed his eyes tiredly and sighed. "I'll go to the *Bibliothèque Sainte-Geneviève* tomorrow morning."

"Why would you go to a library when you have the diary? Just use the internet."

Hénri sighed again; "I haven't signed up for the internet, which I'll do when I move into the studio. Besides, I don't think I'll find historical documents online."

"All right, but let me know if you need anything. I love you," Frances said in a maternal tone, and Hénri replied with a grin.

"Love you too, mom."

After Hénri hung up, he went to bed. He was exhausted, and with a big day ahead, he wanted to be rested to face it head-on. He often fell asleep on his couch, but he slept in his bed that night, and all he could think about was Cécile.

★★★

Hénri was so vested in the story he even dreamt about her, and when the dream turned into a nightmare, he woke up. He blinked slowly, trying to make sense of his bearings. His eyes did not adjust to the sunlight peeking through the curtains, temporarily blinding him. He stared at the ceiling for a few minutes before checking the clock. It was seven in the morning, and Hénri could not remember the last time he woke up so early, especially after going to bed so late. "Great, now I'm having nightmares about Hitler," he muttered as he rubbed his eyes. The imaginary sounds of flying bullets still rang in his ears, and he could not remove the image of burning buildings and smoke from his mind. Hénri was startled when Alice hopped on his bed. "Oh, Alice, you scared me." He picked up his cat and stared into her beautiful green eyes. "Do you think it's strange that I'm dreaming about a woman I've never seen?" Hénri asked her, and Alice stared back at him before she meowed.

"So, you agree." He put Alice down and watched as the cat made her way to the bottom of the bed. He had wound up in Cécile's mind so much that he saw things that were not even in the diary.

After shaking off the nightmare and feeding Alice, he prepared to head out for the day. He wore black trousers and a black button-up shirt tucked around his waist. He grabbed his tweed coat and a scarf since it was colder than usual. Hénri stepped out of his studio and looked up. The weather was deceiving. Not a single cloud was in the sky; the sun blinded him, but the air was crisp and cold.

Hénri got on his bicycle and made his way to the library after a quick stop at a coffee shop. He decided to pick up breakfast on the go after he checked his wallet and sighed with relief at the sight of the few notes. The warm butter croissant and a hot cup of latte warmed him up from the inside.

He reread some of the intriguing tidbits from the diary. He wondered about Élizabeth and what type of life she and her family faced under an alias. Their lives had to be taxing, watching over their shoulders and remembering not to use their old name anymore.

"What did they do if they ran into someone they knew?" Hénri wondered, but Paris was large enough, and moving a few districts away may have solved that dilemma for the family.

After breakfast, he made his way to *Sainte-Geneviève*, one of the oldest libraries in Paris, with the most visually pleasing reading room façade engraved with the names of remarkable scholars, poets, and philosophers, such as Galileo, Copernicus, and Shakespeare. They formed a true gateway between the past and the future, storing manuscripts dating back to the sixth century and rows of computers set up with the internet.

The lofty ceilings were decorated with exposed iron structural elements—a strange mix of modern and old. A vast space in the middle of the reading room had tables and chairs in clear alignment. Every table of four had a small reading lamp in the middle, giving a soft glow, spotlighting the secrets an open book reveals to its reader.

"These lamps remind me of the mushroom the caterpillar sat on as he smoked his hookah," chuckled Hénri as he recalled this scene from his favorite book, *Alice's Adventures in Wonderland.* And this book was the origin of his cat's name. Everything had a meaning; from that perspective, Hénri was not all that different from Cécile.

Being an architectural enthusiast, Hénri knew everything about the building. The structure was unique, even for the architect who shared his first name, Hénri Labrouste. The windows on the walls loomed over the occupants in an extravagant design. Labrouste was very forward-thinking for the nineteenth century, but his ideas stood the test of time and are still remarkable today.

Hénri sat in front of one of the computers after paying a fee, but he knew he was investing his money in something he had already invested his time in, and the results would be worth his money and time. He typed Cécile Dubonnet's name into the search engine and hit enter. He was unsure what he hoped to find, but he believed something would pop up. The machine hummed underneath the desk with a green light blinking, indicating that the processor was hard at work. The hourglass spun around before the search engine spat out the results.

There were no hits for her full name, but the name Dubonnet came up multiple times. That did not surprise him because Dubonnet was a common surname. Hénri sighed, then clicked image search. He realized that going through the sites one by one would be exhausting, and he was unsure what he was expecting to find just by looking at pictures.

"If Cécile were twenty years old in 1938, that would make her seventy-nine today," he muttered to himself as he quickly did the math aloud.

He skipped over the pictures of young women. He paid attention to other older ones, but it did not lead him anywhere. Some looked promising, and he clicked on a few with excitement, only to be let down by them. He hated how image search raised his hopes and then shot them down.

He spent three to four hours in front of the monitor before finally giving up on the virtual research, proving futile. Hénri sat back in the chair, becoming more uncomfortable with each passing second. With a defeated sigh, he decided that he would have to walk through the story of Cécile Dubonnet the old-fashioned way. He will have to go on the journey of this young lady by reading her diary to the end.

Chapter 6

A Changing World

Saturday, 29 October 1938

Dear Diary,

I am finally back to writing again. I am sorry I neglected you for an entire week, but it seems life has its strange ways of throwing all of us off track, or I am not good at staying true to my commitment. Either way, I could not find solitude for long enough to write my thoughts. I am still distraught and confused about what happened in *La Gaston* last Saturday night. I met the man of my dreams, but I also almost lost a friend.

I suppose I did 'lose' a friend by acquiring a 'new' one, but I am scared of what I pen here for fear of being labeled a traitor lest someone, someday, finds this diary. My memories were linked to Esther, not to this person, Élizabeth. It feels like I am talking about a stranger, but Élizabeth assured me she was still the same despite the new name. I hope that believing her will help me remember, and we will eventually create new memories as Élizabeth, Agnes, and me.

The question I had repeatedly been asking myself was, how did we all get here? How did this happen? It could have happened overnight, or I had not realized the growing tension in the air until last week, and I am afraid it will not go away soon. I see a different side of Europe, and I now see that Élizabeth was right, and she had been scared for all the right reasons.

When Papa and Mama discussed politics a few weeks ago, I excused myself to my room to read my book. Now, I sit through their discussions after dinner and listen to every word they say. Papa does the talking most time. Mama sits quietly, listening to him rambling as she anxiously attends to her crocheting. While Papa is off on a tangent, I browse through the news articles in the paper, and all I see scares me. It makes me wonder why the Germans harbor such hatred for the Jews. What have they done?

★★★

"Oh, Cécile," said Hénri and adjusted the cushion behind his neck. "You cannot even imagine what is about to happen." He knew. Hénri also knew what Cécile did not, that the Jews had been mistreated more than any other group in the world. That anti-Judaism is probably the longest hatred in the world, going back to ancient Greece. As the group adapted, this strong aversion became a snowball rolling down the hill, growing larger, picking up social and economic excuses only to crash in Germany during World War II. While Hénri learned the facts from his history books in school, Cécile was about to witness it all.

Hénri paused for a second in his thoughts. Will Cécile actually, see it? He wondered and was very tempted to flip to the last page, but he stopped. He still saw himself as an intruder, but his strong desire to learn more overpowered his morals. Thus, curiosity can be considered a weapon rather than a handy tool.

Hénri rationalized that curiosity leads people astray from their principles from time to time. He knew he was not committing a crime. However, he still felt anxious as the battle between his curiosity and morals climaxed. He decided to continue this journey with Cécile on his side, and with another flip of the page, Hénri traveled back to 1938. He stepped into the life of a love-struck woman, Cécile Dubonnet, and soon forgot everything around him.

★★★

I cannot fathom how Paris can live its busy life and rest easy at night, while the reality is not so simple for Élizabeth, and it may not be for a while. She rang the *Tabac* a few times last week, but I do not see her as often now, and I miss her. I must remind myself that she is the same friend I have loved dearly. Élizabeth is not a stranger, and she will never be.

I miss seeing her every day. Or at least to have the opportunity to see her whenever I want. I accept that she is busy settling down into a new home and a new job, but I am selfish enough to want to spend the same amount of time with her as we did while she lived close by.

She quit her nursing job in the hospital for that looney bin. She is wasting her potential. She deserves a better workplace, but she told me she had no other choice. It was either working at the institute or not working at all. I told her there was still time to become an actress. That made her giggle. I had said that in jest because I needed to hear her laugh, but I could still sense the worry and fear lingering in her voice.

It is difficult for her to be happy; I see that. She moved to a new place and entered a new neighborhood. Being surrounded by strangers can be hard, especially since that change was abrupt but necessary. From what I could see, she did not get enough time to prepare herself for this shift in her life, which affected her, but she was in no place to complain about it since she knew it was for her safety.

Élizabeth and her entire family gathered their belongings and moved to a new apartment from the 20th district to the 17th district two days after she told me the news. The move was sudden and surprising, but everything about this change seemed abrupt to me—the name, the move, everything. I feel like Sleeping Beauty, who had been awakened after years of sleeping, although it was not a charming prince who kissed me but a tyrant whose actions shook me awake.

61

First, I thought she would move to a place far away from Paris, but it is just a few districts, so it is not as remote as I thought it would be. Before everything changed, Élizabeth and I used to meet whenever we wanted. Now, it takes some planning to see her. I do not mind it, but it bothers me how politics interrupted our lives. Maybe it put some distance between us, but it sure would not cause a rift. I cannot help but admire her strength to do all this without breaking down. What would I do? I know I would not be able to handle it as calmly as she does. I want everything to be where it was a week ago. For her. For all of us.

Monsieur Bossard, Élizabeth's papa, has the same plan as his daughter. He will set up his practice around January in his new neighborhood. He is waiting for things to settle down a bit, which gives him and Élizabeth plenty of time to establish their new lives.

They are indeed the kindest people on earth, and seeing them facing such barriers is heartbreaking. Mama decided it was best if she did not follow them to their new location and work for him anymore. She says it is the safest option, and *Monsieur* Bossard agrees.

As a parting gift to Élizabeth's father, Mama had the whole family over for dinner on Tuesday. We sat in the living room while Papa and *Monsieur* Bossard lectured us on what to do and what not to do, which agitated me a little. I felt overwhelmed but also annoyed at the same time because I wanted to go to my bedroom with Élizabeth and listen to the radio. I wanted to spend all the time I could with her while she was with me, but Papa and *Monsieur* Bossard continued to discuss the conditions and rules with us throughout the rest of the night.

Élizabeth's sister, Ruth, or Mimi as we call her now, is nine years old and looks different from her sister. Mimi is a lot shorter for her age, but her heavy black curly locks that bounce with every move she makes will make up for that when she becomes a fine young lady. Mimi was excited about moving to a new home and going to a new school despite the family's hardship. For her, this was an adventure, but she also does not see the world for what it is.

Children are pure, and they have no worries in the world. They are confined to their little world, and I envy them. I wish I could also ignore everything terrible around me. I wanted to be like Mimi, clueless and happy. Mimi is a sweet child with spunk, and she loves her new name. She skipped around the dinner table, saying, "Mimi, Mimi. My name is Mimi." I was delighted to see her like that. I could not help but think how the new name suited her as she danced around with her ragdoll in her arms, with her sass in full display. The ragdoll had a round face with pink cheeks and curly jet-black hair—a complete copy of her. Her mother named her "Mimi" as a reminder. Very clever, I have to say.

I must be secretive regarding their identities, even in my thoughts. Keeping you, my Diary, under the floorboard was good, but I needed to make it impossible for others to find, although I am afraid I will be part of the 'others' and as forgetful as I can be. Still, I needed to find a more secure place, so after a few hours of looking, I discovered that if I removed a couple of bricks and hid the diary in the cavity, no one in this world would ever find it. It is impossible to see. I must lay on the floor and reach deep with my arm until I feel it. The space was perfect. I took one of my older shirts and wrapped the diary in it to protect the leather, just as I needed to protect my friend. Oh, I may have to admit how close I grew to an object. I almost think I should register myself in the loony bin. What a perfect idea! That way, I can see Élizabeth every day! She would tell me not to joke about this if she were here, although we would laugh about my silly joke. But it can happen, can it not, Diary?

Only if I had someone to share this humor with, but you are more than enough for me now, and I will do my best to keep you safe. Surprisingly, I did not end up moving the furniture like I thought I needed, but I slid the carpet over the board. The hiding area is in the corner of my bedroom, near the window, and entirely out of sight. No one will notice it, not even Papa, which is important since Papa is very observant. Still, I am trying to figure out how I have not been caught smuggling mortar in my coat pocket every morning. I am as discreet and clever as possible when I throw it out of my pocket after getting off the *Métro* on my way to work.

Speaking of work, I completely forgot to tell you. I was so caught up in Élizabeth and her new life that I lost sight of telling you about mine. Ludwig came to see me in the *Tabac* on a Friday morning. I would have been happier if he had not visited me unexpectedly, and I had something or someone to look forward to, but that man had the nerve to stand by the entrance again before I even opened the shop. Why does he keep coming by before the opening time?

It was gray outside that morning as clouds covered every inch of the once-blue sky. It is still October, but it reminded me that winter is just around the corner. I was annoyed by the drizzle and held my umbrella in one hand while I used the other to dig into my purse for the keys. At first, I did not see him standing there; I was too occupied with my thoughts, but when I looked up, I caught his gaze. My heart skipped a beat. He smiled with a cigarette between his fingers and leaned against the wall next to the front door. I stared at him, bewildered. I watched him smoke leisurely like he was at the beach.

However, my bewilderment soon turned into shyness as he greeted me cheerily.

"*Mademoiselle* Cécile, it's nice to see you again. You are just as lovely on a gray Friday morning as on a hot Saturday night on the dancefloor," he said and kissed my hand.

"*Bonjour, Monsieur* König," I said, but my voice choked. I forgot to breathe for a moment as I stared into the eyes of this handsome stranger, trying to make sense of the "hot Saturday night." My head spun around faster than I could blink.

I must remind myself not to refer to him as a stranger because I learned quite a bit about him that night. You see, Diary, Ludwig is a diplomat, which I think is a very fancy job, at the *L'Ambassade d'Alle-magne à Paris*, the German Embassy. I have never met a diplomat before. Besides being handsome, he is polished and very polite. Although he is

German, which scares me a little, I know he is a kind-hearted man. I feel it.

Chapter 7

Ludwig

Tuesday, 1 November 1938

Dear Diary,

I always felt as if the world were against me. I have never had anyone who yearned for me, and only in my dreams have I imagined being on the arm of a man like Ludwig; yet, here we are. Someone I am fond of fancies me back. He lifted me up in his palm and gently put me on the puffiest cloud in the sky, where I intend to stay forever.

I, Cécile, will finally, finally experience *Affaire de Coeur*. All the romantic moments I shared in my life came from stories, but this love affair will go beyond all the films I have ever watched and all the books I have ever read. I, who never dared to talk to a boy in my younger years, let alone a man, will finally be in a real courtship. I knew I was not delusional when I told you Ludwig is charming. He is handsome, charismatic, and chivalrous and has a swoon-worthy smile.

I forget about everything when he looks at me. He puts me into a hypnotic daze, and my thoughts flutter like a butterfly flying from flower to flower. The reality slowly finds its way back after he leaves the store to quickly remind me of the 'silent war' against Jews in Germany. And at that moment, my once soft white cloud turns into a raging thunderstorm that thrashes me around like a bronco its rider.

Strange how we perceive time. We were in the *La Gaston* a week and a half ago, yet, a lifetime's worth of events happened in this short period. I wonder how Élizabeth is holding up; nevertheless, I look for Ludwig's face in the crowd every waking moment.

I wonder whether the new place she settled into is as great as she imagined, but I cannot help but dream of walking down the street with Ludwig as my friends turn their heads with envy. I still wish some things would go back to normal—back to a week and a half ago when Ludwig swept me off my feet, but then, none of the trouble in the world existed. A selfish part of me wants Élizabeth and Ludwig to be with me, but the sensible part knows it is better if I keep quiet about one another. For now.

I spent every moment with Élizabeth since we met in school, so it feels strange not to have her in my life as I previously knew her. I wish she relied on me more, but I do not fault her. Despite being the only child of my parents, I still cannot take charge of my life all that well, although I have become a little more responsible these past few days. God only knows what kind of nightmare she is living in while I chase my fairytale. Oh, what paradoxical world do I live in? No surprise that people end up in the mental ward—this world is madness!

I travel from one world to another in a blink of an eye when Ludwig comes by the shop, but I do not seem to end up either in the past or the future, unlike the protagonist in H. G. Wells's novel, The Time Traveller. It is the same day but only different. I certainly hope that is what true love is supposed to feel, or else I will end up in the looney bin under the care of Élizabeth.

It was raining yesterday morning as I rushed through the last October shower and quickly opened the store to step inside. When I closed my umbrella, I realized that Ludwig had been standing outside, leaning against the wall as usual, in a uniform, standing bravely against the rain dripping down on him. I could not help but stare at him for a second through the glass. His uniform made him look taller, more sophisticated, and more charming. You could say I was star-struck for a moment, Diary, but none of the actors on the silver screen made me feel the way I felt at that moment. I snapped out of my stupor and opened the door. He tipped his hat to greet me.

"Good morning, *Mademoiselle* Cécile." He smiled at me despite being drenched in the rain.

"Oh, *Monsieur* König! What are you doing there standing in the rain? Don't you have an umbrella?" I asked him while holding the door. Briefly, I saw a look I could not recognize flashing through his eyes. For a moment, Ludwig almost looked vulnerable. "You'll catch a cold at the end." I trailed off as Ludwig gave me a lopsided grin that made him look more boyish than a man. Darling, I thought as Ludwig spoke.

"I didn't even realize it was raining. The memory of your beautiful face kept me in the sunshine," Ludwig said with that wonderfully deep voice of his, which made me blush.

"Don't make fun of me," I told him, feeling uncomfortable with the flattery he was giving me. I was not used to hearing charm from anyone, let alone from a handsome man like him.

Ludwig only shook his head, "It's true, *Mademoiselle*. I cannot bring myself to stop thinking about you."

I only gaped at him because I did not know how to respond. I turned to stone, and Ludwig did not look like he wanted me to reply to him, so I quickly changed the topic. I could not bear to watch him stand under the rain, and I certainly did not want to get wet either.

"Please come in and dry yourself. I will not open for another fifteen minutes," I said and opened the door wider. Ludwig was dripping wet, as expected, but I paid little attention to the puddle forming by his feet. "You can hang your jacket and your hat on the coat hanger," I told him as I pointed toward the corner of the room where the coat hanger stood next to the armchairs. The way he stood there made me more aware of his presence for some strange reason. Much more than when we met him at the *La Gaston* or any other time he came by. Ludwig was strangely intimidating, or perhaps his uniform was a constant reminder of who he was. I did not know diplomats wore uniforms, but I am nothing but a commoner who works at a tobacco shop. I reminded myself as I tried to find something to busy myself with. What do I really know?

"Would you care for a cup of coffee or some tea?" I asked him while trying to avoid looking straight at him. I was petrified that I would do something silly again.

"That is kind of you, Cécile. A cup of coffee would be wonderful, and I'll take it black, with no sugar," he said calmly and unbuttoned his jacket to let it dry. My eyes met Ludwig's, and a shiver went through my spine. It is just the weather, I told myself. It was certainly not the intensity hidden in his eyes as he gazed at me. Of course not. That would be daft, right?

I looked away as quickly as possible and cranked up the heat since my clothes were slightly damp despite having an umbrella. I went over to the counter to hang my coat in the back along with my hat. I placed the percolator on the tiny gas stove, grabbed a few cigarette cartons, and returned to the front of the counter. Ludwig was leisurely sitting in the armchair, looking out the window, smoking his cigarette, and watching people rushing by. He jumped up like a child caught stealing candy from the tin box when I stepped back in.

"Thank you so much for your hospitality, Cécile. I did not mean to be a bother today, and it was foolish of me not to be able to predict today's weather," he said as he put his cigarette out in the large, heavy crystal ashtray.

"It was kind of foolish of you," I said bravely with a giggle, and Ludwig seemed puzzled for a moment before he looked away. I thought I had offended him, but I noticed the slight smirk at the corner of his lips and relaxed.

"I know you are at work here, Cécile. Don't let my presence pester you," he said as he lit another cigarette and looked at me sideways.

He did it so elegantly that the cat took my tongue, and I could not respond. Silence fell, wrapping the air around us in its silk. The muffled pitter-pattering of the rain suddenly became loud as it hit the shop's windows, but even though that racket, we still heard each other breathe, which bothered me a little. No, maybe 'bother' is not the right word here. It made me feel different. I felt more aware of him, which heightened my senses so much that I felt his warm exhalation on my neck from across the counter. I closed my eyes as my knees nearly caved.

"*Monsieur* König, …" I said, breaking the stillness to avoid fainting, but Ludwig interrupted me.

"Please, call me 'Ludwig.'"

"Y-yes, please make yourself comfortable, Ludwig," I stuttered. Addressing him by his first name seemed so personal and almost romantic. Oh God, I felt as if his stare were burning straight through my soul.

For some unknown reason, I was far from being as confident as I was in the La Gaston last week. The way I had casually talked to Ludwig seemed like a faraway dream. Having my friends there with me boosted my confidence. Or the champagne. Or both. My voice was a little shaky now, but as much of a gentleman as he was, Ludwig, did not call attention to it.

The percolator coughed a few times, indicating that the coffee was ready. I quickly ran back and poured a cup for him, then I turned the door sign, indicating the shop was open, but there were no customers in sight. The rain always kept most customers away, and only the ones down to their last cigarette braved the elements. Not having others around us made my mind blur over everything except him, and my ears only heard his words.

He walked over and stood by the counter while sipping his coffee. After another blanket of awkward silence, I stood across from him and watched him nervously. Ludwig must have noticed my uneasiness when he glanced down at my shaking hands. I quickly hid them behind my back, but I was not fast enough as Ludwig gently grabbed one.

"You don't have to be so nervous around me, Cécile," he whispered as he smoothed his thumb over my knuckles. I could feel the electricity seeping through his touch. Pins and needles were running through my veins, which is how one must feel when lightning strikes.

"It's just a habit of mine," I replied.

"Ah, I think I understand. You are an only child, are you not?" He inquired.

"Yes, yes, I am an only child," I frowned at him and did not understand where he was going with this conversation or how he knew.

"I heard it's harder for an only child to interact with other people."

"I think I just can't interact with strangers," I blurted before I could even stop myself, but Ludwig only smiled instead of being offended by my statement. Of course, this was far from the truth, but I could not have told him that.

"We are not strangers, are we?" He asked with an apparent comfort in his voice.

"Er, I wouldn't say so," I replied hesitantly.

"Why is that?"

"B–Because we only met a couple of times." My face burned as I stuttered, but Ludwig only chuckled.

"I suppose it's true, but I feel I have known you for a long time Cécile, although I still do not know enough about you."

"You know where I work and that I am an only child. Why don't you tell me more about yourself, about your family?" I asked him shyly, wanting to shift the attention from me.

Ludwig sighed, "Well, I have a sister who lives in Germany with her husband. My parents perished a few years ago, and I work as a diplomat, which you already know," he told me with a bright smile, and I nearly melted. "Now it's your turn."

"Uhm, well," I looked down at my hands, "there's nothing much to say about me that you don't already know. I enjoy going to the cinema, spending time with my friends, and reading books."

"Cécile, you're far more interesting than you can imagine," Ludwig said as he heard the hesitation in my voice. "What is your favorite?" he asked, not letting go.

"Films. If I must pick, I think I could spend all my wages on cinema tickets, but that would upset Papa, I am certain," I said, and just like that, all my insecurities disappeared like a puff of smoke in the air.

"Oh, we have a film enthusiast here!" Ludwig's eyes lit up. He looked eager to know more, and we soon found ourselves lost talking about films. My nervousness flew out the window as soon as Ludwig and I fell into a comfortable conversation. I am captivated by the silver screen and know everything about it.

"I still remember Papa taking me to my first film, *Ben-Hur*, when I was seven. It was a silent film, but it mesmerized me. My obsession began the moment the lights went out. I wanted to be Her, and I wanted to be there. Wherever it was, whoever she was.

As we talked, I forgot about myself, or maybe I became who I was. Ludwig listened as I chatted his ears off, but he did not seem to mind. He stood there quietly, soaking up everything I said with a ghost of a smile lingering on his clean-shaven face. That was when he asked me for an official rendezvous!

"Cécile, may I invite you to the cinema?"

I blinked owlishly, waiting for him to repeat what he said because I clearly had misheard him.

"I beg your pardon. Can you repeat what you said?" I asked him with a blush.

"As you wish, *Mademoiselle* Cécile. I asked if you would like to watch a film with me. I have two tickets for *Pygmalion* on November 19. I bought two, hoping you could accompany me. That is one reason I came here today. I ran out of cigarettes, and I could no longer stop myself from seeing your beautiful face. Please come watch the film with me." He held my hand closer to his lips before gently laying my hand down on the counter. "That is if you haven't already seen that film."

"Oh," I sighed, "yes, I would love to. I have been trying to go with my friends, but none of them has had time to spare. It would delight me to accompany you," I gushed and hoped I did not sound too eager. I spoke what my heart told me to say, but I am now worried that I may have revealed my fondness for him. Before I could ask him why he chose to go so far out, his smile widened.

"It's settled then. I think I have stayed here and occupied your time long enough. I need to go back to Berlin for now, but I promise I will stop by again as soon as I get back."

I just let him hold my hand as he gazed at me endearingly. My mind seemed to have malfunctioned as Ludwig showered me with so much attention. I could feel the giddiness dancing in the pit of my stomach as he kissed my knuckles, like the gentleman he always is, for one last time. He thanked me for the coffee, tipped his hat, and walked out of the shop with a longing look.

Not many customers came in after Ludwig left—not even after the rain stopped, which left me daydreaming for the rest of the day. According to the paper, there would be no sunshine in sight for weeks, but my entire being seemed to be in an eternal summer. I felt like the luckiest girl in Paris. No. The entire world. Oh, Diary! All I wanted to do was sing and dance down the avenue, telling the world I was going on a rendezvous with Ludwig! An actual date with a real man who has walked out of my dreams, which cannot be possible, I told myself repeatedly all afternoon. A part of me thought I might have made up the whole encounter in my head, but the other part of me was still dancing down the street.

I do have a confession to make. I lied to Ludwig; I had seen *Pygmalion*, but I thought this little lie was acceptable. If I had not lied, he would consider it a rejection and probably assumed that I was not interested in him. But I will watch anything for the hundredth time to be with him. We will sit side by side in the dark while watching a romantic film. I wonder if he will hold my hand. If he did, my whole body would tingle, and I would not be able to pay attention, but it would be worth it. Nineteen agonizing days I must wait.

★★★

Friday, 11 November 1938

I cannot eat, and I cannot think. The more time passes, the more I will fall in love with a man when I know I must not. My first love will be a forbidden one before it even begins, which cannot be happening, but it is.

I know that I cannot tell my parents about him. Mama may understand, but Papa would be disappointed in me if he found out. He has been speaking against the Germans for months. If only Papa would see beyond the headlines and see Ludwig for what he is; a true gentleman, a caring and charming person. One day, Papa may have a change of heart.

I cannot tell Élizabeth about this blossoming love either. Not yet. The news would crush her. Oh, Diary, what am I going to do? I must keep my rendezvous and Ludwig a secret from everyone I care about, which is breaking my heart. I feel like I am neither asleep nor awake. How can a heart feel the warmth of love and the coldness of the pain with each beat? But fire always melts ice, and there are dreams between being awake and fast asleep.

Diary, you are now trusted with another secret to keep. I am in love with a German.

CHAPTER 8

MAN WITHOUT HIS UNIFORM

Sunday, 20 November 1938

These last couple of weeks without Ludwig felt like years. He came back from Berlin earlier this week, and while he was away, I fell for him more and more with each passing day. I fell for him harder and harder. It is true what they say: that distance makes the heart grow fonder. It made the rest of my time lonely, but the wait was worth it.

I thought love comes in the springtime, not when it is raining, foggy, and just outright miserable, but love is strange. There is no schedule, no right time for love. It will find you when you need to be found. You could know a person for months and realize you are in love with them when they give you a small smile. I never knew that being in love could be so different that it could change your life. No, this was not about elementary school boys chasing girls around the schoolyard. I thought love was stupid when someone chased another, but this is different.

Ludwig was not chasing me around, but I was the one chasing him. It was silly and childish, but I still felt grown-up. I know my boundaries, and the best part is that I am not in second grade, and Ludwig is not some schoolboy. He is a man, and a prestigious diplomat no less, who carries himself with great dignity and elegance. This man had such a strong appeal that people would have no choice but to notice him. He exudes a powerful aura that requires utmost attention. Or, well, that is what I believe it to be.

The love I developed for him felt even more romantic and earth-shattering than what I read in my novels. We could have the whole wide world if we wanted. It might be a far-fetched idea for now, but if Ludwig returned my feelings, I would do anything for him. We could get married, move to Berlin, settle, and have children. I know of the possibility of my parents rejecting him, but they would understand once I told them how I felt. How this love burns up my entire being and makes my spine tingle whenever I imagine those lips of his kissing my hands. This love was slowly driving me toward the edge of insanity.

I do not want our love to end like an ill-fated Shakespearean play, but I cannot have the best of both worlds yet. Not when I am unsure of my parents' and friends' reactions. What would Élizabeth think of me if she found out I was in love with her enemy? I know Ludwig did nothing to her or her family, but he is still German. In Élizabeth's eyes, he is against her very existence, which is terrifying.

But what is more terrifying is not knowing how Ludwig feels. Does he miss me as much as I do when he is not with me? Does he think about me before going to sleep? There is always the possibility of Ludwig not loving me back. I must keep my longing for him a secret until I know his intentions. I would be humiliated if he found out. I am not ready to risk everything when our future is uncertain. 'Us,' 'We.' Can we ever be a 'we'? Sometimes, I am a little doubtful. Come to think of it, he has not declared his love for me, but the time we spent together was enough for me to feel that he liked me.

On Monday, Ludwig came by the *Tabac* to ensure I had not changed my mind about seeing *Pygmalion*. We agreed to meet in front of the cinema on Saturday at five o'clock. The film started a couple of hours later, but he wanted us to have supper in the nearby café beforehand. It was so hard for me to tell Agnes and Élizabeth that I would not join them to visit the Louvre that day, and I told them I had to go to the library. They hesitantly accepted it, but I was unsure if they believed me. They knew my favorite part of the Louvre was the Egyptian exhibit, and I would not miss the opportunity to go, no matter how many times I had seen it.

I missed my friends, but I committed to this date weeks ago, which I could not reveal. Should I have gone with my friends? Was I too selfish for not going with my friends? I had been waiting for this moment to go on a date for a lifetime. I had even lied to Mama—something I had never done in my entire life. She believed me, but part of me felt like I was breaking her trust.

Lying always makes me feel guilty, and it makes me feel awful. I cannot believe I set my morals aside to avoid ending up as a single woman, living with a thousand cats for companionship. Knowing how forgetful I am, I now need to remember the lies I told. How am I going to keep doing this? If I do not lie to my friends, at least for the time being, I will miss my chance to kindle a relationship with Ludwig.

Mama commented about how particular I was about getting ready. "It's only the library, Cécile, not a ballroom dance," she told me.

I was spending hours on my hair, trying to tame it but the only thing I could do was pin the strands away from my face. It was not silver screen ready, but it did not make me look like a mad woman. I even ironed my clothes that day, which I had never cared to do before. I was very fussy about what I wore and went through my wardrobe twice, trying to find a decent dress to wear. I realized that I did not have a single beautiful piece to wear. Nothing rendezvous worthy. It was too late to go shopping, and buying a new skirt or a dress would have definitely made Mama suspicious. It is embarrassing, and I must update my wardrobe, but before that, I need to save money.

I may even ask Mademoiselle Morel for a pay rise. That is precisely what I will do because my pay is not enough. I always have to choose between going to the cinema, buying books, or new dresses. But then I would spend most of my money on films and novels and have nothing left for my wardrobe. I must ask her for a raise on Monday. She typically comes at the beginning of the week and when I close on Friday. I am sure she will not mind because I am a hardworking employee.

After much debate but not much confidence, I picked a dark green plaid wool skirt while internally beating myself for being so unprepared for the rendezvous. If we were not in Paris, someone would think it was a Scottish kilt. I had this skirt for at least five years, but I looked after it. You could not even tell that it was old. The black sweater and coat were only from last year, nearly in style but not as fashionably dated as Agnes's wardrobe, but it was far from old-fashioned. I desperately wanted to borrow Mama's new hat, but she had already been a little wary about my alleged library visit. I could not risk asking for it. She will quickly catch on to my lie if I become too persistent.

I had to be careful around her, which made me feel bad. I never kept a secret from Mama. I always thought she would be the first person I would ever tell if I fell in love with someone. Mama would try to understand, but even if she did, she would still be against it if my father were against it. His word always won.

Mama would never have had the mental resources to support me if my father had said no. Some days or weeks, she is full of energy and restless. I could hear her moving around the house at night, unable to sleep. But then she would slip into eternal despair and pick at her food. She would even skip her favorite radio shows.

Luckily, like the sun lightening up the sky after a storm, she always returned to being happy. I was worried about Mama, but Papa told me that she falls into sadness sometimes but always bounces back. The doctor called it *folie circulaire* and gave her medication to help her sleep. Papa also said it was only natural when someone had witnessed so much pain; however, the doctors are unsure whether her periodic highs and lows are caused by the trauma she experienced as a frontline nurse in the war.

I wish I could share my blossoming affair with her, and it would be such sweet news that just ended there and would not continue with a 'but.' But unfortunately, it does, so I lie.

As I said goodbye and stepped out the front door, I reached over to the coat rack and took Mama's new hat. It was a quick reflex, and I did not even think twice before sneaking the hat away with me. Horror dawned on me when I stepped outside the house and realized what I had done. I cannot believe that I am becoming a liar and a thief within two weeks. Love does make people do strange things. Whatever it is, I hope that my love is worth it.

★★★

Hénri put the journal on the ground, closed his eyes, and groaned at an oncoming headache. He was sitting in the corner of his studio where he imagined Cécile's room would have been. Bringing the diary back to where it was found gave a new light to the story in Hénri's eyes, providing it with more flavor and authenticity.

The room quickly transformed into Cécile's bedroom. Hénri saw the chest of drawers and the leaky radiator exactly where he sat. He saw her sitting on her bed, writing in her beloved journal. Maybe she was even biting the end of the pencil as she recalled her days. Hénri tried to picture her and how she looked based on her writing and some old movies he watched with his grandmother when he was a young boy. He vividly remembers his grandma loving the black and white films but could not remember any but one. The movie *What Ever Happened to Baby Jane?* made a lasting impression on him since he was only six years old when he saw this film. Grandma did not seem to care that a psychological thriller about a now adult child actress, Baby Jane, emotionally torturing her paralyzed sister was not the most appropriate genre for young Hénri. It was a scary movie for a young child, even if it was released in the sixties. That is as far as Hénri's filmography knowledge reached. Cécile would beat him in Trivial Pursuit if it came to movies. That was certain.

Hénri's headache slowly intensified. The crew was busy putting in new floors, but their noise was just a distant hum.

"Are you okay, boss?" Jakov asked him in a concerned tone.

"Oh, yes, I'm fine. This journal you found is giving me a headache," Hénri said as he emerged from the daze he was sinking into.

"Oh, it's a journal, eh? Whose is it?" Jakov asked. He was very short and very factual, which Hénri liked about him. He often wondered if he was like this in his native Croatia. Or did his not having a broad French vocabulary give him the impression of being so brazen?

Hénri did not want to get into the details, so he gave just enough information to Jakov to satisfy his curiosity.

"The diary concerns a woman who lived here a long time ago. She was madly in love, and that is all she wrote about. I was hoping to learn more about her and maybe track her down. If she is still alive, that is."

"Ah."

Hénri immediately knew that Jakov had lost complete interest in the treasure they found. He hoped the rag hid a valuable item, and Hénri would give him a finder's fee. It, being a book, dissipated all his hopes for some extra cash.

Hénri leaned against the wall and closed his eyes. He suddenly understood his mother's question about reading the thoughts of a twenty-something woman. It was more than eerie, Hénri realized; it was overwhelming. He just wanted his headache to disappear before continuing this journey with Cécile. The deeper Hénri dove into the journal, the more he felt he lived in a parallel universe.

Hénri walked outside to the *Cluny La Sorbonne Metro* station. It dawned on Hénri that Cécile rode this line almost all the time. The *Odéon,* where she got off on her way to work, was the next stop, and her favorite cinema was less than a five-minute walk from *La Sorbonne.* Hénri needed some fresh air, so he thought to look for the cigarette shop where Cécile worked, which may still be there. The sound of the screeching breaks did not ease his headache as he realized he was retracing Cécile's steps to her first rendezvous with Ludwig.

***

I could feel my stomach tingling in anticipation as I walked to the *Cinéma Le Champo* from the station. Ludwig was waiting for me there, and to my surprise, he was not in his uniform. I was a tad disappointed because he looked very handsome in it. Handsome but intimidating. However, I realized that he looked sophisticated in everything he wore.

He looked fascinating in his uniform, but he was even more sophisticated in regular clothes. Tonight, he wore a dark gray suit with a black turtleneck sweater (and we wore matching sweaters! Oh, the coincidence was lovely!). There was a cigarette between his long-tapered fingers, as usual. I stood a few feet away from him as I watched him smoke. He could easily be mistaken for a celebrity. I wondered why he did not wear his uniform for a moment, but the thought was just as faint as the moon trying to peek through the foggy night sky.

Ludwig turned his head around, and I watched his eyes light up. There was his charming smile that made my heart jump every time. I patted my skirt nervously as I approached him. We exchanged a pleasant greeting, and Ludwig held his arm out for me so we could walk to the Café. My hands entangled around his arms, with him telling me about his trip. Nothing could stop me from feeling insanely happy. It was already dark, although it was barely half past five. I do not like how early the sun sets in the winter, but this was still the most romantic walk I have ever had in my life. The streetlights reflected the fog, creating a golden globe around them. Cars were driving by, and couples were walking arms in arms while looking for a quiet place. Some shops were still open, selling their goods to late customers. *Le Café Soleil* was only a few minutes' walk from the cinema, but I wished our walk lasted longer. A lot longer. I wanted this moment to last forever.

We entered a mid-size café that served freshly brewed coffee and pastries. "It is never really too late for coffee and croissants," I said as I took in the aroma, and Ludwig smiled.

"That's what I love about Paris," he replied, and I swear I felt a little pride swell in my chest.

We sat by the window next to another couple. This shop was smaller but more spacious than the *Café de Luna* in the park. It had fewer tables and a long counter with endless pastries on it. I was hungry because I missed dinner but was too nervous to eat. I ordered *Café Au Lait* and soda water while Ludwig ordered a double espresso.

"Do you care for a cigarette, Cécile?" He asked me and pulled out a pack of *Gitanes* from his pocket. I hesitated for a minute and pulled a cigarette out of the packet. Ludwig watched me intensely as I held the cigarette up to my lips, and he lit it up immediately. I gazed into his eyes a little before I drew on it and hoped I did not look like a fish stuck on a hook. As soon as the smoke entered my mouth, I coughed a little.

"Working in that elegant tobacco shop. I would not have taken you for a non-smoker." Ludwig said as he gave me a small smile.

"*Gitanes* is a strong brand for my liking. I prefer Job," I pretended because I did not want him to think I hardly smoked.

Ludwig could find me too dull or unadventurous, and I wanted to be far from boring. I tried to recall how Agnes behaved and how she drank and smoked. She always carried herself elegantly. I tried to remember her demeanor to mimic every movement of hers. I wanted to be the *femme fatale* tonight.

"Ludwig, tonight is already wonderful," I said while trying to look as seductive as possible as I took another hit from the cigarette with squinted eyes. He smiled in response, and I resisted my urge to swoon. I was cautious not to inhale too much smoke; I would have made a fool of myself in front of Ludwig. He reached for my hand and squeezed it gently.

"Thank you for saying that, Cécile. I missed you, and I could not wait to return from Berlin. My days and nights were filled with thoughts of you. There was no way I could bring myself to forget about you, even if I tried. Remembering your laugh, passion for films, and sweet smile kept me up most nights. Your beauty lifted me to the stars and stayed there the entire time I was away. It is the most incredible feeling, and

I have never felt this way for anyone before. I will never forget this delicate face of yours," he said in a soothing voice.

Ludwig reached out and cupped my face tenderly. I looked into his blue eyes and got lost in them. They always reminded me of the ocean and dragged me straight there.

The world around us ceased to exist. It was the moment when I could only feel, see, and hear Ludwig. The people around us slowly vanished, and their constant chatter was reduced to nothing but a hum. I could only see him and his sincerity sparkling in his eyes. My head spun, and I felt like Alice when she jumped down the hole after the White Rabbit. The sensation of falling swam through my head, and I felt dizzy. Excitement like no other, whipped through my body at that moment, but I was in a daze after Ludwig confessed his feelings for me.

I tried concentrating on the news before the film, but my body and heart were under Ludwig's spell. I still felt his gentle hands on my face, and my thoughts bounced around. I promised myself I would pay better attention to the world around me, but comprehending the full extent of what was on the screen at that moment was nearly impossible. I only remember the images and the main headlines from what the news said. Ludwig's associate was assassinated here in Paris by a Jewish man, which sent the Nazi paramilitary into a frenzy. Everything was on fire in Berlin and all over Germany. Jewish businesses, shops, and even synagogues were broken into and burned to the ground. People were screaming and running down the streets while trying to escape this living nightmare. It looked like life itself caught on fire. Thank heaven that Élizabeth and her family are safe here in Paris.

I cannot imagine them living through that hell if they were in Germany. As I sat there with my thoughts going back and forth between what I saw on the screen and Ludwig's sweet voice, it suddenly hit me. Ludwig is a Nazi officer! That is why he was away in Berlin, which probably was why he was not wearing his uniform. Ludwig is hiding from the public to avoid any possible assault. He is hiding the fact he has something to do with *Kristallnacht*, the Night of Broken Glass, the widespread hatred, and the racial persecution of Jews.

This is it; it must be! He is ashamed of who he really is. Ludwig is just doing his job like the rest of us are, whether we like it or not. It is not easy to change your job, and Ludwig was here to take his mind off the fire that had engulfed his entire nation, but I could tell the news was not helping to ease his mind.

The tension I felt about him earlier eased, and I returned to my romantic thoughts about us. The movie suddenly had a whole new meaning. I was the lower-class flower girl, Eliza Doolittle, and Ludwig was the charming Professor Higgins, transforming me into a proper lady and falling in love with me at the end. I do not consider myself déclassé, someone who fell into a lower class or speaking as she did, but it was still a lovely daydream. Her hair was a little out of control, just like mine, before she became all proper. At least we have that in common, except I will not pretend to be a duchess.

My world slowly faded away and transformed me into Miss Doolittle. Films and books tended to affect me, but I felt like a real female protagonist in my own life for the first time. I was no longer a background character but a heroine. That lifted my mood, and I enjoyed the film all over again until it all ended in a flash—much sooner than I had hoped, meaning I had to rush home. I did not want Mama to suspect me of not being in the library. Ludwig escorted me to the *Métro,* where we parted ways. I asked him not to come with me all the way, and I had to confess to him about the library.

"I just don't want my mother to think I'm out doing something I'm not supposed to," I told him, "It's not because of who you are or anything. It's just, I've never really ...," I trailed off, and my *femme fatale* act fell apart.

Ludwig only chuckled under his breath, "Cécile, you're silly, but I understand why you would lie to your parents. I will do as you wish." He looked a little hurt as he said this, and I hoped he did not find out the real reason I was keeping 'us' a secret. "I had the most wonderful night with you," he whispered as he lifted my chin and looked me in the eye.

"Thank you, Ludwig." I became breathless as he leaned closer. "I did have the most wonderful night with you, too," I whispered. And then it happened.

One second, I saw my reflection in his eyes, and the next, he leaned over and gently kissed me. I closed my eyes and let the whirlpool take me down the rabbit hole. My knees gave away as he tenderly pressed his lips against mine. It was such a soft kiss that it made me wonder whether I had imagined it. I leaned closer to his body, and he wrapped an arm around my waist. I could feel the heat his body was emitting despite the cold winds surrounding us.

There it was. The boyish grin was on Ludwig's face as he gently traced his thumb down my cheek.

"Good night, Cécile. I hope to see you soon," he whispered huskily and pecked me on the lips one last time before he stepped back. He lifted his hat to say goodbye, and I watched him walk away from me.

I was stuck in a world I had not been to before as I mumbled, "Good night," to him. I did not want this moment to end, so I stood there for a second or two longer than necessary, seeing his gray silhouette blend into the night before I turned around. I rushed down the stairs to the *Métro* to catch the train.

I quickly found an empty seat by the window and caught my reflection. I looked at my face and tried to figure out what Ludwig found so attractive in me. It can't be my wiry black hair. I have a flat nose, which I think is too large, but my eyes are pretty. A little bit, maybe? No, I do like my eyes. Perhaps because Agnes is so envious of them, she always says she wished she had black eyes like me. I placed a hand on the window, and my fingertips felt the coldness of the glass. I touched my lips and looked back at my reflection with a wide smile.

"My first kiss," I whispered to the image, and my warm breath covered up my face on the window, like the fog surrounding the streetlamps outside.

Here I am, lounging on my bed, recounting tonight's events, and I desperately need someone to confide in. I am happy, excited, afraid, and scared to deal with all these emotions alone. I want to introduce Ludwig to everyone, and I want him to become part of my world. But I am afraid he will become my world, which worries me more than I realize, but I cannot explain why. Love can blind a person and make them do things they will regret later.

CHAPTER 9

DATING A GERMAN

Tuesday, 13 December 1938

It has been almost a month since our first kiss. After being pulled back from the spell Ludwig had me under, I thought about everything with a clear mind. As clear as love, let it be clear, but instead, I spent most of my time with fearful thoughts about my present and my future... our future, and it kept getting more difficult to live like this.

I know I love him. There is no doubt in my heart. My love for him consumes my body like the hellish flames flickering in the underworld. I know there is a huge possibility I will end up hurt or lost, but then there is this gleam of hope that Ludwig will never let me burn. I know he likes me. No, I know Ludwig loves me. Why else would he kiss me the way he does?

But then, my thoughts circle back, and the little voice tells me that I do not know what is on his mind, and with that, I can feel the doubt creeping back in. I thought I had made peace with my appearance that evening on the train, but my self-esteem was lower than expected.

I cannot believe a man as handsome as Ludwig would be interested in me. I am plain as day; I am bland and a dreamer. I am just a regular, middle-class girl living in the middle of the ladder. Why would someone so sophisticated and worldly fall in love with me?

Did Ludwig even like me as me, to begin with? I doubt everything. I fear Ludwig might have kissed me because I fooled him with my femme-fatale act. It is hardly possible he would be fond of a dull girl like me. Was a kiss enough to convey one's feelings? The girl he saw in the café, who smoked and tried to seduce him, was not the same girl who read novels and watched movies as a hobby. What if Ludwig realized that I was not the woman of his dreams after all?

I let doubts creep in one by one, but Ludwig is still here. He comes by the *Tabac* at least twice a week now, much more frequently than he used to. I realize all my worries are just the result of my vivid imagination, which I am blessed with, but now I consider it a curse, and everything is fine. His romantic words still ring fresh in my mind, but Ludwig has said nothing that amorous again. He comes around noon, and we end up spending our time together, having lunch in a nearby café.

Ludwig is always his charming self. I am foolish to doubt him since he sometimes brings flowers for me or bonbons to "sweeten my day," he says. He expresses his 'love' for me through his actions, but I want to hear him say it. I have already declared my love for him to you, my Dear Diary, but I cannot just profess my love to him first. That would not be ladylike, and it would be highly improper. Ludwig and I spend more time together, and I have not yet stopped falling. I hope he is beside me long enough to catch me before I hit the ground.

For the past three weeks, we have been eating lunch together and getting to know each other better with each passing day. He kisses me every time before he leaves and promises that he will be back another day. His kisses are like little promises of love for me, making our romance feel true.

A detail that I have yet to come to understand fully is why Ludwig had not worn his uniform since the night we ran into him in the *La Gaston.* Maybe he is trying to hide his identity, as I thought, but perhaps he thinks I would be irrational and blame him for something his country is responsible for. Or maybe I am afraid to know. Ludwig is only doing his job, and that is that. I doubt he is like other Nazis I saw in the news. Those men look ruthless. I have concluded that Ludwig is genuinely embarrassed that he is German. If he were proud, he would never hide who he really is from the public. But it does not matter, I suppose. As much as I yearn to see him in his uniform, he is always a treat for my eyes.

I discovered a lot about Ludwig through our lunch dates together. He told me about himself more openly, which made me ever so comfortable in his presence. He was certainly not a stranger anymore. His eyes showed no hesitancy as he pulled me into his life story. Ludwig seemed a little ashamed as he confessed that he had lied when he told me about his sister living in Germany with her husband, and his reason for lying was too simple.

"It was our third encounter, and I did not want to bore you with my life story."

"I doubt your life is boring, Ludwig."

"It depends," he said with a wandering tone, almost as if he thought of a different life, before he continued, "I don't have any siblings, but I always wished I did."

"That's not to be sad about. You're lucky to have your parents' love and attention all to yourself," I said confidently, having grown up in the same circumstances.

"I did, but they all died, along with my parents. My childhood was not always wonderful, but it started that way."

Suddenly I felt awkward and sad, but Ludwig continued with a faint smile. "I was born in Wilhelmshaven, in northern Germany, on 9 May, 1907, to a Dutch immigrant sailor who madly fell in love with a local telephonist. I don't remember much of my early years or our move to Berlin," he said, "but I do remember the start of the war, and it was terrifying when I was only seven."

Ludwig told me his father joined the German army out of obligation because he felt he owed the state so much. His patriotic spirit led him to defend and protect the country he called home. He was sent to the front lines in early 1915, where his father later died in the trenches. I cannot even imagine what kind of pain Ludwig must have endured because of such a significant loss at an early age, but he did not want to discuss that. He seemed upset, and I did not want to spoil his mood by pressing him on the matter much. The memories of bloodshed put Mama in deep depression every time, so I certainly understood. Sadness did not start or end there for Ludwig, however.

Before losing the love of her life, his mother had to endure the loss of eight children to various illnesses like typhoid, polio, and cholera. He was the youngest and the only one who survived, but he, too, had his fair share of infant diseases to last him a lifetime. Soon after his father passed, another tragedy struck when his mother died of cholera, leaving Ludwig an orphan at eleven. His mother's aunt, who was childless and married to a Jewish lawyer, took him in and raised him until Ludwig was old enough to follow in his late father's footsteps.

He joined the *Reichswehr*, the German army, where, because of his dedication and loyalty, last year, by his thirtieth birthday, he was promoted to *SS-Obersturmbannführer*, a Lieutenant Colonel. I made him write this word down on the napkin to remember. He often travels back and forth in-between Paris and Berlin, but he has spent more time in Paris lately because of the assassination of the German ambassador last month. The murder itself brought an onset of problems for the Jews.

Élizabeth called me the day it happened, and I remember it all so clearly. I could hardly understand her because she was panicking as she told me the story about some Jewish boy shooting the ambassador. She tried to tell me what this meant for them all, but she did not make much sense at the time. They were not related to the assassin, so why worry? I did not understand what she was trying to tell me, but my secret and forbidden companionship with Ludwig made me acknowledge it.

I wanted to understand her fear. Although it all sounded irrelevant and unimportant, I still pretended to care. I realize now that it was daft, but Élizabeth knew me better than I knew myself. I suspected she called Agnes after cutting the call with me, but I was not bitter.

Agnes is the calmest and brightest among us, much more level-headed than I will ever be. Of course, learning that Ludwig is an army officer and an advisor at the embassy makes this memory of the assassination even more complicated. It is sad to think about how I am neglecting everyone for him, but I cannot be so forthcoming about us. Not yet.

Ludwig is sweet enough, always trying to soothe me and constantly asking about Élizabeth and Agnes. He wants to be part of my world, and my world contains both of my dear friends. I promise one day, we will all be sitting in the park drinking our coffee, with each of us having our man by our side. Maybe not Agnes, but it is still a nice dream. I keep telling Ludwig all about us until we can make this wish come true. He knows how we all met, grew up together, and all the silly things we like doing. I feel that Ludwig probably knows all of us just as well now as if he were with us in person. I even feel pride in how connected and posh my friends are, especially Agnes and her papa. He loves hearing about him and his police work, and I am sure he and *Monsieur* Girard will be good friends one day.

Army men think differently. You can learn a lot about someone through somebody else. I am surprised that Ludwig is not running for the hills yet. I get overly excited when I see him, but thankfully I do not have butterflies in my stomach these days. The more I see him, the more I can be myself around him. The fear of letting him know who I really am has disappeared completely.

I always learn something new about Ludwig when we are together. German is a truly awkward language, but I started learning it for his sake and my amusement. Of course, I cannot practice at home, but I try my best to recall words in my head whenever my thoughts do not wander off. I agree with Mark Twain, who said in his book, *A Tramp Abroad*, *"In German, a young lady has no sex, while a turnip has. Think what overwrought reverence shows for the turnip and what callous disrespect for the girl."* He is so right, and I often joke with Ludwig about it. "But Ludwig, German is impossible. How can a Gretchen be an 'it,' but a turnip be a 'she' in a sentence?"

"Oh, do you think German is difficult? There are so many letters in French words that are not said. My tongue broke the first time I took lessons, and I nearly gave up learning it," Ludwig said in response, and we laughed at the oddities of our languages. I am glad he did not give up because I adore listening to his wonderfully flowing French with a hint of German authority.

Ludwig is changing me for the better from the inside out. I am happier and more confident now than I ever was before. I am letting my hair grow longer, hoping to tame this wild mess, and I pay more attention to my clothes and what I wear. Although I have not bought anything new recently, I fuss over the garments I own, so they match perfectly. I must have lost some weight recently because everything fits so much better. I feel a lot less like an Easter ham, I tell you. I have also been browsing Agnes's *Vogue* magazine to keep up with the recent fashion trends. Ludwig may even turn me into The Woman I always wanted to be.

Diary, if you still wonder how I find time to read, I must confess, it is difficult. I had one reason to keep up with politics: to make sense of Papa's rants. With Ludwig, I now have two reasons for trying to educate myself. I read the headline in the newspaper, but I become starry-eyed halfway into the article. Frustration dawns on me as I push myself to continue, but I always give up.

I am just not meant to read boring and dry political articles, and I always end up slamming the newspaper down and going to my room to pick up what is meant for me. Books. My world is much better when filled with romance, mystery, and faraway lands. I finished reading *Death on the Nile* shortly after my birthday, and this detective story was truly difficult to put down. I am a few chapters into *Le Tour Du Monde En 80 Jours, Around the World in Eighty Days* by Jules Verne. He is an absolute genius to write a masterpiece like this!

The story started rather slowly, but that was because these adventurous novels were new to me. Indeed, my romance and murder mysteries often occur in foreign countries, but it took me a little while to adapt to this new fast-moving genre. But adapted I am, and I am fairly obsessed with this globe-trotting Englishman.

I wish I could be wealthy enough to circumnavigate the globe like Phileas Fogg, although I would do it in more than eighty days. Why rush through it if you have the time? If I were rich, it would not matter much either way. I, for sure, would take my time to savor and soak up everything there is while visiting a new place. In the book, *Monsieur Fogg* is in Egypt as he races across the world, and I realized I am quite familiar with the land of endless dunes and deadly mirages.

I experienced most of the world without ever leaving France. Faraway landscapes and cultures are familiar to me now, but love ... oh, I was feeling romance on a whole new spectrum like never before.

It is the middle of winter, yet, I feel hot sand under my feet and the warm sun on my skin while reading the book. See, Dear Diary, Ludwig does have a profound influence on me. Even my imagination is on a wild ride. I want to tell my friends about this remarkable man I know, but I cannot. Novels always make forbidden love appealing and mysterious, but I can assure you it is worrisome in real life. I am anxious about what would happen if my parents or friends found out about him. Not only would they be disappointed, but it would crush Élizabeth to know that I was dating a German soldier. She would think I am siding with her enemies, and I would not want her to feel like that.

Oh, what agony! I do not know what to do. Maybe doing nothing is the answer, but I would not know that either. I hope Ludwig declares his love for me soon because he does not realize how much I need to hear those words to believe him.

Chapter 10

A Confession Before New Year's Eve

Saturday, 31 December 1938

I did not realize how this affair would change my commitment to writing. Just over two months ago, I thought I would record every minute of my day, but now, weeks go by without a single pen stroke. Once I also did think I would become an old maiden, knitting sweaters for orphans; yet, this is no longer my destiny. Some dreams do come true, while some remain an idea.

The same can be said about my feelings. They are confusing, and I cannot make heads or tails of them. I feel as though I live a double life. I am overjoyed and frightened. Bottling up these emotions creates a dangerous concoction, an ecstatic pain I cannot describe. I fear this glass will soon crack and break into tiny pieces if I cannot get this off my chest. Someone might just as well throw me in the ocean and see where I washed ashore. A little girl playing with her kite on the beach would find me and read the secret message I had been harboring all this time. I had to tell someone before I went mad, so I confided in Agnes.

I was in despair, hoping to finally put down the weight I had been carrying, but instead of relief, I am now condemned to hold it for eternity.

Telling Agnes only made me realize the severity of the affair with Ludwig, and I cannot help but drown in regret.

We were all to meet this morning for the last coffee of this year. The three of us had created a tradition of sharing our final cup of coffee of the year. We also always met up at someone's place to celebrate the end of another year, but Élizabeth canceled on us. She was scheduled for night duty at the loony bin and wanted to catch up on her sleep before heading to work. A nurse came down with croup and being new puts you at the bottom of the medical pecking order. The hospital asked her to start in mid-December, almost a month earlier than she intended to, because of how shorthanded they were.

She did not mind that part but was a little agitated about New Year's Eve because we all wanted to stay together and not worry about a thing. We fancied celebrating, saying goodbye to the old year, and welcoming the new one. Agnes has moved into her two-bedroom apartment a few blocks from where she used to live, and none of us have visited yet. I admired her ability to grow independent and her constant desire to show the world what women are made of. She was busy moving, having furniture delivered, and generally setting up her new place in the past few weeks. Her apartment has one kitchen, two small bedrooms, and a living room. But despite still being very empty, we were thrilled for her and excited to see it, no matter how bare it was. It was hers!

Agnes and I met in the *Café de Luna*, and Élizabeth not being there gave me the opportunity and privacy I needed to confess 'my sins.' Although the three of us were best friends, I was closer to Élizabeth than Agnes, but confiding in Agnes was the safest option, my only option. It was almost as if I were confessing to a priest and looking to Agnes to absolve me of my sins. Only if it were that easy, but it was not easy by any means.

"Agnes, I have something very important to tell you but promise me you won't get mad at me," I nervously said as I lit my cigarette with a fidgety hand.

"Is everything okay?" Agnes looked concerned as her eyes flickered between my shaking hand and my timid face.

I exhaled the smoke nervously. I was scared, wondering whether I was making the right decision by telling Agnes about Ludwig or making a huge mistake. Agnes is my friend, and she loves me, I told myself. There was a time when I could tell her anything without thinking twice, but this fear of being judged, embedded deep in my heart, made me nervous.

"Please promise me," I begged her because I needed some confirmation.

"There is no way I would be mad at you, Cécile. Do not be silly. You over-analyze everything. Can I get a cigarette from you?" She asked me with a smile. "I left mine at home, rushed out in a hurry, and left my pack in my other purse."

"Oh, yes, of course. Please, go ahead," I said as my agitation was halted briefly. I smoked more often than occasionally at the bar, so I carried my pack now. Smoking is part of this new image I desperately want to build. As I handed her the pack, my hand shook, and I saw the concern growing in Agnes's eyes.

Agnes placed the cigarette between her red-stained lips and tried to light it up, but the wind extinguished the flame a few times, which was a perfect time to reveal my secret to her.

"I have a companion," I finally blurted out, and there was no going back.

For the first time, Agnes choked on her draw of smoke. She coughed, and I handed her my glass of water. Agnes took a sip and looked at me with an astonished look on her face.

"Cécile?" Agnes raised her voice. "A companion, as in a man?" She asked but did not wait for my answer. "I can't believe it! Good heavens, you must tell me all about it. How could you keep this a secret? How long has this been going on?"

I sighed in relief when I finally understood that she was happy for me. She kept firing questions at me like a squad leader would during an interrogation. I felt the burden lifting off my shoulders, but my relief was short-lived, and fear found its way back in. "You know him, or you met him once, rather," I said, trying to avoid looking her in the eye. Agnes frowned in confusion as she questioned me or her memory.

"Did I? You may be mistaken; I would remember if I met your prospect!"

"Remember that night in the *La Gaston*? The night we all swore to keep a huge secret?" I asked with a blush.

Agnes sipped at her coffee, flicked the ash of her cigarette in the heavy crystal ashtray on our table, and I could tell she was thinking, flipping through her memories like a picture album.

Her smile faltered as I caught her gaze. "I remember now," she intoned, then she looked me in the eye with an expression I could not comprehend. It stung. If looks could kill, it would have speared me in the heart. No, it would have drawn and quartered me as if I had just attempted to assassinate a medieval king. She was waiting for me to deny that I was talking about Ludwig, but all she received in response was my silence.

"NO!" Agnes shouted, and everyone in the café turned around to look at her. Agnes gritted her teeth as she ignored the onlookers, "Cécile, don't tell me this is true." She admonished me while shaking her head. She leaned closer across the table with her elbows resting on the table, "You cannot date a German, especially not now." She said firmly but lowered her voice to a whisper so only I could hear it.

"Ludwig isn't evil. He is a caring, gentle soul, Agnes. You'll see when you meet him again." I pleaded after finally finding my voice, but Agnes would not have it.

"Have you thought about your family? Have you thought about Élizabeth, for goodness' sake? What do you think will happen if he finds out about her?"

"You don't understand, Agnes. He is not a soldier. He's an adviser at the German embassy, that's all," I said in a faint voice, only telling her half the truth because, at that moment, I was trying to convince myself more than I was trying to have Agnes believe me.

"That's even worse!" Agnes said with a firm voice, her eyes blazing with anger like an inextinguishable fire.

I shrunk in my seat just as my heart sank in my chest. "You promised you wouldn't get mad at me," I said in a low voice. "Ludwig is a gentleman. I do not think our secret is in jeopardy or we are in any danger. He does not even wear his uniform in public. That is a sign, isn't it? I think he's ashamed of his country." I defended him as quietly as possible, but my whisper could have been played on the gramophone. It was that loud and brazen for Agnes.

"You're naïve, Cécile, but I beg your pardon. You're right. I promised you I wouldn't get mad, so please continue," Agnes said after taking a deep breath. I ignored the critical tone in her voice. "Please tell me everything about your suitor. Are you in love with him?" She asked, and I know she hoped I would reconsider in answering.

"After our night together in *La Gaston*, he kept coming by the *Tabac* and eventually invited me for a film," I started nervously, "then, after that, we spent more and more time together during my lunch hours." I told her with a small smile, "I love him, Agnes, I do," I said passionately, but by the end, my voice became weak. I had tears in my eyes. Why does love have to be so painful, I asked myself.

"Have you told anyone else about him?" she asked, and I sensed compassion in her voice.

"No, I haven't," I replied honestly and took my handkerchief out of my purse to wipe my eyes. "I love Ludwig so much. I don't know what to do and how to tell Mama and Papa about him," I mumbled.

"I know you love him, Cécile. I can see it in your eyes and the way you talk about him, and I want to be happy for you. Believe me! I wish I could be happy for you, but I am worried. Do you know how dangerous this could be? You do not see him that way, but he is dangerous. You don't know what he could do if ..." she trailed off, and I shook my head.

"No, Ludwig won't ever hurt my loved ones or me," I said stubbornly.

"Promise me you will keep Élizabeth's secret safe from him, no matter what. You must never tell him about her, no matter how much you love him. Promise me," she said and took my hands in hers.

I finally looked into her green eyes and nodded, "I promise, I promise," I sniffled, "I swear I will never, ever break that promise. I swore that night, and I do not mind swearing again. But what should

I do, Agnes? I know it can be dangerous, but I love him. Every time I think about him, my heart quivers. I know this is love, and I can feel it. I'm weightless, like a feather flying in the air. I don't want to hurt anyone, but I would hurt myself the most by leaving him."

I finally felt a deep fear lifting off my chest as my confession neared its end, but the worry stayed.

"It is a hard decision to make, and I can't tell you what to do when you want to do the opposite. Your heart is telling you to be in love with him, but your brain should tell you to stop it before it is too late. Be in love, Cécile. Only death can stop a heart from loving. It is what our hearts do, but please be careful. Please be cautious and aware. If you see or hear anything that poses a danger to any of us, you, or your family, you need to leave immediately and bring this affair to an end." She let go of my hands slowly and leaned back in her chair with a guarded expression. "What does he know about you?" Agnes interrogated.

"He knows where I work and what I like, but I don't think he knows where I live. But I suppose that is easy to find out, isn't it?" I asked hesitantly, hoping Agnes would tell me otherwise. Unfortunately, she has confirmed my fear. He knows more about me than I think he does. "What have you told him about us?"

"Nothing, really. Ludwig met all of you in the bar, but we don't talk about us," I lied, and Agnes gave me another spearing look. "I swear, Agnes," I said, resting my right hand on my chest above my heart. "He is interested in me," I continued humbly, and I did not tell her that Ludwig often asked about them. She shouldn't know, so I continued focusing on myself. "We talked about our childhood, films, books, stars, and where we would travel if we were rich. We daydream, and by doing this, we get to know each other. I believe he is genuine with his feelings toward me." I knew Agnes needed an explanation to understand my side of the story. At that moment, I hoped she understood that I loved him.

"Be careful, Cécile. Do not say a word to your parents about him and seal your lips in front of Élizabeth. That is the only advice I can give you. And from now on, you need to keep me updated, which you must promise. From this moment forward, this will be our secret."

"Okay. Our secret." The words sounded bitter in my mouth, but I already knew there was no way I could tell anyone else.

Soon, Agnes and I fell into a light chatter for the rest of the morning. We talked about *Le Réveillon de la Saint-Sylvestre*, our New Year's Eve celebration.

"Élizabeth canceled because they pulled her into the night shift, but you know that already. Do you still want to come over?' she asked me with a pout.

"Yes, very much so. I still would like to come! I would love to see your new place and celebrate the end of 1938 together with you." I smiled. "1939," I said with awe. "I feel this is going to be the best year ever. I feel it, Agnes. All of our wishes will come true," I said in a dreamy voice, then remembered to ask, "Is anyone else coming to the party?"

"Yes, two girls and two men from work. You have never met them, but I think you'll like them," she said as she took another cigarette out of my pack.

We sat there all morning, catching up on our life from the last few weeks. Ludwig has officially become a 'suitor' or a 'him' for the rest of the morning, and this was the last time 'he' ever came up in a conversation. He became a ghost for the rest of the year, or what was left of it. I still do not know why I referred to him as my companion or why I have not told Agnes the entire story. Maybe it's because I knew that she would make me end the relationship if she knew it had not started yet, or that we talk about us ladies often. I want him to know all about me, and Agnes and Élizabeth are all part of it, but can he be my suitor without even declaring his love? Does he love me at all?

I arrived at Agnes's apartment just like she had asked at six o'clock. I did not want to take the bus and opted to take the thirty-minute walk. The night was milder than usual, and it was not snowing or raining. I just wanted to be with my thoughts and catch some fresh air. I could see couples walking together, arm in arm, no doubt going to parties in their fancy coats and furs. They laughed and hoped the year ahead of them would be better than the year they would leave behind. A new beginning. I thought about Ludwig and if we could ever walk as openly as these couples under an open sky.

I opened the gate to Agnes's house and hit the main light switch. It short-circuited a little when I switched it on, and then it buzzed like a dying fly before being dimly lit. I slowly walked up the stairs to the fourth floor, the top level of the building.

The house looked like any other house in the area, but this building seemed to have more apartments than ours. The stairway swirled up, passing floor after floor. I liked how this house had private balconies on each floor, like a ring going around. I leaned over the iron railing and looked up at the night sky when I reached the top. It was a perfect square. It was a little overcast, and the stars were not so bright yet, but the moon shone through a layer of thin clouds.

Staring at this white winter crescent, I wished Ludwig were here with me. We could have kissed at midnight out here under the moonlight, but he had an official engagement at the embassy. Besides, even if he were available, I would not have been able to bring him here with me, so maybe this was for the best I hope he was thinking about me as much as I was thinking about him. I wondered if he also wished to kiss me at midnight as I wished to kiss him.

I could not understand it, but I missed him already. I reached into my coat pocket and picked out a piece of paper with Agnes's address written down. 15 *Rue de Tourelles, fourth floor, Apartment No. 3*. I did not know if I should start from left to right or from right to left, but I decided it did not matter because I would get there anyway as it just circled back around. I turned right and was lucky because Apartment No.3 was right there.

Agnes' front door was just like ours, a big brown oak door with two small panel windows in the middle of the gate with some iron rails to prevent burglars from breaking in. I tried to see through the opaque glass but could only see shadows. I heard a radio playing soft music, and

I could hear chatter coming from inside. I rang the doorbell and saw a silhouette approaching the door, becoming larger and sharper with each passing second.

When the door opened, Agnes was standing there in all her glory. She wore a knee-length white and red dress and her signature red lipstick and light blue eye shadow.

"Cécile, at last. Come in. We have been waiting for you. Emil, Guy, Irene, and Rose are already here and are excited to meet you," she said and hurried me into her apartment, closing the door quickly behind me.

"Let me get your coat," she reached out, helped me take it off, and hung it on the coat rack.

"*Merci*," I thanked her with a smile, and Agnes only hugged me in response.

"You can put your shoes right here." She moved back and pointed at the wall radiator. Her apartment had a hallway leading to the kitchen, and her kitchen had a window facing the balcony. A bathroom was on one side of the hall with a full-size bathtub. The place was very spacious for an apartment. I could not help but be a little envious, but mostly I was happy for her to buy her apartment at such a young age.

The hallway led into the living room with three large windows facing the street. Her bedroom opened from there with a large double-wide door, which Agnes kept closed. Overall, I admired her place and aspired to buy one like this one day.

The party was lovely, and I quickly became acquainted with Agnes's other friends. She was right about one thing. Her friends liked me, and I liked them back. They were a lively bunch and made me feel like I was a part of their group. I wished Élizabeth were here with us. I wanted her to celebrate the end of this strange year together, but I knew she had other priorities to look after now.

I enjoyed my night but felt a little lonely when the clock struck twelve. My mind wandered from Ludwig to Élizabeth until it faded into the montage of jazz, chatter, and midnight happy cheers from the streets. On my way home, I told myself I would get to kiss Ludwig next New Year's Eve, which helped me return from this pit of sadness.

I knew telling Agnes about Ludwig would be risky, but I was glad that at least one person knew my secret. That was all I needed… someone else to hold my secret as close to their heart as I was holding it.

CHAPTER 11

A LOVELY NIGHT

Saturday, 7 January 1939

Dear Diary,

1939. A new year, a new me, a new life. That is what I wished for when the clock hit midnight. I still have ambivalent feelings about whether confiding in Agnes was a clever idea, but today, a week after my confession, I am glad I told her about Ludwig. Talking about him with someone eased my anxiety somewhat because it made him real, but I still feel nervous about his status. Maybe I am just scared because everyone else is concerned. I overanalyze everything. Agnes is right. I know we will get through this, and the world will calm down.

Agnes worries about me, although she tries not to show it. I saw how uncomfortable she became during our conversation. She hated that Ludwig was German, even more so that he was a high-ranking officer. In her eyes, he was the enemy. But as I told her how sweet he was, she was beginning to like him more and more. So, I thought.

Don't you think trust is more significant than any treasure we can give someone in this world? I always believed that having someone you could trust and be trusted in return was a matter of honor. I trusted Agnes with this secret the same way Élizabeth trusted us. Agnes remained true to her word and did not tell a soul about my secret–not even Élizabeth. It was better to keep this away from Élizabeth because I did not want to endanger her, even though I believed with all my heart that Ludwig was harmless.

How can a man as gentle and sweet as Ludwig even be harmful, to begin with? He is the most caring man in the world. At first, I only found him attractive because he was tall; he had an aura that made people notice him immediately, and of course, he resembled a film star. His stature and handsome looks would make any girl swoon. Even men would become self-conscious whenever they saw him walk through the door. It was his appearance and the way he walked that turned necks around. He was attractive physically (do not even get me started on it, Diary, or there will never be an end to it), but it was his heart that I fell in love with. It was his sweet gestures that made me fall for him.

He not only carries my heart in his palm, Diary, but he also holds my entire being in his hand, and I have already given myself to him in a way I have never given to anyone. He has all my pieces with him, and if anything ever happened to him, I would not only lose him, but I would end up losing myself.

The love I have for him grows steadily, but now it has reached the point of no return. I can never go back now. It is exciting to know that I have someone like him in my life. Ludwig is strong, and I know he will always keep me safe. He will never let anything happen to me. He will protect me and will forever love me. All I could think about was the beautiful night we shared for the first time. This year 1939, is going to be perfect.

Our most recent outing sealed my feelings and was no different than any other day. I worked my shift at the *Tabac*, and the crowd was average. The day ended, and I was getting ready to close the shop. I was behind the counter, leaning over to put the pipes onto the shelves. I heard the bells chime as the door opened. Here we go again, I thought to myself. I had to wait a few more minutes because of this late customer. I wish I had known who had walked in through the door.

It was five minutes to six o'clock, and I just wanted to go home. Hearing that jingle meant that I would have to miss dinner again. My parents always hated it whenever I came home late from work. Dinner is our sacred time together, as we huddle around the table, share our days, and listen to Papa's latest rants. Then, we all retire to the living room, where we listen to the radio or read our books. I like this time of the day, and it makes me sad when I miss it.

I sighed and brushed my skirt as I straightened up. I turned around, and Ludwig greeted me. He looked as handsome as ever as he stood there in a long black coat and a hat neatly seated on top of his head. I noticed the colorful bouquet in his hand. He had been patiently waiting for me to turn around so that he could have my attention. But I could only stand there like a fool with my mouth open in surprise. I should have smiled, and my current expression made Ludwig laugh.

"Cécile, I suggest you close that pretty little mouth of yours before you catch a fly," Ludwig said as he guffawed.

With embarrassment crawling up from the base of my neck to my cheeks, I closed my mouth. I had too many embarrassing moments to last a lifetime. In a way, I realized that Ludwig would always look at me with a tender look in his eyes whenever I did something I considered embarrassing, and he thought it was innocent.

However, I felt indignant as he laughed at me at that moment. I stood there frozen in time before he walked over to the counter and handed me the largest and most colorful bouquet. He had brought me flowers before, but this bouquet was something I had not seen before. There were so many flowers, so wide varieties. I felt he had picked an entire field of flowers to assemble this beautiful piece. I took the bouquet excitedly and held it up to my face. I wanted to smell them, but I also wanted to hide the wide grin that refused to leave my face. There were so many kinds, and I did not know which one to pick as my favorite: lilies, hyacinths, or roses. Besides, where did Ludwig get all these spring flowers in the middle of winter? I wondered.

"Do you like it?" Ludwig asked me with a grin, and I could not help but think how cheeky he looked, like a schoolboy who was happy to know that he had succeeded in stealing candy. I found it endearing as I looked down at all the white, pink, and purple shades blending in.

"I love it," I replied after I regained consciousness and found my voice. "What's the occasion?" I asked him shyly.

"I thought we could be together tonight. Alone, just the two of us," Ludwig said with a warm smile, and that was all I needed to hear before I found myself calling home to let Mama know I would not be home on time.

Of course, that meant that I would have to lie to my parents again; and I had never done something like that in my life before I met Ludwig. Lying never came easy to me, and I was lousy at it, but I knew I had to lie. That was a skill I had to master, which made me sad.

Papa would worry if he ever found out that I had spent the night with Ludwig. No. He would not worry, he would be furious, so I told them I was spending the night at Agnes'. I told my friends little lies before, but it only was because I could remember them, and they were harmless. However, this was a lie of biblical proportions I could never forget.

I lied to my parents and spent the night with Ludwig, and he took me to a charming restaurant a few blocks away. The place was marvelous. The restaurant was dimly lit with candles that created a soft glow around couples huddling over the table, and the ambiance was perfect.

Everyone seated inside looked sleek and quite elegant. The sleek chestnut-brown tables were meticulously organized, with plenty of spaces between them for extra privacy. A few were placed in front of the large panoramic windows framed by heavy maroon velvet curtains, looking out to the streets. I was nervous at first that I would not fit in, but having Ludwig by my side eased my mind, and I soon found myself lost in just how romantic the place was. We tried seafood cuisine, a treat that I would rarely have in my life because of how expensive it was. The dinner was delicious, and Ludwig ordered everything. It was partially my fault, though.

"What would you fancy, Cécile?" he asked while browsing through the menu.

I scanned the pages and could not make up my mind about it. "I don't know what to pick," I replied, and Ludwig raised a brow in question.

"Why? Do you not like seafood?" he asked me curiously, and I shook my head quickly.

"No, no, it's not that. It is—that I rarely have seafood with my family. We don't eat out much," I told him since I did not want to admit even to myself that we were too middle-class to have dinner in posh restaurants or not-so-posh ones.

Everything was expensive, and I was a little embarrassed to admit that I did not know some of the items, so I pretended to be hesitant.

"I just can't make up my mind about what to eat."

Ludwig nodded and looked at the waiter before requesting nearly everything on the menu. He ordered *bouillabaisse*, a creamy fish stew, mussels, and lobster, and it was so much I could only gape at the dinner as the waiters set them up.

"This is too much, Ludwig," I said with a shy blush.

Ludwig only chuckled, "I want to spoil you tonight, Cécile."

We soon ate, and I felt too full to be able to move. I could not possibly finish everything on the table and felt terrible, but Ludwig did not mind. He was happy to be here with me, and it showed. After an hour of walking around and discussing our dreams, Ludwig took me to his apartment.

He lived in an exceptionally grand one-bedroom apartment, larger than the two-bedroom I shared with my parents. The windows were wide enough to feel like you were looking over the entire world, not just Paris. The trees by the roadside provided enough shade during the summer but still let in plenty of light. The whole apartment felt trapped in a world of its own.

Ludwig came up behind me as I looked outside the window, mesmerized by the city lights. I painfully knew of his closeness. All my senses registered him when we were alone and away from the noise of this world. It was just the two of us, and I felt like every part of my body was on fire.

I had only turned around and found Ludwig's lips landing on mine. I do not remember what happened next, but I could only feel my heartbeat rise. Soon, we moved from there to the bedroom, where Ludwig and I made love for the first time. I am blushing as I write. I am not a prude but shy. It happened spontaneously; I am so glad it did because the anticipation would have surely killed me. Instead, our emotions took control and guided me through this beautifully erotic night.

The night was perfect, and we only whispered words of love at that moment with each other. I had all of him, and he had all of me. We were perfect together and fit like two pieces in a puzzle. I knew that I would never be able to forget this lovely night. Not now, not ever. We were bound to be together forever.

CHAPTER 12

WHITE DREAMS

Tuesday, 2 November 1999

Hénri felt completely taken aback when he came across the torn-out pages in the diary, although he remembered noticing it when he flipped through it the first time Jakov handed it to him. By now, he was so invested in Cécile's life that these lost pages disappointed him. Complete or partial sheets were missing from January 1939 to April 1939. Hénri wondered what happened to Cécile that made her tear out the pages. Or did someone else try to destroy it? He tried guessing what had happened in that missing period. Did Cécile break up with Ludwig after they became intimate? Why were the pages even missing? His curiosity demanded answers to these burning questions.

Hénri sadly sighed as he placed the diary on the wooden table before sitting on the sofa. He stretched his back and eyed the journal with a frown on his face. He never thought he would devote so much emotional energy to Cécile, which was different from the book he read as a teenager, *The Secret Diary of Adrian Mole, Aged 13¾*, a fictional comic story about a teenager and his hilarious coming-of-age problems. Hénri chuckled as it brought back fond memories. But that was fiction, and he was a teen. This journal and the story were real, and Cécile was real.

The diary also had historical importance, he thought. Hénri was only a young boy when his grandparents passed, and he never knew anyone who lived through the horrors of an impending war. Still, Cécile's diary proves that people still found love and intimacy, which was missing from all his school's history books.

Hénri waited for the suspense of Cécile's life to unfold in the diary. World War II was on Cécile's doorstep, and she was playing with fire. He knew this, but she did not. Cécile was a sweet and sensitive woman who read too much between the lines. She lived in a world of made-up fairytales for so long that she started believing in them… "She would tell me I was like her father," Hénri chuckled at this thought. She was direct but naïve.

Hénri was scared to read the end of the story, but his excitement felt like an irresistible itch one could not forget about. As tempted as he was to dive back into Cécile's life, he got up from the sofa and rubbed his eyes after placing his spectacles on the table. Hénri could not believe that he had been reading the diary for three hours, but his hunger remained unsatiated. He did not realize Cécile's life was about to change, and he was in for a lifetime surprise.

***

Thursday, 27 April 1939

Dear Diary,

Mama always told me our worlds look more colorful after falling in love. I asked her how she fell for Papa since he was such a tough man to have a good relationship with. Papa was strict and a man of few words, but Mama told me that it was what attracted her in the first place. I sat before her while she was knitting, like an eager child who wanted one more bedtime story. The world Mama talked about seemed like a magical place to be in.

"Do you still feel that way, Mama?" I asked her when she was talking about falling in love, and there was a ghost of sadness in her eyes as she smiled down at me.

"Love can only take us so far, and it never goes away. It transforms," she plainly said as if it were simple, but I only sat back with a frown.

I was not expecting such a response from Mama, and I thought she would reassure me that the flame always stays the same no matter how long we spend together. Love cannot be waned down by the simple passage of years, can it? I wondered about that as I thought about Ludwig and me before falling asleep that night.

I knew Ludwig loved me, and I loved him, but there was a strange sense of approaching chaos. Ludwig became busier at the embassy and traveled far more to Berlin than I had hoped. I hardly saw him at the shop anymore. He showered me with attention when he had the time, but it was proving difficult for us to be together. While I missed his regular visits, we talked over the telephone for hours. We talked about movies, music, and art. I told him about Élizabeth's experiences in the loony bin. He loved hearing about her stories and often asked about my friends. He thought Agnes was non-conforming for wanting a career and nothing else.

At times I became a little jealous of my friends and Ludwig's keen interest in them, but that soon dissipated, as always, because I knew Ludwig loved me with all his heart. He had yet to ask for my hand in marriage, which sometimes confused me. I had not spoken to him about my angst, and I feared he would run away if I talked about our nuptials. I fantasized about our life together and always pictured myself in his arms as I looked out the bedroom window.

Would Ludwig and I become blind to the colors of love with time, just as Mama said? I was not sure anymore, and it was making me uneasy. Thankfully, I had my friends who, even if for a short time, yanked me out of my worries. Agnes was concerned I would break our pact and tell everyone our secret, but I told her Élizabeth's secret was safe with me.

There was no way I would ever betray Élizabeth and reveal her identity to Ludwig. She was my darling friend. Slowly, I introduced the idea of including Ludwig in our get-togethers to her and Agnes because he assured me that he would be in my life forever, so my friends should get to know him, too. He is right. I cannot keep us separate forever, and this quarrel would be silly once we were married.

We met up with him on several occasions, but there were times when Élizabeth would get wary around Ludwig. He sometimes had some strange behavior, which I could not explain. I did not like how Ludwig would look at Élizabeth at times or when he pestered Agnes about her and her papa's work. That conversation was rather dull, so I never really paid much attention.

At times I noticed some strange spark in Ludwig's eyes whenever Élizabeth was around. I saw that spark when we kissed or held hands, but it became fainter as time passed. Élizabeth did not like him, and I knew why very well. Like many others, she felt intimidated in his company by his tall stature or handsome dark looks that beat all the actors of our times.

But of course, Élizabeth had other reasons for not wanting to be around him. She would try to excuse herself and leave early whenever I arrived with Ludwig, but he always insisted that she stay, and it was almost as if he did not want her to leave.

"I must go to work early in the morning, but please don't mind me. Carry on," Élizabeth would say gracefully before leaving.

I would get up and hug Élizabeth because she knew how much her approval meant to me. I could tell she was scared to be around a man like Ludwig, but I hoped she could see the man without his uniform. In my eyes, Ludwig was righteous, and he would never harm anyone like Élizabeth just for the sake of duty. He was compassionate, and men like him always put their values ahead of their orders.

"I'll see you around," Élizabeth whispered in my ears every time before she left, and I would see her off sadly.

Even though she made such promises of meeting more often, I knew Élizabeth and I would hardly get enough chances to meet. Sometimes, I would go to her place with my family from time to time, and her family would come over to mine for coffee, but even that became less and less frequent over the months.

A part of me knew that Élizabeth did not like seeing me with Ludwig from the way she always avoided his gaze. I felt that Ludwig started to like her more than he liked me. This thought crept into my mind and made my heart jealous, and my heart now sees what it wants to see.

My mind is fighting my emotions, and I sometimes feel I grabbed a slowly deflating life preserver. My mind assured me that Élizabeth feared Ludwig enough to stay away from him, but my heart saw her stealing the man I would die for.

Élizabeth's life has been filled with angst since they moved, but the political events throughout Europe leave everyone feeling a little nervous. Some days she is more agitated than usual, but then she is her cheery old happy self again. Those times reminded me of when we were little girls and walked to school together, skipping and laughing. She was a lot better student than I was. From a very young age, she was determined to become a nurse. Her mother was a nurse in World War I, just like Mama for a short time, so looking after the wounded must run in the family. Except I did not want anything to do with blood and guts. No, thank you!

While Agnes and I always wanted to play 'house,' Élizabeth just wanted to play 'hospital,' where she would be the nurse, and we were her obedient patients. We always had to have some injury, and she made us lay down on the ground in the park, her imaginary hospital, and she tended our wounds.

The psychiatric ward does not have that type of need for a nurse, but Élizabeth still loves it there. She tells me funny stories about what her patients do, but some are scary. I often wonder how they can lose their mind and what makes them end up behind bars because she told me there are bars on the windows. Patients were generally on electroshock treatment twice a week, but she said the maniacs were often strapped into a bathtub full of cold water to calm them down. This is terrifying.

I know one thing for certain. I do not ever want to end up in a looney bin.

But enough of reminiscing. Diary, I could hardly contain my excitement to tell you what happened today. Something that made all my worry seem to be a trick of my mind. Ludwig wants to meet my parents! I nearly died of excitement because I could not believe he wanted to marry me. What other reason would he want to meet them? I have longed to hear these words for a long time. I had dreamt about our marriage over and over again. I spent every waking minute imagining my dress and focused solely on those advertisements in the newspaper. Every detail of my dress was meticulously thought through. The material, satin, of course. The veil, long and sheer, and the bouquet of white lilies only. A spring wedding, naturally. Wouldn't it be wonderful if Ludwig decided to ask Papa's permission to marry me? Oh, I would melt to the ground. The hardest part was convincing my parents to meet up with Ludwig, but I believe Mama would approve. She had been suspicious about me meeting up with someone for a long time, and I will finally tell her about Ludwig tomorrow.

I know that sleeping now will be impossible, but I will think about my wedding until I fall asleep. Ludwig is finally taking a step forward, and I cannot help but respect him more for being a man of his word. He had promised that he would make me his, and it was finally time for him to fulfill my dreams of becoming his bride. Tonight, my dreams will be white and pure.

***

Hénri decided to head off to bed as well. He had to drop by his studio early in the morning, and he decided to call it a night. Although he was exhausted, he, too, had a hard time falling asleep. He could not stop thinking about Cécile and the mystery surrounding her and her diary.

Ever since he stepped into Cécile's life, he dreamt of her, and the journal came to life through a blurry lens. He saw a blood-stained wedding dress, flowers being thrown around, and a couple standing at the altar surrounded by a bizarre crowd that looked like the gargoyle statues looming from the top of the Notre Dame cathedral. Nazi aircraft were buzzing above the wedding party. Still, instead of bombs, they were dropping more grotesque-looking creatures into the crowd that eventually grew so huge it formed one giant wave and washed the whole party away.

Hénri woke up with a jolt and squinted at the sunlight that poured into his room through the bedroom window. He checked the time on the clock on the side table and groaned in annoyance. He was already late to his studio and quickly showered up. He rushed out of the apartment and decided many times in recent weeks to have breakfast on his way. He hopped on his bike and headed to the nearest local bakery.

The aura of freshly baked goods, from pastries to loaves of bread, filled the air, and he felt warm inside. The bakery owner, *Mademoiselle* Chloé, smiled at Hénri when she noticed him entering through the glass doors. She fancied the young man, and since Natalie no longer accompanied Hénri, Chloé felt she could be more forthcoming with him. She liked Natalie too, but their breakup gave Chloé an opportunity she would not otherwise have.

"Hénri, what a pleasure to see you every day," she said with a cheeky tone as she batted her eyelashes at him when he approached the counter. "What can I get you today?" She asked with a bright smile, and Hénri felt tongue-tied.

Chloé, a young woman, owned her shop with pride and ordered her staff and customers around like an admiral, his seamen. It was a family business handed down to her by her grandfather. Although the bakery was reputable because of her family, Chloé was an excellent baker and chef. Still, above all, she was an innovative thinker that made this bakery packed with people. After taking it over from her grandfather *Monsieur*

Petit-Didier, she extended the bakery to include a small but charming dining area, and *Café Du Monde* was born.

Despite the number of clients, Chloé always made time for Hénri. She was a pretty twenty-four-year-old with long, light brown hair, green eyes, and fair skin. Hénri had always found the playful woman beautiful, but her bold personality reminded him too much of Natalie, and the last thing he needed was another heartbreak.

"I'll have a cappuccino with a cheese croissant, please," Hénri finally responded as he ran a hand through his unruly curls.

Chloé smiled, "Cappuccino, cheese croissant coming right up," she said as she jotted down his orders, and Hénri took a seat near the counter with a nod.

'If I'm going to be late, I might as well take my time,' Hénri thought. Living in a rented apartment was convenient but always felt temporary. Jakov did not need him there this morning, but Hénri insisted that as the owner, he be there. He wanted to make sure everything was going according to plan. Hénri was a perfectionist, a trait he inherited from his mother. He had dreamt of owning his place for a while, and each day, he came one step closer to making this dream a reality. Some might even believe that Hénri was overexcited, but the truth was that he was just eager to live and work in his place without worrying about anything else. It was the next step he needed to take in life.

Chloé approached Hénri with his food after a few minutes and looked around to see that the place was already packed. Chloé always served Hénri his food quickly, and Hénri decided to let loose a little as he gave her a sweet smile as she placed the plate in front of him.

"I tried a new recipe for the croissant this morning, and it's straight out of the oven too. I'd love to hear some feedback," she said, and Hénri nodded.

"I will, thank you," he replied with a small smile, and Chloé deeply blushed before she hurried away.

Hénri almost laughed at her adorable behavior and wondered if the diary was getting to his head or if it was true what people said, 'Only time can heal a broken heart.' But what if time stood still since Natalie left? He shook this thought out of his head.

He always considered Chloé a good friend, but recently he started seeing her in a different light. He began to see things he had never noticed before. He caught her eyes a few times, and she decided to come over to chat with Hénri a bit. Chloé was a beautiful woman, and honestly, Hénri did not know what she saw in him.

Chloé could have anyone she wanted, but somehow, she took an interest in Hénri. Maybe I am being too presumptuous, Hénri thought to himself. Maybe Chloé does not like me that much, and I read too much between the lines. "Let's hope that time will heal the broken heart and not break a waiting one, too, in the process," he thought and rolled the cutlery out of the napkin.

Hénri dug into his breakfast and heartily ate while conversing with Chloé in between. She seemed happy to have his attention for a change, and Hénri no longer wondered if he were saying the right things. He felt strange confidence this time, and for the first time in months, he enjoyed a beautiful woman's company while eating breakfast. Soon, he found himself lost in the green-eyed beauty's tale of baking adventures.

Hénri decided to keep reading the diary once he was back in his apartment at the end of the day. He did not know how uncertain this life can be and how quickly our worlds can change once we allow someone new into our lives. Hénri was unaware of the chaos waiting for him at the apartment in that little diary, but he seemed to enjoy the rest of his day while bathing in blissful ignorance. After all, Hénri has been sensitive to others' feelings since childhood, but he had no idea that the diary had been slowly changing his life from the moment he opened the cover.

CHAPTER 13

WORLD WAR II

S unday, 3 September 1939

Dear Diary,

I woke up today, unaware of the news, and noticed that Mama and Papa were not themselves. Instead of finding Mama standing before the stove making toast, she was huddled in front of the radio with a stricken expression. Papa had abandoned the morning newspaper on the table and stood beside Mama—not pacing the room with his cigarette in his hand. They had forgotten about their regular morning routine as the radio blared. The broadcast cracked, and the correspondent sounded monotonous as he delivered devastating and life-altering news.

"In response to Hitler's invasion of Poland just two days ago, Britain and France declared war on Germany."

Mama emitted a frightening gasp as she covered her face. I had just walked in when the news had been delivered and was confused to see them look terrified.

"Papa, is there any coffee?" I tried to ask as quietly as possible, but Papa hushed me into silence without even looking at me. His full attention was focused on what the man on the radio was saying. I stood by the kitchen door and heard the declaration of war, and I felt like someone had instantly snatched the ground beneath my feet.

War? How? Why? I do not understand how a war could break out right now. I wondered if I had to go to work today. Will the café be closed? What about the cinema? Oh God, will I ever get to see Ludwig today? He told me he would come by today to meet me at the shop.

I honestly wished he would give me his telephone number. I would worry about him a lot less. He was such a gentleman who could not see me lift a finger. He did everything for me, but I know little about his life in Paris.

I was also worried about our marriage now. Ludwig had asked my father for my hand in marriage in April, and my parents, reluctantly, I might add, have agreed. I was so worried Papa would say no. His obvious aversion to Germans did not help, but I hoped he would see how much his approval would mean to me once he met Ludwig. I still have difficulty believing he agreed, and now I cannot help but wonder why a sudden change of heart, but I dared not ask.

I could feel my heart shatter at the thought of my wedding being canceled. What will all my friends think? I was supposed to be worrying about my wedding dress and venue, not about war and the impact it would have on us. There cannot be a war now!

Mama and Papa had decided to keep the wedding news quiet. Now, I knew why they had done that. They predicted that this would happen. That one day, we would all wake up to the news of France being at war with Germany. Oh, I was terrified now but for all selfish reasons.

Papa went to work early today, and I rode the *Métro* in a fog that did not clear. My mind had been scattered as I tried to tend to the customers, but it was hard to keep my mind focused when all I could worry about was my wedding. Everyone was agitated and wanted to talk about the war, but I was elsewhere in my thoughts. We talked about our wedding last when Ludwig met my parents. After that, no one uttered a word about marriage. Mama had told me not to tell anyone yet because she was unsure when the wedding would be held. Just having my parents' approval sent me over the moon. Now, I wondered if Ludwig would even marry me before being deployed.

I wanted to see Ludwig, and I almost thought he had given up on his promise to meet me today until I saw him enter the shop. I immediately moved around the counter and engulfed him in a tight hug.

"Oh, Ludwig, I thought you forgot about the promise you made me yesterday." I nearly cried tears of joy and moved back to give him a bright smile.

However, Ludwig's expression remained passive as he leaned down to kiss me on the forehead. His grim expression worried me, and I bit my lower lip out of habit. I gently touched the side of his face, "Is everything okay, my love?" I asked him quietly.

Ludwig looked at me for a moment, his dark eyes swirling with too many emotions before he shook his head.

"No, Cécile, nothing is ever going to be okay," Ludwig stated, and I felt my heart drop to my stomach at that statement. What did he mean by that? "Are you closing the shop right now?" he asked, and I nodded.

"Yes, I was just about to close. Give me a few minutes," I said, and Ludwig quietly walked out of the shop.

It was strange to see my Ludwig being so worn down. He looked lifeless as he stood beside the door with a cigarette hanging between his teeth. He always looked handsome whenever he smoked, but today, something was sad about him.

"We shall go to my place," he stated as he took my arm in his, and we walked away.

"What about dinner?" I asked him with a frown. I was expecting him to take me to a restaurant.

Ludwig sighed, "Do you know how to cook?" he asked as we walked down the dark alley. Ludwig lived near the shop and always walked back home instead of taking the *Métro*.

"I can," I replied hesitantly. "Well, Mama taught me how to cook, but I don't know if my cooking is that great yet. The only thing I can make perfectly is soup and bread."

"Then, let's have that for tonight," he informed me tiredly before he finally smiled. "I want to know what my future wife's cooking tastes like before I go into war," he said, and I felt my biggest fears coming to life.

What did he mean by that? I was too scared to ask him why he looked so upset, but I held myself back as we finally entered his spacious apartment. Ludwig helped me in the kitchen as I looked more like a fish out of water than a confident housewife. Despite being a clumsy cook, I still had so much fun that I forgot what he had said when we went to his apartment.

Ludwig and I had a simple dinner, then stepped outside onto the balcony. The world was on fire, and our countries were at war, but the warm autumn evening air surrounded us like a blanket as we smoked a cigarette and gazed up at the starry night. I felt content and at peace, but it was soon shattered when Ludwig spoke up.

"There's something I need to tell you, Cécile," Ludwig slowly said as if he was talking to a child.

"What is it?" I asked him in a small voice. I was afraid of whatever news he wanted to give me.

Ludwig led me back into the living room and he handed me a glass of red wine before he sat beside me.

"We need to postpone the wedding," he told me, and I felt as if all the blood rushed out of my body.

"You're saying this because of the war, aren't you? You're saying this because you're going to be a part of this war," I accusingly said as I felt myself tear up. My dreams shattered when the broadcaster broke the news, but it did not become a nightmare until these words left his lips.

"Yes."

We sat silently for a few moments before I looked up at Ludwig. "I don't care whether or not you're going to war. I know it is your duty, but I want us to marry before this war takes over our lives. Ludwig, please, let us get married. I do not care whether I have the perfect wedding dress or not; I just want us to be married. I want us to be together." I begged, but Ludwig shook his head.

"It's not that simple, Cécile. We cannot get married right now. It's not... it's just not that simple."

"It is if we just do it. All we have to do is exchange our vows and sign the certificate. We can—we can go to the court tomorrow and get married. I do not want to postpone the wedding. It can just be you and me." I begged and felt like a child pestering her parents for an extra candy bar. But I was desperate and did not want him to leave without giving me something.

"Why would you want to marry a man who will probably die in this war? Do you want to become a widow that badly?" Ludwig snapped at me angrily, and I shook my head.

"Don't say that! You're not going to die."

"What if I did die? What will you do then? Will you spend the rest of your life as a mourning widow? I am doing this for your sake, Cécile, not mine, and I do not want to ruin your life." He snarled at me and stood up.

I stood up as well and grabbed him by his arm. "We can run away. You don't have to be a part of this war."

"Cécile, no! The army would find me if I decided to run away. Serving is my duty, and I am not a coward or a traitor."

"I don't understand!" I wept, and disappointment was evident in my voice as I looked at him past my tears.

The thought of losing Ludwig in this war was killing me but not marrying him was even worse. If he loved me, then he would do anything for me, and I did not want to send my love off to a war where he could be killed or injured. This was not our war, to begin with.

"We love each other, don't we? I gave myself to you, and you promised me we would get married. You told me we would settle down together and start our own family. We can still do that, Ludwig. We can run away to Switzerland, buy a house in the Alps, and raise our children there. We do not have to live through this war. We can leave everything behind. We can leave everyone behind!" I cried out, but Ludwig only seemed angry now as he held me back by my shoulders tightly.

"What don't you understand, dammit? It is a war, Cécile. For heaven's sake, try to think with a sober mind for once. I knew you were naïve and never had your priorities in order, but you must pull yourself together. It is not that easy, and I would never run away from something like this. Do you want me to live the rest of my life in shame?"

"Living in shame is better than dying too early," I shouted angrily.

Ludwig's dark eyes brewed with anger, and I could tell he was losing his temper; he clenched his hands into fists, and it almost looked like he wanted to hit something. He finally relaxed after a moment and ran a hand through his hair.

"We're postponing the wedding. We do not know how long this war will last, and I will not get married right before I walk into a battlefield. You are still as naïve as ever, and you can live in the clouds, but I cannot, Cécile. I am a man of honor and will carry out my duties."

"But Ludwig—"

"Enough! Let us not talk about this anymore. I will come over tomorrow to inform your parents about our decision. You need to go back home. It's getting late," Ludwig said, and his words felt like a punch to my stomach. "I'm going to be a part of this war, and I don't want to involve you in this any more than I already have."

"It is not my decision. You just don't want to marry me!" I said as the realization settled down. Ludwig talked about postponing our marriage as if he had been contemplating it for months, and it seemed as if he had thought about it before the war started.

"It's not that I don't want to marry you, and I would never ask your parents for your hand if I did not want to marry you. It's not the right time to be married," Ludwig lied because he did not look convincing. His eyes screamed at me to get out before I said something I would regret.

But I was not as naïve as he thought I was. I had noticed everything: Ludwig's eyes would wander over Élizabeth with interest. I noticed how he seemed to stare at her whenever she was around me. Élizabeth was prettier than I was, and she was smarter as well. His hesitancy over our marriage made it obvious that Ludwig liked her and had taken a keen interest in her months ago.

"It is because you like Élizabeth, isn't it?" I asked him suddenly and immediately regretted it as Ludwig slowly turned around to glare at me. I knew I had made a terrible mistake, but my emotions clouded any judgment I had ever had, and I was not about to let it go. I had nothing and everything to lose. "Or is it because you like men, too?" I continued firing my provocative questions at him, and the flicker of fear and fury in his eyes made me sick to my stomach.

I knew Ludwig was scared. He had always been afraid of me finding out. I had observed him for a while and always felt odd whenever we made love. Something just was not right. I wanted this love over anything I ever had. I saw him staring at male customers at the shop and striking up conversations with younger men at the club whenever I did not bring Élizabeth. I did. I saw it but brushed it off because I wanted 'us.' I desperately wanted us to be a couple. After some time, it felt that only these two things mattered to him: his lust for Élizabeth and his fondness for men. Unfortunately, these two things also scared him the most. I was no longer his focus, or maybe I never was.

I stepped up to Ludwig with my head held high, "I know all about you, Ludwig. I know the man I love the most, and I know you like Élizabeth. I also know you are interested in men..."

Ludwig cut me off as he suddenly pushed me against the wall and grabbed me by my neck. I squeaked in pain and grabbed his hand, holding my throat before I glared back at him. Ludwig was shaking with anger. He reminded me of a raging bull in the way he stared down at me with tightened lips. His eyes were wide with rage, and I could see the fear swimming in those dark eyes. His breath felt heavy against my face, and I knew I had hit a nerve.

My mind became numb once I realized that I was right. A shock like no other slid down my spine as I stared at Ludwig with a dumbfound expression.

"Ludwig," all I could say was his name as I ventured into forbidden territory.

"If you ever say that again, I will kill you. You hear me!" He whispered angrily, but I did not realize at this point that it was not Élizabeth that pushed him into such rage.

"Liar. You won't kill me because you love me." But even as I said it, I sounded unsure. I looked Ludwig straight in the eyes as I desperately looked for assurance, but I could find none. "I thought I was wrong, but you love Élizabeth. How could you do this to me?" I shouted at him before I struggled to push him away from me.

Ludwig only slammed me into the wall harshly before he backhanded me so hard that I felt the warm blood running down my nose. I heard something crack and realized that he had nearly dislocated my jaw. His punch had been powerful enough, and he did not know how strong he was as he let go of me. I slumped down on the floor in defeat as I felt my world crashing around me. It was as if my very existence had been shattered into million little pieces at that moment.

"You're insane, you whore! Of course, anyone would like Élizabeth over you. She is prettier and smarter than you. Unlike you, she is a classy woman. You sound like a sniveling little peasant. You are a disgrace, Cécile, and nothing but filth on the sole of my shoe." He thundered, and I felt my sanity snap that very moment.

I blurted out the words before I could even stop them.

"Élizabeth can never be yours because she's a Jew, you idiot! Agnes's father gave the whole family fake identity." I gasped when I realized what I had said and felt like someone had thrown a bucket of freezing water all over my body.

Ludwig seemed stunned for a moment before he reached down to grab me by the hair.

"Ludwig, stop!" I pleaded with him, but he pulled my hair harshly to stop me from struggling under his grip. My head throbbed horribly under his tight grip. I looked up at the man who swept me off my feet. An ugly expression covered his face, making him look like a monster, not the man I once loved and adored.

"What did you just say?" Ludwig asked as if he did not hear me, but I knew he did. It was clear that he heard me loud and clear. I could see it in his eyes, but I also saw a strange grin. It maddened him to know that he loved someone who was a Jew and someone who belonged to a group of people he hated the most. I could see the goosebumps on his skin as he stood there like a statue.

His mind was spiraling down into a dangerous rage as he tried to comprehend what he had heard. All I could do was sob as I realized what I had done. I broke the promise I made to Élizabeth and Agnes. I told Ludwig something in a fit of jealousy without realizing that I had placed my best friend's existence in danger.

Ludwig slowly let go of my hair as he pulled me up by the arm. He grabbed my hat and coat and threw them at me, and he opened the door and kicked me out like some lowly beggar.

"Get out of here, Cécile, and don't you dare ever come back."

"Ludwig, please." I cried, but he only gave me one last push.

"Cécile. You still do not understand. My job was to find out who was helping the Jews in Paris, and you gave me exactly what I needed to know. Just get out. Get out of here before I kill you with my bare hands!" He said with a clenched jaw and slammed the door shut. The last expression I saw on the face of the man I loved was disgust, which devastated me.

I felt like I was a million miles away as I slowly walked out of the building and looked around the empty streets. The world was on fire, and my dream was burning with it. I could feel my face swelling horribly, and I saw my cheek was turning a gruesome blue color when I passed by a glass window. I took a handkerchief out of my coat pocket and wiped the dried blood off my face, but I could not go home like this! I felt disgusted and horrified as I tried to comprehend what had just happened.

Ludwig used me. He used me and threw me away like a piece of garbage after I betrayed my friends. But he did have feelings for Élizabeth, and he did like men. I was right about those things, and I do not think Ludwig expected me to uncover his secrets, but what will I tell Mama and Papa?

The pain and shame I felt gave me a moment of clarity. I quickly tore off pieces from my skirt and coat and threw some of the money into the nearest dustbin so I could be disguised as a robbery victim.

I needed my thievery story to work because I needed an excuse for looking so disheveled and bruised. I went to the nearest police station and filed a report before telephoning Papa. I waited for him at the station. When I spotted him, I ran straight into his arms, and he hugged me tightly. Then, I burst into tears.

"What happened, Cécile?" he asked me with concern, but all I could do was sob in his arms.

How could I possibly tell him that I ruined everything? That the man who I was going to marry hit me? The man who they trusted, who I trusted and loved, was a monster? I stood there engulfed in my father's arms, wishing I were dead.

Ludwig hated me, but I realized that my love for him turned into hatred after everything he did to me. In a split second, my most cherished emotion turned. I was afraid of what would happen now and could only cry helplessly. I knew the crime I committed tonight was too big, and there was no way I would ever be forgiven even if I tried.

I had made the biggest mistake of my life, and regret seemed to eat me up from the inside out. As Papa took me back home, the only thought running through my head was that I wanted to die. I could not stop crying, and Papa thought the robbery had been too traumatizing. If only he knew. I could hardly think straight as that one agonizing thought kept me imprisoned for the rest of the night.

What have I done?

Chapter 14
Vel' d'Hiv

Hénri could feel his heart racing in his chest, his breathing increasing. Anger rushed through his body and put him into fight or flight mode only; he wanted to fight Ludwig. No man should ever treat a woman like Ludwig treated Cécile. He used her, beat her, and this poor woman, out of desperation, betrayed her best friend. It must be done.

Hénri was agitated to read on. He desperately wanted to know now what happened to Cécile, but his determination was doused when he noticed the date of the next entry, which read 1942. Hénri sat up and flipped the journal around, looking for signs of tearing.

"Ugh. Another missing period," Hénri murmured in disbelief, but he could not find any sign of destruction this time. Cécile did not write for nearly three years. With a disappointed sigh, he turned the page.

★★★

Thursday, 16 July 1942

Diary,

I do not know where to start or where to continue. Hitler had set the world on fire, but I struck the match that burned my hopes to the ashes. It has been almost three years of utter agony and hell. I could not bear to write anymore after that fateful night. I was scared of my thoughts. I was scared for my friends, and I was scaring myself. All I wanted was to die. It took me a long time to work up the courage to even look at you again, Diary. There have been days and months when I wondered why I was alive. My heartache has led me back to you, and I will again bear all my sins as I fill you up with my regrets. After all, shame has become an abiding part of my life.

It has been three painful years since I last saw or heard of Ludwig. The night had sealed my faith and shattered my dreams. It was as if the man had fallen from the face of the earth. I searched for him everywhere, but it was as if Ludwig never existed. His lovely home now stood empty and cold. I worked every day in hopes of him coming by. I waited for him to walk through the door. I clung to this foolish hope that he might come back and apologize. We would kiss and cry together. I hoped I could tell him that I was lying about Élizabeth—that I was angry and clouded by jealousy.

Mama and Papa were genuinely concerned about my injuries after the 'robbery,' but those healed in no time, and although they did not say, they did not miss Ludwig. We were at war! I prayed for three years as I spent every day in utter agony believing, hoping, as much as it hurt to admit, but hoping, that Ludwig loved Élizabeth enough to let her be. Sadly, I cannot say the same for my heart because I know it will be forever broken. I do not know what to say because no words can amount to the terror I still feel at this very moment.

Élizabeth and her family went into hiding shortly after Germany invaded Poland. We cut all contact with them, and I had not had the chance to lie about my injuries and tell her about my terrifying robbery.

My hands are shaking, writing this down for the first time, as these heavy words stare back at me like a mirror of my actions. Élizabeth still did not know, only Ludwig and I did, that I had betrayed her. To my horror, I woke up today to the news that the Gestapo found the Klotz family hiding on a nearby farm on the outskirts of Paris, and they dragged the entire family out of their beds, dreams, and lives. I handed my best friend over to the Gestapo on a silver platter.

The Klotz family will be killed, and I know it would be entirely my fault. Élizabeth and her family would not have been discovered if it were not for me. My hands will forever be tainted with blood if I do not do something about this. I can hardly write because tears blur my vision as they run down my face and soak the pages.

When I heard about the roundup, I ran to the stadium, the *Vélodrome d'Hive*, and I saw my ultimate fear coming true. Jews were everywhere by the hundreds and thousands, just scattered in front of the large gate. Other non-Jewish people loitered around as if they were sizing up the opposite team's fans before getting ready to watch a wrestling match.

Despite Mama's disapproval, Papa took me there in the summer of 1924 for the Olympic games. I was only six, but I remember the excitement and laughter. Today now I saw confusion.

My eyes caught Élizabeth, and her disheveled appearance drove a stake through my heart. Her face was soaked with tears as she held Mimi close in her arms, protecting her from getting lost in the crowd. Her parents all wore brown coats with a yellow star on them. I felt a scream lodged in my throat as I tried to get past the people. I wanted to do whatever it took to get close to them, and my guilt nearly ate me alive.

It was my fault. It was my fault that the whole family was about to be plunged into a deep nightmare they were unaware of. There would no longer be any days where I would talk to Élizabeth during my lunch break, and I would no longer be able to hold her close and hug her tightly. My best friend was there in the crowd, looking utterly terrified.

The reality and fear I had avoided in the past three years were staring at me through Élizabeth's eyes. It made me nauseous as my knees gave out, and I fell. Élizabeth, who had always been brave and confident, stood there looking petrified. I had never seen such nauseating terror on her face. Her fear was the manifestation of my own. I was scared, shaking, and heaving, and as I was getting off the ground, it hit me. I had to get her out of there. I had to, even if it meant being in that crowd filled with angst. I was trying so hard to get closer to them. I did not care how heavily the police guarded them. I only wanted to hug Élizabeth and tell her everything would be okay.

But a stranger held me back as I screamed for Élizabeth. The misery of every sleepless night, and waking moment of the last three years came crashing like a tidal wave. I have to make this right somehow.

A thought came to me suddenly. Could I explain that this has been a terrible mistake? I knew the ones at the desk would not have the authority; if nothing else, I learned this from Ludwig. However, I could find the officer in charge if I were inside the stadium. Although it is risky, I am completely useless from this side of the gate, but the only way I could get inside is if I became a Jew.

This budding plan gives me hope, but I have a significant obstacle to overcome. The obstacle is that I must confess if I involved Agnes and her father's connections to obtain Jewish identification papers.

★★★

Hénri put the diary down as he felt his chest filling with emotions, and his heart was beating in his throat. He could feel Cécile's devastation through the pages, which weighed heavy on him. He finally knew what it felt like to be alone, harboring such a secret. Cécile did not have anyone to confide in but her diary, who would listen to her worries without judgement. This diary was her everything, and it was disheartening. She was alone despite having friends. They would not have understood, would they?

It was unbelievable how deeply this diary was affecting Hénri. He had never honestly thought about World War II other than what he studied in school. He was the nineteenth-century-romantic type of man who believed in the exaltation of emotion over reason and of the senses over intellect. Still, Cécile connected to him through her pain, and the diary put him through an emotional rollercoaster of love and anger.

After reading about the argument between Ludwig and Cécile, he wished he could step in and punch Ludwig in the face. Cécile loved him more than the world, and he had betrayed her love so easily as if it meant nothing. Cécile had almost fooled herself and Hénri when she talked about him. Hénri was hoping for a happy ending, in a truly romantic way, maybe he wanted to read about her marriage and her children, but he was instead plunged into the world of war and terror.

***

My Sweet Diary,

After I saw Élizabeth and her family by the stadium with all the other Jews, I ran straight to Agnes's apartment and told her everything. Three years later, I could finally bring myself to say what I had done that night. For three years, I have been carrying this pain.

If it were not for the war, she would have noticed my agony after that ghastly night with Ludwig, but she attributed my pain to the anxiety the entire world was carrying. I finally confessed my sins. I lied for my happiness, and I lied to hide my sorrow, but finally, confiding in her made me feel better, and I needed her help.

I was not expecting her to slap me across the face, but I knew I deserved much worse as I stood before her with my head bowed in shame. Agnes was livid and sat back down on her living room sofa as she cried into her hands. We had not seen or spoken to each other for a month, but Agnes called me to her house in a panic once when the Gestapo made threats against the Jews.

They were forewarned of the danger, but since their name was changed from Klotz to Bossard, they had nothing to fear —or so they thought. They should have been safe, and they would have been safe if I had not betrayed them, which was a heavy burden.

"Cécile, what in God's name have you done?" Agnes asked through her choked tears, and I stood there in silence.

I knew I had done the worst thing a person could do. No one would do this to their worst enemy, and I had done it to my very own friend. Élizabeth, who was like a sister to me. I never felt like an only child because I always had Élizabeth by my side, and this is how I repaid her friendship.

I was the lowest degenerate in this world, and standing before Agnes in humiliation only made me feel worse.

"What have you done?" Agnes asked hysterically and repeatedly as she got up and grabbed me by the arms. She shook me uncontrollably, and I could only cry in response. I stood there like a ragdoll as Agnes demanded answers. Her grip was so tight that I could feel her nails digging into my skin and bruising me, but this did not hurt as much as watching Élizabeth's pained eyes did. These years taught me nothing is worse than the pain tormenting the heart. Nothing could hurt me anymore. I would rather take a thousand beatings over and over than feel this miserable ever again.

"I don't know, Agnes, I don't know. It was an accident." Words spilled out of my mouth, and that was all it took for me to break down. "Remember the night a couple of years ago when I was mugged on the street? I was not. I was in Ludwig's apartment, and we were arguing. He wanted to postpone the wedding, and I was angry. It slipped out because I suspected that he liked Élizabeth. I was jealous, and he hit me. He called me all sorts of names I am too ashamed to repeat. I told him Élizabeth could never be his because she was a Jew, and it was as if everything inside him snapped. He is a monster, Agnes! I thought he loved me, but he was only playing with me all this time. Oh God, I've ruined everything." I sobbed in her arms, and Agnes let go of me as if she had touched fire.

"Now it makes sense why the Germans raided my father's office. You told Ludwig he helped Élizabeth," Agnes cried out as she stepped back.

I nearly fell to the floor, but Agnes caught me and helped me sit on the sofa. I could hardly speak as the sobs made their way out of my throat. Agnes gave me a glass of water to calm me down and handed me a handkerchief.

"We can't do anything now, Cécile," Agnes sobbed and wiped her nose.

I shook my head at her, "I know what we can do. I have an idea, Agnes, but I need your Papa's help."

Agnes frowned at me, "The Nazis have already rounded up Élizabeth and her family. There is nothing we can do now. It is too late. We could have done something if you had told me the truth right after it happened, but it's too late now." Agnes said in a firm voice as she tried to stop weeping herself. I knew she was furious at me and would never forgive me even if I begged for it.

"I need your Papa to help me get a new identity. A Jewish identity."

"Haven't you done enough damage? What makes you think my father can still help? What exactly are you planning?" Agnes fired her questions at me at a rapid pace.

I looked into Agnes' eyes, "I need papers to get inside the *Vel' d'Hiv*. I'll find the officer in charge and explain their arrest was nothing but a colossal mistake," I explained patiently, and Agnes looked at me with bewilderment.

"Have you lost your mind?" Agnes snapped at me angrily. "Do you even know what would happen to you if you did make your way there? There's no way anyone can get you out once you're in."

"There's no other way! We cannot do anything from here, and I need to get inside."

"And then what, Cécile? What are you going to do once you're in?" She asked in a frustrated voice. I was unsure what angered her more—me betraying Élizabeth or this less-than-ideal plan. She knew I did not have this thought out, and she was impatient with me. But I knew I had to make things right.

"I don't know, Agnes," I whispered as I tried to wipe my tears. "I don't know, I, I ... I'll explain to the Gestapo that it is all a misunderstanding, and they will let us go," I improvised quickly, and Agnes shook her head in disbelief.

I could tell she already thought I was going insane, and she was not wrong, either. This deadlock of a situation was driving me mad. I wanted to break out of this eternal hell, and do right by her, even if I had to throw myself in the line of fire to rescue her.

I had sinned, Diary; sinners like me cannot live peacefully in this world. There is no place for someone like me. Mama and Papa were also terrified. Papa kept a close eye on me, but he also cared for Mama as her mind was rather unstable. None of this was fair, and I would not run away from this like a coward.

"You're not making any sense, Cécile!" Agnes said before she placed a hand on her forehead to keep the headache away. "What about Ludwig? Do you have any idea where he is or what he's up to?" She asked me.

"He disappeared after we fought. I have not seen him since. Why?"

"We need to know he won't be coming after you now that he's taken Élizabeth" Agnes said, but she did not believe her own words.

I thought about it briefly before looking at Agnes with shame. "There is something I haven't told you, Agnes. I found out that Ludwig likes men and women ... sexually. He may be homosexual, but I can't be sure," I explained to Agnes, who listened to me with interest.

I looked at Agnes wide-eyed. "I can call the embassy and tip them off anonymously. I can tell them Ludwig is queer, and they will sentence him to prison. He will never hurt anyone again," I said slowly, but Agnes did not look happy with this plan either.

She stared back at me as if my idea had gone from bad to worse. Maybe I did lose my mind after arguing with Ludwig that night, and I cannot think clearly anymore, which would not be far-fetched. These three years had taken a part of my sanity, the same way Ludwig robbed me of my heart. I had been living like a freak, like Frankenstein. Just a body of flesh without a soul. I wanted revenge, and this was the first time I felt revenge was the right thing to do. Agnes tried to convince me that I was on a suicide mission, but her words fell on deaf ears. I made up my mind and told her I would get Jewish papers with or without her help.

Before I got home, I walked up to the nearest phone booth and called the embassy anonymously. I told them about Ludwig and his secrets before cutting the call.

I was in command now, but I did not realize it was just a matter of time before everything spiraled out of control and started taking its own course. I do not regret turning Ludwig in for being homosexual, and my desire for revenge is strong. I knew the Nazis would imprison him since being homosexual was not part of their master plan of producing a pure race, which was only the first part of my plan, and I finally felt the guilt easing. I could finally breathe a little easier, but I was far from being absolved of my sins.

Obtaining fake documents without Agnes's help was much more difficult than I thought. I attempted to steal papers I could falsify later, but I am a lousy pickpocket. I am yearning to see Élizabeth and her family and clear up this mess. I am confident my plan will work, but time is running out, and I need to get them out of the stadium. I will not be able to live if I did nothing. I am the one who got her into captivity, and I will be the only one who can get her out of it.

Agnes told me I was naïve if I believed I could help Élizabeth. She was mad at me and said that my plan was nothing but a death wish. But I am determined, and there is no way I will let anyone stop me from getting inside that stadium.

CHAPTER 15
PLAN IN MOTION

Tuesday, 28 July 1942

Dear Diary,

This is it. This is when I give up everything to make up for the single mistake I made at the spur of the moment. I allowed my emotions to get the best of me and spilled a secret that never should have been revealed. I risked the life of someone I loved for someone I thought I loved. I risked Élizabeth's life for Ludwig's sake and lost both. I have too many questions running through my mind. Questions without answers, like a future without its past.

Paris looks different under the Nazi occupation. Soldiers walk the streets, drinking their coffee in the café like everything is normal. But nothing is normal. Not to me, not to Élizabeth or the other hundreds of Jews in the stadium. I kept looking for Ludwig's face in the crowd for a while, but the last hope of ever seeing him again waiting for me by the shop vanished with that call to the embassy. The last hope of ever reconciling was gone; all I was left with were memories, but I must stop reminiscing and stay focused. If I give in to Ludwig's memory and the love I had, I fear I may not carry out my plan.

Agnes convinced her Papa to arrange a new Jewish identity for me after seeing how determined I was and how many times I failed on my own. Agnes knew the inevitable, but she let me go through with my plan anyway, as an approval of my path to redemption. She was crying as she handed the papers over.

I do not know what is waiting for me in the stadium or if I will even make it out alive, but I will figure everything out once I am inside.

I have my fake documents tucked into my stockings; it is the only place I can think of now. Doubts are slowly creeping in as I look around my room. Nervousness sets in, and my hands tremble as I write these words. Was Agnes right when she said it was too late to help Élizabeth? What if I never found Élizabeth and her family? Oh God, I no longer know what I am doing and am nauseated, but I need to remind myself that I was doing this for my friend. I am becoming Cécile Eisner for Élizabeth, and everything will be fine.

That thought alone comforts me enough to solidify my plan. My mind continues reeling with second thoughts, but at least I know my heart is in the right place. Before I leave it all behind, I need to dispose of this diary. I tried setting it on fire in the kitchen earlier, thinking it would burn to ashes quickly, but I had to extinguish it because of the smoke. I did not want to alert the neighbors, let alone set the entire house on fire.

Mama and Papa have already gone to work. I told them I was feeling sick today so that I could put my final plan into motion. I kissed them goodbye and hugged them, but not too tightly. I could not reveal anything to them now, not even by my actions. I knew they would do their best to stop me if they found out what I was up to, but I would be back by dinner. It was unnecessary to make them worry for no reason, I told myself repeatedly.

I leave you here to rest, my sweetest Diary. If my parents had not found you under the floorboard, you would be safe here. Please keep my secret until I come back tonight.

Oh, and pray for me.

★★★

Hénri sat up at the abrupt ending of the diary. He could not believe that Cécile had gone this far. Indeed, this was a suicide mission, and he feared that Cécile had fallen victim to the Holocaust with millions of others. Hénri could almost see this faceless woman stepping out of the apartment to carry out her mission. He pictured her taking one last look at the building before making her way to hell, leaving everything dear to her behind.

Hénri could not believe how his world had collided with Cécile's. He felt connected to this woman, but at the same time, they were worlds apart. Hénri wanted to know what had happened to her. Did she die as he feared? Did she help Élizabeth escape? What happened next? As much as Hénri hesitated to start reading this journal, he was disappointed that it ended. He could not believe how emotionally invested he had become.

At first, he told himself to treat this just like any other story, a work of fiction, mainly to soothe his conscience for intruding. But the story became personal to Hénri, which did not surprise him. Hénri was the type of man who would easily get attached to things or people, but most of all, books and movies roped him in with ease, like a cowboy roping wild cattle. Reading a book or watching a film put Hénri in a trance. The stories put a spell on him, and he became one with them, and in that sense, he was a lot like Cécile.

But this diary had left him with feelings that changed from one page to the next. He felt love one day and rage the next. The ending of the journal left him feeling anxious, like a junkie who cannot get the next fix. He wanted more, but he was scared to know more. His previous attempt to find Cécile was in vain, admittingly that he did not put too much effort into it either. Now, he realized he felt the same determination and force Cécile felt about helping Élizabeth. He needed to know if she perished in the war or made it out of the stadium alive. Was her mission successful, or did she fail?

"Damn it," Hénri said aloud without realizing he was vocalizing his thoughts. There were so many questions, yet he was unsure whether he would ever get the chance to find answers.

Hénri checked the time and saw it was only one in the afternoon. He decided to continue his search, even if he had to visit several libraries to find whatever information he could.

Hénri took the diary and headed to the other famous library in Paris, the *Bibliothèque Mazarine*. Hénri was more hopeful and determined since he left *Bibliothèque Sainte-Geneviève* empty-handed a couple of weeks ago. He had faith in *Mazarine,* whose equally impressive collection focused on French history from the twelfth century to the present. It had thousands of rare medieval manuscripts, such as the Gutenberg Bible, that date back to 1250 and are kept in a secret vault.

This library was also one of the best places to find historical information. Hénri locked up his bicycle at the rack and walked into the grand building. He did not know where to begin, but he decided to start his search on 3 September 1939, the date Cécile wrote down in her diary when she heard the news, although she also made an entry on 16 July 1942, the day of the *Vel' d'Hiv'* roundup.

Based on these entries and that it had to take Agnes's father a few days to get her the fake ID cards, Cécile must have gone to the stadium after the 16th but starting from the beginning of World War II seemed more logical. He knew facts about the war, but now he looked at them differently. He was not trying to memorize date after date as he did while preparing for a history test in high school. He now needed to read between the lines and find stories deeply hidden among them.

Hénri sat in the corner of the microfiche room, blindly following his gut instincts. He went through one paper after another, hoping to find something about the Klotz family, the Bossards, or even Cécile Eisner. Hénri could not believe that he was partially terrified to find out the rest of the story. What kind of fate did they face? Hénri was beyond curious now and knew he would not rest until he found some information.

He spent hours combing through page after page, article after article—a tedious task, staring at the screen, turning the dial, and scanning the documents. His eyes were tired, and his mind wandered off from time to time, almost as if he were in a lucid dream.

Right before the library was about to close for the night, he came across an article after the Red Army liberated Auschwitz in January 1945 that asked the public to help identify some survivors and called for relatives. He skimmed through the papers before a familiar name caught his eye. Cécile Eisner # 23871 read the tag under a grainy picture. He paused for a brief second and rubbed his eyes. Can it be? His heart pounded so hard inside his chest that Hénri thought he would faint. The picture showed a woman's sunk-in face with very short dark hair, almost bald.

Her eyes were open but lifeless as if her soul had departed her body. This was not the face of a bubbly young French girl Hénri had imagined so many times, but instead, he saw pain and a hollow pair of eyes looking back at him. His stomach churned. He read the blurb under the photo.

According to this article, Cécile had been found lying on top of a pile of corpses outside of the gas chambers in Auschwitz II-Birkenau, barely alive. She was rescued and taken to the *Hôtel-Dieu,* the oldest hospital in Paris. He grabbed a notebook from his pocket and wrote down information before he rushed out of the library.

Hénri felt like he was on a manhunt, except he was not going out there to find someone to kill. He was on a hunt to conclude this story and return the diary to Cécile or her living relative. He knew this was beyond maddening, and whatever he did was not ordinary. He had never met this woman and had no connections; yet, he felt strangely tied to her. He was drawn to her, and just like a puppet, he was being strung along in her direction.

Around eight o'clock in the evening, he arrived at the *Hôtel-Dieu.* Hénri walked up to the reception impulsively, and he did not even think twice before approaching the nurse's desk but instantly got tongue-tied when she turned her attention to him. He just realized how insane he would sound.

"How can I help you, *Monsieur*?" The nurse asked Hénri, who panted crazily before checking the time out of nervousness.

"Hello, my name is Hénri, and I'm looking for a... relative or information about her. She was brought here after World War II was over." Hénri lied, and the nurse held a hand up before telling him to head downstairs to the basement and the archives. Hénri's world shattered for a moment. "It was too good to be true," he murmured as he skipped down the stairs. The smell of formaldehyde hit his nose, and he nearly gagged. His dinner would have landed on the linoleum floor had he eaten. The Office of Archives was next to the morgue, which did not help ease his fear of this lead ending before it could even begin.

Hénri met up with two more staff who were much less friendly than the one he met upstairs. They constantly reminded him that it was far too late in the evening for such research, but they finally found some records on all the French nationals who were brought to the hospital from Auschwitz. The nurse flipped to "E" in a large and thick book, which reminded him of a guest book he sometimes saw in hotels, but this was much larger. It was twice the size of a briefcase and twice as thick too.

"Cécile Eisner?" The nurse asked Hénri in confirmation, and he nodded.

"Yes, that's the one," he said eagerly, and the nurse disappeared to the back of the room to bring the file. Of course, it is only he who knows her as Dubonnet.

"Let us see. Cécile Eisner. Hmm. She was brought in from Auschwitz on 5 February 1945. She was around twenty-five to thirty years old at the time, but that was the nurse's best guess. The Nazis destroyed most of the records, so they had to rely on the patient's statement for some details."

"Yes, twenty-five is about right," Hénri confirmed before the nurse continued.

"The file here says that she was released from us and taken to another hospital for psychiatric evaluation. She showed severe trauma and hysteria," the old nurse said before she closed the records, "That is all, I am afraid. They had to process a lot of people, so there aren't many details."

"Can I please know where she was taken?" Hénri asked hopefully.

The nurse shook her head, "I'm afraid I cannot share that information with you," the nurse said stiffly. "It's against our hospital rules."

"Please. I'm her relative!" Hénri lied and pleaded, but the nurse only gave Hénri a dubious look.

"Do you have any proof that you're related to her?" She asked him sharply, and Hénri sighed in aggravation.

He was so close to finding Cécile. He was close to finding the truth and the ending of her story, yet, he felt like he had just jumped ten steps backward. He could not fight against the hospital policy or prove that she was related to him. He almost gave up before an idea popped into his head, hoping it would work.

"I have her diary," Hénri carefully said as he grabbed the frayed diary from his bag. He opened the page where her name was written, and the nurse looked surprised. "My mother passed this diary down to me. Cécile was my great-aunt, and I am the only family member who came this close to finding her. Please help me find out what happened to her," Hénri pleaded, and the nurse looked perplexed.

"Sure, I'll give you the details," she said guiltily, and Hénri did not sigh in relief until she showed him the records, and he quickly wrote down the details of her whereabouts in his notebook.

"Thank you, *Madame*," Hénri said before walking out of one hospital just to make his way to another. He was beyond excited, but he headed home instead. He knew he would not have a minute of shut-eye, but it was nearly eleven o'clock at night. As he was riding through the dark streets, it started to rain. The cold, November drizzling rain and the darkness of the night blurred the buildings and taillights around him. Cécile survived Auschwitz, which gave Hénri hope, but there was no guarantee she was still alive.

***

The sight of *Centre Hospitalier Sainte-Anne* sent shivers down Hénri's spine because it was not an ordinary hospital—it had an extensive psychiatric ward that housed many mentally ill people. Hénri walked up to the receptionist, where a nurse greeted him.

"How may I help you, *Monsieur?*" she asked Hénri.

"Yes, I'm here to find out what happened to a relative after World War II. *Hôtel-Dieu* guided me here. They said my great-aunt was sent here after she recovered from her injuries around February 1945. My family thought she died in Auschwitz, but I am working on our family tree as a school project, and that led me here," he explained and gave a detailed story to make it sound convincing.

The nurse nodded, "Oh wow, 1945. That was a long time ago, but let me check. Name of the patient?" She asked him.

"Cécile. Cécile Eisner," he answered, and the nurse stared up at him with a struck expression.

"Cécile Eisner?" She repeated the name to make sure that she heard him right.

It confused Hénri, and he expected resistance but did not bend. "Yes. Was she here?" He asked the nurse with his heart thundering under his chest, mostly with excitement and because he had not lied so much in his life as he did in these last two days. He suddenly understood Cecile's angst about not telling the truth and realized he was not cut from a different cloth. Everybody lies.

Hénri came all the way here on pure impulse to find a woman who was not related to him in any way, and he prayed to whatever gods were out there that he could find out what happened to her. Secretly he hoped she was still alive, and after he found out she survived the concentration camp, this quest was even more promising.

"Was she?" the nurse asked rhetorically. "She is still here. No one has visited her in the past fifty-four years, so I beg your pardon if I am a little taken aback by your visit," the nurse said in a stunned manner as she guided him toward the ward.

"She's been in here for fifty-four years?" Hénri asked the nurse as they walked toward the rooms through the steel double door, leading to a locked one that separated visitors from patients, the nightmares from dreams. Hénri tried to keep up with the conversation, but his emotions overwhelmed him, making concentrating difficult.

"Yes, and she's one of our oldest patients here. The *Hôtel-Dieu* tried locating her relatives, but they couldn't find anyone, and no one came forward, so they transferred her here," the nurse explained before she stopped in front of her room. "You're lucky; it's visiting hours, or you would have to come tomorrow," she said before she opened the door slowly.

"*Mademoiselle* Cécile, you have a visitor," the nurse softly announced before she opened the door widely.

Hénri felt like he was almost struck in the face. The young woman he imagined was nowhere to be found in the weakened woman. Her white hair was stringy but neatly tied in a loose braid, and she wore a white nightgown.

The old woman made no indication that she heard the nurse or anyone else for that matter. Hénri thought he was staring at a statue as Cécile sat in a wheelchair before the window and silently watched the raindrops running down on the window.

"Has she always been this quiet?" Hénri asked the nurse, who nodded.

"Yes, she only speaks when she wants to, and even then, it's mostly incoherent. At times she has a breakdown, but she has been oddly somber today," the nurse whispered to Hénri as she did not want to disturb the demons haunting Cécile. "I'll leave you two here. Press that button on the wall if something happens, alright?"

"Thank you, umm … Brigitte," said Hénri as he quickly peeked at her name tag pinned to her uniform.

He entered the room and approached the woman quietly, but he did not know where to start or what to say as he stared at her. The young, vibrant, life-loving woman he got to know through her diary is not the woman sitting in this bare room. The wrinkles on her face marked years of torture she lived through, and the horror in her eyes only spoke volumes of her nightmares. Cécile Dubonnet sat there as still as a stone. She did not move even when Hénri pulled up a chair and sat in front of her. He made sure he was far enough from her reach, just in case.

"*Mademoiselle* Cécile. My name is Hénri," he introduced himself, but he was just as lost as she was. He had no idea how to begin, but it seemed like none of it mattered anyway because Cécile made no indication that she heard or saw him in the first place.

"I don't even know what I'm doing here," he started on his tangent, which he thought would probably turn into a monologue, "I guess you could say that I made an impulsive decision to find you. You would be surprised, but I know a little bit about you, or a lot about you, actually," Hénri uncomfortably chuckled before he grabbed her diary from his bag. It was a strange moment for him. He never thought he would meet up with the woman who poured her heart and feelings out on these pages. He oddly felt like a fan meeting up with their favorite star for the first time, except that this rendezvous was laced with pain.

It was clear that Cécile survived Auschwitz, but it was still unclear whether Élizabeth made it out of there.

"I came across your diary by chance," Hénri said in another attempt to snap the old woman out of her stupor as he unwrapped it from the rag in which he kept the journal.

He placed the diary on the bed so she could see it, but it seemed that Cécile was too stuck in a loop of memories to notice what was right in front of her.

"I just wanted to know what happened to you. What happened to Élizabeth?" Hénri pressed impatiently, but Cécile stayed still.

Hénri stood up with a sigh. "I guess this was pointless," he muttered but quickly realized how selfish he was.

"I'm so sorry I disturbed you, *Mademoiselle*," Hénri apologized, placing the diary in Cécile's frail hands. He had no right to be here, and he had no right to demand an answer from a woman who had suffered enough horrors to last her a lifetime. She was stuck in her nightmares, and Hénri only made it worse by springing this out of nowhere. He felt he knew her, but he did not realize that Cécile knew nothing of him. When Hénri set off on this journey, he wanted to find the owner and give the diary back, which he has now accomplished.

Hénri turned around and walked away before hearing a faint voice whisper something.

"Élizabeth, Élizabeth, Élizabeth," Cécile murmured, and Hénri turned around to see her clutching the diary in her hands tightly.

"Cécile, do you know what happened to Élizabeth?" Hénri asked her, but Cécile only kept rocking back and forth in her wheelchair while chanting Élizabeth's name. If Hénri did not know any better, he would say that Cécile was the personification of guilt and regret.

Seeing the woman wound up in the past tugged at his heartstrings, and Hénri sat back down again. He placed a hand above her hand, and Cécile stopped suddenly. Her eyes were wide, and she was murmuring something inaudible under her breath.

"What happened to you, *Mademoiselle* Dubonnet?" Hénri asked her, and Cécile finally looked into Hénri's eyes. The sound of her real surname made her acknowledge his presence for the first time.

"Save Élizabeth," Cécile whispered in a raspy voice. She grabbed Hénri's hand and squeezed it tightly.

Hénri felt helpless as he stood up and looked down at Cécile. He knew it would take a long while to figure out her story, but he was ready to do whatever it was going to take to uncover the secrets hiding beneath those frightened eyes.

CHAPTER 16

CHASING A GHOST

Thursday, 2 December 1999

Hénri remembered the feeling that left him nauseated. Meeting her for the first time had disturbed him because seeing her confirmed that this was a living, breathing person. Cécile was no longer just a character from some book he randomly stumbled upon. Cécile was a person, and she was still very much alive, which was more than Hénri ever thought he would achieve, but he still felt incomplete. He still felt that he needed to know what had happened.

The problem was that Cécile was stuck in a part of her past that no one had been able to penetrate, not Hénri and certainly not the medical staff. Her eyes were full of sadness, broken dreams, and evils of World War II, and other than Hénri barely scratching the surface of it, no one knew the extent. He wanted to give her some redemption, a little peace—even if it meant freeing her mind, which could be dangerous in her fragile state. It could just as easily push her deeper into her nightmare as much as it could help. Cécile was suffering, but her story was one of those worth telling.

Hénri knew that Jews were not the only ones who suffered from the war. Gypsies, the handicapped, homosexuals, the mentally ill, or anyone who did not fit the idea of a biologically superior Aryan race fell victim to the Holocaust. However, Cécile was just an ordinary French girl; yet, she had endured the same fate as them. She had been through something so frightening that it left her stuck in the past. Hénri guessed that she did not successfully reveal her true identity and prove she was not Jewish as planned on that fateful day when she entered the stadium. Is that why she ended up in Auschwitz? What else was at play?

***

Hénri did not give up. He visited her every day for weeks, but Cécile was still far away in her mind. She was still adrift in the vast sea of pain, which frustrated Hénri. He wanted answers, so with a determination that even surprised him, Hénri decided it was time to bring Cécile out of her past. He knew he had to tread lightly.

Hénri knew that he needed to take it slowly, so he did not scare her, and most importantly, he did not hinder any treatment she had been receiving. His curiosity and unquenched thirst led him this far, and he was not about to stop. Hénri had always been curious and eager as a child. Some habits die hard, Hénri thought to himself as he approached the nurse at the desk.

"Good morning, *Mademoiselle!*" Hénri greeted the woman with a charming voice, and the nurse looked back at him with a soft smile.

"Here to visit your great-aunt again, *Monsieur?*" She asked him as she handed him the visitor's pass.

"Well, I hope she finally speaks to you today," the nurse said, wishing him well. She knew about Cécile's condition, and her heart always softened for this young man who so tirelessly had been coming by.

"I have a feeling today's the day," he replied as he took the pass and turned around.

Hénri had become a regular visitor ever since he met Cécile over a month ago. He always showed up with something, and Brigitte smiled at the box of pastries he had in his hands.

Hénri passed through the hall until he came across Cécile's room. It was just as quiet as ever. One could even mistake her quarter for being empty as it was silent. Cécile only stood out because of her wheelchair near the window, just tall enough to peek over the ledge. Otherwise, she would easily blend in with the white walls. Hénri entered the room with a smile on his face.

"Good morning, Cécile," Hénri chirped as he always did. He had been trying to coax Cécile out of her stupor, but she barely even moved a finger. She sat as still as a statue, her fading eyes staring out the window with longing. "I brought some pastries for you today, *mille-feuille*. I know that is your favorite," he said and paused when he realized how strange he sounded. The only reason he even knew her favorite pastry was because he had read her journal. He caught himself now and then realizing how many intimate details he knew about Cécile, which sometimes made him feel ashamed.

His eyes flitted toward her lap as he thought about the diary. She still clutched it with her fingers as if she feared someone would rip it out of her hands. One night, a nurse tried to put it on the nightstand, but Cécile screamed at her. No one tried to touch the diary again, and Dr. Pelletier, her psychiatrist, allowed her to carry it everywhere. He thought it could help her with her therapy.

Dr. Pelletier has been seeing Cécile once a week for the past ten years, and just like many of his colleagues before him, he was not successful in getting her to talk. Hénri's sudden and unexpected appearance with the diary gave them much-needed hope. Dr. Pelletier went as far as giving her a pencil, a risky move in a psychiatric hospital.

Hénri felt as if Cécile had started to come out of her past a little bit. He also felt that this was turning out to be a borderline obsession. He knew it was unhealthy to visit Cécile every day, being a stranger who had nothing to do with her. She did not owe him anything, especially not her life story, but Hénri knew that if he never got anything out of her, he would at least reunite her with her diary. He could rest in peace, knowing he did at least one good thing for her.

"Anyways, the weather is lovely today, isn't it? It's hard to believe it's December," Hénri started his daily monologue as he stood beside her wheelchair and stared out the window. He did not feel as awkward as he did the first time; quite the opposite. Hénri found some level of comfort in chatting aimlessly or recapping his day.

"Winter is nice, but autumn is my favorite season. Rain or shine. I often go to the cemetery early in September before the leaves fall, but this time of the year is just as nice. Walking the streets on a misty, foggy night is so romantic," Hénri paused as his thoughts drifted away. Cécile just sat there blankly. He decided to open the window and let some fresh air inside the room. He carried the thin blanket from her bed and draped it over her shoulder.

"Do you mind if I have a quick smoke?" He asked but knew she would never answer, which is how their weeks have been. Hénri was talking, and Cécile was sitting by the window in silence. He grabbed the packet of *Gitanes* from his jacket and took out a cigarette, but before he could light it up, Cécile's hand shot out and startled Hénri. Her reflexes were slow, but she surprised him as she grabbed his hand. Cécile was staring at the cigarette packet.

"Ludwig," she whispered and slowly let go.

Hénri felt like someone had shaken him from a peaceful slumber and poured freezing water all over him. He felt goosebumps rise all over his body as he stared at Cécile.

"I'm not Ludwig," Hénri said, but he did not receive any reply.

The truth is that Hénri does not smoke. He bought the cigarette on a whim to see how Cécile would react. He knew she loved watching Ludwig smoke, and he hoped the smell of tobacco might trigger something in her. Scents have feelings and places attached to them, just like maps' coordinates, but these memories can be wonderful or painful, Hénri knew. Now and then, he catches a molecule of Natalie in the air, although he knows she is in Africa. Still, it makes his heart skip a beat.

If Dr. Pelletier knew, he could ban Hénri from visiting Cécile, but that was a risk worth taking, and Cécile was bent on surprising him today. She nodded at him, and Hénri reeled back.

"Do you know who Ludwig is?" He asked her slowly, and Cécile choked.

"Bad," she replied in a whisper.

Hénri felt like the room had started closing in. He nodded slowly, and without Cécile noticing, he pushed the help button. "Do you remember anything else, Cécile?"

"23871." Cécile whispered in a raspy voice. Hénri frowned for a moment before his eyes widened.

"That's the number they gave you," Hénri replied slowly. He knelt before Cécile and looked up at her. "Is there anything else you remember?" he quietly asked her in the most soothing voice as a nurse entered the room. Hénri gestured for her to stop.

Cécile gasped. "Everything," she clutched her diary to her chest. "Everything," Cécile repeated in a shaky voice. The nurse immediately rushed out to grab Dr. Pelletier.

This is it, Hénri thought to himself. This was the moment they all had been waiting for. They had finally managed to crack the walls. He felt excited, but he was also afraid. He did not know what would happen next. Some stories are meant to be left alone, and some are better off without an ending, Hénri thought to himself. But not this one, his conscience told him.

And so, Cécile grabbed the pencil Dr. Pelletier had given her, opened the diary, and continued writing where she left off fifty-seven years ago.

***

I approached the stadium with my heart thundering in my chest. I passed people standing around, watching the remaining Jews of the round-up queuing with their suitcases, holding their children's hands. Every part of my body knew that I was being foolish. Agnes's voice rang as I remembered her telling me this was a suicide mission. But the moment Élizabeth's name crossed my mind, all of the doubts disappeared from my mind. I took the papers from my stockings and put them in my pocket.

"This is going to work. Just get Élizabeth out, and we can put everything behind us. We will laugh, go to the cinema, and gush over handsome actors like we used to," I muttered under my breath, trying to soothe my ever-increasing anxiety.

"*Halt!*" An SS officer yelled at me to stop. "Papers, please," he said. I took a deep breath, slowly reached into my pockets, and pulled out the false identification. My hands were trembling, and my stomach was in a knot.

The officer took the papers, and I watched his expression change. His face became firm as his eyes filled with anger, and he grabbed me by the arm, and I yelped in pain. He took me to the stadium entrance, striding to the tables where Nazi officers were still registering Jews after two weeks. Long queues coiled in front of the tables, but the officer cut into the line to take me to the front.

"I found this one wandering around without the *Judenstern*," the officer said to another sitting behind a desk. I realized he referred to me not having the yellow star on my coat. "She must have stepped out of line. Make sure you get her inside before she goes astray," he said, shoving me toward the table.

I winced as the table tugged into my stomach before I stood up straight. The man behind the table nodded at the officer and quickly filled out my forms to take me inside the stadium. I felt like I had walked into a pigpen. The air was humid as the odor of sweat and urine filled the place. But there was something else besides the stench—the fear that weighed everyone down and terrified me. No fans were shouting or cheering on the athletes, no sense of victory and tears of accomplishment; only Nazi officers ordering prisoners around who did not understand their crimes. Old, stained cots and mattresses were stacked next to each other, following the curve of the stadium with little space between them. I saw no water or food. I noticed a few buckets behind a white sheet hanging from the wall, which probably served as makeshift toilets. These conditions were appalling, but I knew I would not be here long.

Several processing desks were lined up in an orderly manner in the middle of the stadium floor. I knew exactly where I would need to go to clear up this situation. I only needed to find the officer in charge and clear up this major misunderstanding. I was relaxed and confident that this was a brief stay and that my plan would work. After all, Agnes had my real identification, and her Papa could confirm that the Bossard family had no reason to be here.

The officer assigned me a cot, and I took my coat off before I started looking for Élizabeth and her family. Despite the densely placed beds, they were sparsely occupied. I hoped to glimpse familiar faces in this unfamiliar world. I never thought I would be stuck in a place like this all by myself, even temporarily. My desperation was evident as I scanned through the crowd when a man stopped me in my tracks.

"Whoever you're looking for, *Mademoiselle*, they aren't here any-more," a scratchy voice said. An old man sitting in the corner with a cigarette in his mouth looked at me flatly. Based on his dirty, unshaven, and broken look, he had to have been here for weeks, at least. "Every other day," he continued, "the officers take people from this room in groups, and you never see them again once they walk through that door," he pointed to the back of the stadium. "Whoever you're looking for has already been taken."

It was as if someone had struck me in the face. "That can't be."

For the first time, I realized my mistake. I should have known what I was getting myself into, which was much bigger than me and Éliz-abeth's family. Suddenly, everything felt too real, and I needed a new plan.

"I made a mistake," I muttered as I grabbed my coat and walked to the front entrance. I needed to get home and talk to Agnes, and she will be able to help with a new plan.

I reached for the door before I felt something hit me on the side of my head. My ears rang as fists and kicks rained down on me. My head swam around, and it felt like I was on a merry-go-round. I felt my consciousness slipping away before the pain jolted me awake. I thought Ludwig's beating would be the worst thing to ever happen to me, but several officers were kicking me as I lay on the ground.

This hurt, I thought to myself. I opened my eyes slowly and saw the men glaring at me with contempt.

"What are you doing, you stinking Jew?" One soldier screamed at me as the others dug their boots into my back and stomach. I could hardly breathe.

"You don't understand," I managed to say shakily, but the soldier kicked me in the throat. I choked on my saliva as he dug his boot into my throat. Tears filled my eyes as he nearly crushed my windpipe. "I'm not a Jew." I choked out, but the soldiers only laughed and kicked me in the stomach again.

"You hear that, boys? This woman says she is not a Jew. Right, why don't we just let her walk away?" They joked around like a bunch of knuckleheads.

I gathered some strength, sat up, and glared at the men. "I'm not a Jew," I repeated through clenched teeth. The soldiers stopped laughing abruptly as one of the soldiers grabbed me by my hair.

"We don't listen to Jews," he spat in my face, and instead of anger, I only felt fear. My stomach coiled with repulsion as I looked at them surrounding me like wolves closing in on their prey.

"Please," I whispered, but my heart was beating too fast in my chest. My ears were ringing, and my head kept swimming in circles. The only thing that kept me awake was the fear of what would happen if I passed out in front of them.

The soldiers went back to beating and striking me. It felt rhythmical, as if they tried playing a tune from the radio. It felt like hours before they finally stopped. My body shook with pain that I had never encountered before. It felt like they had broken every bone in my body and pushed me around like a rag doll. I tried to speak and tell them this was just a misunderstanding, but every kick knocked the air out of me. Every strike pushed me a little closer to unconsciousness. I could no longer cry or make a sound.

After they were satisfied, they glared down at me. "You can't leave," the officer yelled at me, and I cringed as his boot collided with my face. He nearly crushed my head into the ground. "We've only just begun," the officer whispered in my ear before he grabbed me by the hair and threw me back. The last thing I saw was the blurred silhouettes of retreating officers before I passed out from the pain.

I realized I had made a mistake, but it was already too late. I was in the deepest part of hell, with no way out.

Chapter 17

Unwanted Journey

I was in and out of consciousness for days. I do not know how long I lay on the ground. Eventually, someone put me on my bed. Day and night blended until I could no longer tell them apart. I wanted to scream because my entire body burned from head to toe, yet, the only sound I made went unheard. My consciousness kept slipping away. Every day, new people arrived only to leave after a few hours, minutes, or days—I could no longer tell.

I thought Ludwig's beating had been the worst part of my life, but I was wrong. I thought I was stuck in some nightmare, but every slight movement of my body reminded me that this was my new harsh reality. My lips were sealed together by dried blood. I could not talk, but at least it muted my pain. I could only see through a thin crack of my swollen eyes. My vision was blurry, but occasionally someone sat beside me, put a wet cloth on my forehead, and tended to my injuries.

Suddenly, my mother's face appeared out of nowhere, and I started crying. Was that blurry figure her? Was I lying in my bed with scarlet fever, and this was just a dream? I reached out, but I touched nothing. The hope vanished as abruptly as my mother's face, which plunged me back to reality. The fever was playing tricks on my mind.

Oh, I missed her so much. I never missed anyone as much as I missed my mother that day. I longed to feel her fingers threading through my hair like she always did whenever I fell ill as a child. I wanted her to tell me that I was going to be okay. But all I was left with was a faceless figure tending to my wounds. At some point, I ran out of tears, and the scream I wanted to let out was painfully stuck in my throat. I was afraid I would lose my mind. I was already on the verge of insanity.

The woman or man caring for me did not say anything to comfort me, as if they could no longer bring themselves to give false hope. This act seemed to be the last act of compassion they were committed to in this dire situation. I felt the wet cloth slide across my lips, freeing them from the dried blood that kept my pain hidden. As soon as I opened my mouth, I sighed. I wanted to move, but my body fought back and stayed still.

I only heard the sound of shouting soldiers and the horrified gasps of women before I fell back into my delirium. Perhaps, it was better that I did not witness the SS rounding up people in groups and pushing them out the back door. I was brought back into reality when I felt my body painfully jostled.

"Ah." I let out a pained whimper, but no one came to my aid. My body felt like it was swinging in a cradle, rocking side to side. Even the clickety-clackety noise I heard vaguely was a lullaby. One thing was certain. I was not in my bed. Through the small crack of my bruised eye, I saw some people sitting on the ground, cuddling their knees, burying their heads. Some stood, trying to peak through the opening as the landscape ran by. I was lying in the corner of a transporter wagon, and every jolt made my body scream in pain as the hard plywood dug into my bones as the train ran over the rail joints. I tried to hold onto reality, but doing so seemed too much. I wanted to ask where I was and where we were going, but the train's whistle muted my faint attempt. Everything was terrifying, and I wanted to escape this place. Sleeping and losing consciousness was my only escape from this hellish place, and I invited darkness with open arms for the first time.

I dreamt about being home. I remember how I woke up every day to the smell of coffee and my parents preparing breakfast in the kitchen. I saw Mama handing me a plate with a warm croissant for breakfast and Papa sitting in the living room in his favorite armchair with a newspaper in his hand. A tear ran down my face, and the dirty wooden plank soaked it up instantly.

Despite my injuries, I was still worried about my parents. Were they safe? Do they know where I am? They must be worried sick. All these questions swirled in my mind, and sometimes my dreams turned into nightmares if living in one was not enough. Most of my bad dreams centered around Ludwig, but sometimes Agnes would appear, telling me how disappointed she was. The anger in her eyes could kill a soul. Then, her image would morph into Élizabeth's, and my entire body trembled with regret.

"I'm sorry, I'm so sorry," I repeated over and over.

I felt disgusted with myself and wanted to claw my skin out as the guilt weighed on my body as much as it weighed on my mind. I betrayed the ones I loved the most. Why did I do that? No, how could I do that? How did I even think it was okay to reveal Élizabeth's identity?

For the longest time, I blamed Ludwig. It was his fault and his alone, but that was all a lie. Truthfully, it was my fault, and I even lied to myself to soothe my conscience. I wanted the pain to fade away along with my last breath. But, alas, I had to wake up from one nightmare to be plunged into another one.

The door slammed with a loud bang, forcing me to leave my mental prison to now confront a new set of physical and psychological horrors. It was not much safer or calmer in my mind, but it was better than my material reality. I faced my frightening real world as seven or eight SS guards stood on the platform, all wearing the same gray-green uniform. One man stood by himself, his hands together behind his back. His uniform was slightly different, crisper, and his knee-high boots were shinier than the others.'

"Get out of the wagons!" One soldier shouted aggressively, and people jumped off in masses, like a flock of birds flying in unison, as all of them kept screaming at us to get off. People started pushing each other, and I slowly stood up. I waited for the crowd to clear out, but I tripped and fell as my feet hit the ground.

The guard screamed at me in German. "Get up, you *Schmutz*, you dirty Jew!" I stood on my shaky legs as the soldier hopped into the wagon, grabbed me by the arm, and pushed me off. I squinted into the sunlight and saw smoke rising from a distant chimney. I did not immediately grasp that I had arrived at Birkenau concentration camp, or Auschwitz II, as it was known.

How will I ever get Élizabeth and Mimi out of here? I thought to myself immediately, but then I realized they might not even be here. A fence with barbed wire on top ran along the train tracks. I followed it with my eyes until it reached the orange brick wall that separated me from freedom. Is this where I am going to die? It became painfully evident that I was truly stuck here with no way out. I could not even say that I was not a real Jew anymore. I had already paid the price of trying to convince the guards in the stadium. They beat me with everything they had, and I was only clinging to this life by a loose thread. I did not know what they would do to me here.

I stood up and tried to blend into the crowd. The SS guards started separating people into two groups as the train pulled away and disappeared into the horizon.

"*Links*!" The guard called out and instructed all the old women, small children, and the weak to stand to the left of the platform.

"*Rechts*!" He screamed and pushed me to the right. Once the sorting was completed, people on the left were sent straight to the gas chambers, as I later found out. The people on the right were also sentenced to death, but our deaths would be slow, prolonged, and painful. I was numb, and I blindly followed the others in front of me, and the others behind me followed me. It was as if my body knew what to do even though my mind could not comprehend it.

"They're going to die," someone muttered beside me and looked toward the people sent to the platform's left side.

"What is this place?" I asked in a muffled voice.

"It's a labor camp. And those over there are the gas chambers," the woman pointed to the distance where I saw smoke earlier. "They call them the 'Little White House' and 'Little Red House,' she whispered before an SS guard turned around to tell us to shut up and delivered a blow to our bodies with his cane.

I stood there, paralyzed, staring at young children in the crowd being led away. They were looking around for their parents, horrified. Some were crying for their mother. Random strangers held their hands to give them the last piece of comfort as they quietly hummed nursery rhymes. Horror gripped my soul in an iron fist and refused to let go. I watched helplessly as hundreds of people were forced to walk toward their death.

Why? Why were the Nazis so cruel? Why were they looking at us with such a hateful look in their eyes? For the first time, I realized what fear of the unknown tasted like and wondered if Élizabeth had felt the same way when her family tried their best to hide their identities. How did she cope when she discovered I was the one who betrayed her? Does she even know? Is she even alive? That thought sent a sharp pain through my chest.

I hunched my back and kept my head down to avoid attracting attention. I wanted to be invisible. The crowd seemed to move, and I moved along with them like one giant wave. I was small, a nobody, just a tiny drop in this human wave, when I suddenly stopped in my tracks.

No, it cannot be! That is impossible! My eyes opened wide in disbelief, and I felt the wind knocked out of me when I saw him standing in the field, barking at a group of prisoners in their striped clothing. I nearly fainted. There, in an SS uniform, stood Ludwig. He seemed as proud and arrogant as ever. Now that I looked at him, I asked myself how I could have missed the lines of cruelty so deeply etched on his face. How did I ever think that this man was gentle and loving? How?

My life flashed before my eyes from when I saw Ludwig leaning against the wall by the *Tabac* to the night I left his apartment battered, running like a coward. Now, my legs were hardly carrying my body, but the wave of people cradled me as we moved along, following orders.

Ludwig was here, and my mind was screaming to run, protecting me by howling at me to get away. Maybe death would have been better for me. He was well and alive. I thought exposing his secret would have landed him in prison or in front of the firing squad, but here he was. My heart wept silently as old wounds tore open. I closed my eyes, hoping he was a mirage.

"I am ill, and the fever is still playing tricks on my mind," I whispered in disbelief as a substantial amount of pain swept through my body. I felt like I was standing in hell, but the flames had turned into ice, and I was forced to stare the devil in his eyes.

"What have I done?" I choked out before I hid behind the other person. Ludwig cannot see me. I knew he would not kill me if he found out I was here. Not immediately, no. He would do much worse. I met this man, allowed him into my life, and now I wallowed in regrets as I walked deeper into Auschwitz and further away from the freedom I once had. I wished being here would help me make up for my sins, but I will never find atonement in this life or the next.

Chapter 18

Hell on Earth

My life had turned upside down in a blink of an eye. My hopes were being beaten down day after day, and my mind slowly gave up on me, little by little. 'Élizabeth, Élizabeth, Élizabeth,' my conscience repeatedly whispered to remind me what I had done to land in this place.

My days were spent trying to be invisible and avoid Ludwig. I still could not believe that he was here. I wished he were just a figment of my imagination, but he was as real as ever. My mind had gone numb for days after seeing him for the first time. I tried to make sense of it all, but I was left with more questions to which I did not have the answers.

Why was he here? Did the SS not imprison him for finding out that he was homosexual? How could they allow him to be here? Why didn't they kill him? He did not deserve to live. Oh, God, he did not deserve to live at all. I was certain they would kill Ludwig for his forbidden desires or put him away for good at least, but it hardly seemed like he had suffered in the past three years. Instead of being buried six feet under, Ludwig was here in his crisp SS uniform and shiny boots and was very much thriving.

I did my best to ensure I did not come into his line of sight. Thinking about what he would do to me if he found out I was here sent shivers down my spine. I was nothing but a number, and I hoped he would not be able to recognize me with a shaved head. I saw myself in a mirror in the hospital one morning where I was assigned to work. I no longer looked like the Cécile I left behind, the girl who loved life, enjoyed films, and dreamt about traveling. I looked like an echo of that person. A shadow. A ghost. My eyes were dwarfed by the dark circles that seemed to get bigger every other day. My face, which had been round and plump, was now pale and sunken. I touched my shaven head, and I wished I could cry. I just kept glaring at the image and the hollow look in my eyes.

I was weak when I arrived in Auschwitz, and my condition had not improved. The food was sparse and tasted horrible. Lunch was putrid, and the soup looked more like dirty dishwater and offered no nourishment. Dinner was not any better, but after a few days, I realized I had to eat it if I wanted to stay alive. It did not provide enough calories to sustain life, but it was something. The hunger I felt for a few days slowly dissipated as my body turned on itself for survival.

My living conditions were just as foul. The barracks must have been assembled hurriedly because gaps between the wooden boards let through the chilling wind, rain, and snow. The uneven rammed-dirt floor was always cold and hard. Two rows of three-tiered bunk beds ran along the walls, with as many as three people to a tier. It was cramped and noisy, but after the first winter, I embraced it as our bodies were the only things keeping us warm at night. I do not know what kept me going. What was my will to survive? The hope I would ever find Élizabeth left with the train I disembarked a few months ago. I was just a ghost, a number.

I was assigned custodial work in the hospital as a cleaner after the SS decided I was 'fit to live.' I thought that working there would not be terrible. I felt luckier than most because at least I was inside, but I soon realized that it was not an average job. It was not apparent initially, but the doctors were experimenting on us. There were a lot of sicknesses and outbreaks throughout the camp, especially during the brutal Polish winters. Pneumonia, tuberculosis, and meningitis spread quickly, caus-ing more devastation and death. No surprise. Living conditions were horrendous; everyone was malnourished, but seemingly healthy people became more ill after their hospital visits. Diseases did some dirty work, and the SS took care of the rest.

I had only been in a hospital once as a patient when I was ten years old and had my appendix removed. I do not remember much, but I have memories of white beds equally spaced next to one another, with only a nightstand between them.

Most rooms looked like what I remembered, but some did not look like hospital chambers. They were equipped with water tanks, compression chambers, and equipment I did not recognize. I heard screaming, and I saw agony, but what I hated the most was silence. Silence meant death. It was difficult to see adults being brought in but seeing children suffering was the worst. It broke my heart to see orphan children infected with viruses and bacteria to see how they reacted. Many did not survive, but those who did were left disfigured or had permanent health issues that either caused them to perish, or the Nazis just killed them. The wagons pulled into the camp every day, bringing more. The supply of test subjects seemed to be endless.

Death was all around me. A hospital is supposed to be where the ill get better, a place to heal, where we cheat death and extend life, sometimes by a lot, other times just by a little bit. But not in Auschwitz. Not here. Not in this camp. The hospital meant torture and pain, the place where everyone came to die. However, Auschwitz taught me a lot about resilience, acceptance, about survival. It was everything I lacked, skills no school would ever teach. The pain was the tuition fees I paid the moment I betrayed Élizabeth.

Auschwitz taught me that there are things worse than death. After all, there is no life after death. So, I believed, but I was wrong, and so was everyone else. Death is not the worst thing on this earth. The worst thing was this—this place where the soul died long before the body. Humans stopped being humans and turned on each other because of an ideology. Death in Auschwitz seemed like a sweet offering, a longing for the end.

My primary duty was mopping floors in the mortuary and operating rooms. I often snuck into the ward to spend some time with the living, but I might just as well have stayed in the morgue. The patients often lay in their beds unconscious or screamed so much I had to leave. I could not bear to hear their agony. I could not escape the gruesome task of cleaning up blood and picking up tissues and body parts. It was nauseating.

The smell of blood always made me gag and gave me a headache. For the first few weeks, I got sick to my stomach and vomited on the floor, and the SS guards just laughed at me. Other times, I fainted at seeing human remains lying around as if they were nothing but trash. I received a severe beating for that and was nearly shot once for knocking over a tray of tools and syringes.

The first few weeks were utter hell, but I slowly turned a blind eye to death over the months. My body went numb; my mind blocked everything, and I learned to steel myself. Sometimes, I would think about my past while cleaning the floors. I did whatever it took to escape my reality.

I would be in the cinema with Agnes and Élizabeth watching films on the silver screen, laughing, gushing over Charles Boyer, although love was far from my mind. I heard he was in a new American film called *Gaslight,* a mystery thriller. Living in this nightmare made me feel like the wife in the picture whose husband slowly manipulates her into believing she is going insane. I would have liked that film. Then, I kept thinking about my parents and our good times. But reminiscing about my family sometimes made things worse. I wanted to find a way to deal with this better and stop feeling queasy.

However, try as I might, there was no such thing as adapting to this life completely. The will to survive, keep going and cherish life over death was stronger than the Nazis had ever imagined. For them, it meant more brutality. For us, it meant more torture. Compliance was beaten into us every day if we defied the rules in any way. Roll call would start as early as three in the morning and last for hours in rain or snow.

Once roll call was complete, the workers would be escorted to their respective jobs. They would take me away with the rest of the cleaners who worked at the hospital. I realized I had it better than other women who lived in the same barracks. At least I was working inside and not in the open fields.

My hope was slowly depleting with each passing day. I tried my best to find Élizabeth and her family, but I could hardly think of a way to do that. Most women I asked did not know anything about Élizabeth and her family, and they were just as desperate to find information about their loved ones as I was.

Auschwitz was vast. It housed thousands and thousands of people crammed into rows of barracks I could not see the end of. Our movement was limited, but I asked every new person I met whether they knew anything about the Bossard family. My faith in finding them vanished quicker than a bullet can kill someone. One woman transferred from Dachau told me that Auschwitz was not the only labor camp. Many similar ones were scattered throughout Europe. That was devastating. Even if they were alive, they could be anywhere, and I was stuck here.

Days turned into weeks, months into years; before I grasped it, it was already October 1944. I spent two years in Auschwitz. I accepted my circumstances, the no-way-outs, and the consequence of my ill-fated actions, but I still had a tough time working around half-dead patients. How could Élizabeth ever be a nurse? How did she leave all that behind the moment she left the hospital? These were the questions I would never get an answer to.

I was not cut out to work in the medical field, even as a janitor. I could not get used to the smell of ether, the sight of blood and tissues, and the wailing that always echoed throughout the hospital. One of the workers told me that the doctors were conducting surgeries on patients without anesthesia. But these people were not patients. They were enemies of the state. Undesirables. They tainted the Aryan ideology but were perfect candidates for experiments. I was now part of the Final Solution, and my existence hung by a thread.

All this time, I thought monsters did not exist in this world, that they were just made-up beings to scare little children into sleeping and obeying their parents. Monsters were not supposed to be real, but I saw monsters' faces in every doctor who passed by me within the walls of this hospital. They wrote the script to be carried out 'all in the name of medicine,' they said. A new Hippocratic Oath.

The worst of them all was Dr. Mengele—the devil himself. He took a keen interest in twins, especially children. He was kind and sweet to them like he was their uncle. Those innocent children adored him and ran to him when he visited them in their barracks, handing out candy—just to kill them the next day. The twins saw slightly better living conditions than the rest, but their future was short-lived. His sadistic experiments ended their lives too soon.

One inmate doctor, Dr. Gisella Perl, told me that Dr. Mengele was fascinated by people with two different eye colors and specifically sought them out. She saw him inject a chemical into a man's eyes to see if he could change his eye color. Then, Dr. Mengele removed his eyes and sent them to Berlin for further study. Before killing him, he made the poor man live blind for a few more days. That was everyday life in the ward, but there was nothing we could do but pray that the person in the surgery room would die quickly and that the next in line would not be one of us.

I managed to make a friend in these two years. Even in the harshest times, we all need a friend to get us through it all. I found a friend in a woman, Jadwiga, who worked as a nurse in the hospital and shared the bottom bunk with me in the barracks. We spent every moment together. Jadwiga was a kind-hearted woman from Poland who still had compassion left in her soul. After my arrival, she kept me alive and nursed me back to health by smuggling food and medicine. She put her life at risk for me. She would have died if she had been caught, but Jadwiga did not care.

"Let me do this for you, Cécile," Jadwiga whispered as she fed me bread.

"I don't want you to end up losing your life for a piece of bread," I croaked out. My voice had drastically changed, and it did not sound like me in the early days of camp. One of the beatings damaged my throat, and I sometimes felt my windpipe twitching. As a result, my voice turned hoarse.

"Then I will die on my own terms," Jadwiga said firmly; I could not help but admire her. She was everything I aspired to be. She was strong and always kept pushing us not to give up hope. After the lights went out in the barracks, she told us that we would get out someday and we would go back to living our own lives. She told us how the war would end. I would get married and have little children playing in the park with a wonderful man who adored me. She explained how I would grow old and that this would be nothing more than a bad dream. Some of the women in the barracks did not like her stories because they gave them false hopes, but listening to her gave me comfort, and I wanted to believe her.

It was October 20th, and my mind flitted back to the diary my mother had gifted me six years ago on this date. I recalled the memories of celebrating with my parents in the safety of my home. I reminisced about our dinner together, about seeing *Algiers* with Agnes and Élizabeth.

The memories left me cold and sent me back to feeling hopeless. I mopped the floor with rage like I tried to punish the tiles for all my pain. My hands frantically worked as I forced my mind to go blank. Do not think, do not think, do not think. My thoughts were crying as my eyes ran out of tears years ago. But how could I not think? How can I force my mind not to remember? I was in and out of this spiral, and that day I allowed darkness to swallow me whole.

My heart trembled as memories kept creeping in, and my mind was fighting to keep them out of my head. Suddenly, a door flung open, and I was startled out of my thoughts. I heard an SS guard and a woman's voice from behind me. I learned over the years not to look or stare. People always go through these doors, so it was nothing new. Sometimes the guards would bring someone healthy, only to be taken out as corpses. I never bothered anyone.

Once I made the mistake of staring at an SS guard dragging a woman with broken legs through the doors. She was in agony, but he still made her walk. He must have disliked the way I looked at him because he hit my back with his baton so hard that I thought he indeed broke my back. It was better if I minded my business and kept my head down. Drawing attention to oneself could have easily resulted in death, yet I stiffened when I heard the woman's voice. Stay put, I told myself, but some unexplainable force made me want to look, and slowly I turned around. I glanced up from the bucket, and my fingers suddenly let go of the mop. The wooden handle hit the floor with a clang, but it sounded like a shattered mirror breaking into pieces in an empty church.

I could not believe what I saw with my own eyes. There, standing near the door, was Élizabeth. Is she a mirage? Have I completely lost my mind? Do I now see and hear things that are not real?

My mind was not playing tricks on me. It was her. Élizabeth. And strangely, she looked fine. She was wearing dark trousers and a clean, white collared button-down shirt. If I did not know any better, I would have mistaken her for one of the people working with the guards. She did not look like a prisoner at all. Unlike the rest of us, she still had a healthy complexion. She did not look ill, thin, or malnourished. Even her hair was decent, given the circumstances.

If anything, she looked healthy as a horse. Her black hair was not tied in a bun like it usually was and was not immaculate, but it was not a mess either. Her hair looked sparkly clean, and she stood there with her left arm in front of her chest. She was cradling it like a baby, and my heart twisted in pain when I noticed her hand was severely bruised—purple and swollen as if someone had tried to break it.

My eyes met Élizabeth's, and I felt like my world was crashing around me. My mind worked in a frenzy as all sorts of thoughts ran through it. Has she been here all along? Was she a prisoner or an accomplice? Why does she look like that? I had so many questions and wanted to jump up to her. I wanted to ask her how she had been, only to fall on my knees to beg for her forgiveness.

We were both frozen in time as we stared at each other. I could tell she had the same questions running through her mind as she looked back at me. I waited to find an ounce of hatred in her eyes, I wanted her to hate me, but all I could see was horror—just horror and sadness in her eyes. The sorrow was so intense and terrifying that it pierced my heart.

Despite her obvious anguish, I could only feel my heart awakening and feeling again. I felt happy and had not felt like this in a while. I never thought I would ever be happy again, but that happiness was short-lived when I realized that we were currently in the middle of a well-orchestrated nightmare. But at least she was alive. Élizabeth is alive, and she is doing well. I was almost jealous that she was not as beaten down as the rest of us. A rush of determination, strength, and relief passed through my body, and I looked at her with a pained expression.

"You are alive," I wanted to say. But my voice was caught in my throat as the SS guard turned around, and I felt my body go cold. My eyes widened, and my lips trembled at the sight of Ludwig standing beside her. Why was he standing beside her? What were they doing together? Élizabeth shook her head slightly at me, but I did not know what that meant. I wanted to grab her and ask her what she was doing with a monster like Ludwig, but my body turned to stone, and I could not move. I felt horrified as I stared into Élizabeth's eyes, but the last thing I wanted was for Ludwig to recognize me.

I no longer knew who she was and what she was doing here. She did not look like a prisoner at all. Was she a friend here, or had she become one of the foes? You cannot judge, Cécile, a little voice whispered in the back of my head. She was only here because of you, and I could not judge her for doing what she had to do to survive. But what did she do? That was the only question swirling in my head as I took a few steps away from them as they passed by. Élizabeth looked uncomfortable when Ludwig placed a hand on her back and pushed her to keep moving. He was so focused he did not notice me at all. Not at first. My body was frozen with fear, but there was a strange rush of strength and hope. I became more determined than ever to get ourselves out of the deepest bowel of hell. I was going to make sure that this nightmare ended—once and for all.

Chapter 19

Encounter

I turned slightly, trying to hide my face as Ludwig walked Élizabeth by me. Seeing her alive and well made me forget everything and everyone around me, including the bucket I left in the middle of the hallway. I heard a loud clang. Filthy gray water spilled all over the floor as the tin can hit the tile floor and rolled around.

"*Scheiße!*" Ludwig swore loudly after he nearly tripped over the bucket. Time stopped at that very second. I was mortified. I looked up as Ludwig turned around, and our eyes met for the first time since I left his apartment bruised and battered. His expression was blank as it was not me who he saw but a Jewish prisoner causing him problems. His eyes were dead, showing nothing.

He took a step forward, and something struck my face out of nowhere. I silently fell to the floor. I held my face and looked up at Ludwig. He gripped his baton as if he were preparing to strike me again, but Élizabeth's horrified gasp stopped him from hitting me. I gulped down the fear as I held my numb face. I knew that it was going to hurt later.

I could tell he had directed all of his anger at that moment. Blood gushed from my mouth, and I felt a loose tooth swirling with the blood. I sat on the floor, trembling pathetically, tears cascading down my cheeks. I never thought I would ever get to meet Élizabeth like this. I could hear someone approaching us. Ludwig firmly held onto Élizabeth's arm as he looked at a nurse.

"We are here to see the doctor," said Ludwig as if nothing had happened. He only glared down at me like I was some sort of insect he had crushed with his boots. He stepped over my body to follow the nurse. I could tell Élizabeth was frightened as she only passed me a wide-eyed look, and she did not say a word or make any sudden movements with Ludwig holding onto her.

I got up from the floor and took a deep breath to calm myself. By now, I was used to the beatings and enduring constant abuse. However, it always hurts. The pain was still real, and my body could not get used to it. My mind told me to stand up and get back to work before an SS guard or an officer noticed me on the floor. I would only get another beating for 'wasting my time.' I got on my shaky knees, looked at the pool of blood on the floor, and wondered who would clean my blood off the floor next time. I grabbed the bucket and got back to work. I could not even imagine how my life changed after this encounter.

I was moving slowly, mopping the floor. Just as I expected, my face had started swelling and was throbbing in pain with every heartbeat. The blood had dried on my face and was itching, but I had nothing to wash my face with. I was somewhat tempted to use the dirty, bloodied water to get rid of the itching sensation, but I still had a little dignity left in this malnourished body of mine. I was already going mad, but I was still holding onto a thin thread of sanity.

"Pst, Cécile!" I heard someone whisper out of the examination room, and I stiffened. I looked up and saw Élizabeth peeking through the door, calling me into the room. I looked around, afraid of what might happen if someone caught me looking in Élizabeth's direction. The hallway was empty, and I decided to follow Élizabeth. I grabbed my bucket and mop before moving toward the door. Élizabeth reached out and pulled me into the dimly lit room. Élizabeth had not even put that much effort into pulling me, but my weakened body stumbled into the room and slammed against her body like a rag doll.

Élizabeth hugged me tightly, but her passion hurt. It hurt my body, but it hurt my soul even more. It drove a stake through my heart. All my pain, hope, and dreams were compressed into that moment.

"Oh, Cécile! Look at you," Élizabeth whispered in horror as she held my face in her palms. "What have they done to you?" She asked as she looked at me.

I knew I looked horrible. My thick wiry hair was nothing but a stringy mess. My skin sagged, and there were wrinkles etched across my ashy face. It seemed like I had aged a century these past two years, and my eyes had sunken into my skull. I looked at Élizabeth, and the concern in her eyes broke me down. No one had looked at me like that in such a long time. Élizabeth still cared about me after everything I had done. That made me want to fall to my knees, and that is what I did.

"Forgive me, please forgive me, Élizabeth! I came for you. I never meant any of this to happen. I am so sorry." My body was wracked with sobs as I held onto the edge of her trousers. Élizabeth knelt next to me and watched me break down right before her. "I betrayed you. I am so sorry. I wish I could have done something, but I ... I …" I was choking on my own tears as my sobs took over, and I could only hold onto her hand.

"Sssh," Élizabeth silenced me as she pulled me into her arms. I could feel her tears soaking my shoulders. "Now, now, Cécile. This is not your fault. The war and these camps; it is not your fault. You cannot hide from evil," Élizabeth said and tried to calm me down. But I could hear it in her voice. I could tell she had hoped they were spared, at least, and it only made me feel worse. Despite everything I did to her and her family, Élizabeth still cared about me, to the point where she was lying to make me feel better. She was a better person than I would ever be.

"But you had a chance! You had a chance not to be here, and I ruined it. All because of my jealousy," I cried out. "How can I ever make this right?" I wept sorrowfully.

"You can make this right," Élizabeth hesitated.

"How?" I asked her hopefully.

"Listen to me now. Mama is extremely sick with typhoid, so I need to get her some medications. They don't search you when you leave, do they?" Élizabeth asked me slowly.

"No," I replied and wiped my tears away. "They don't search us because we're just cleaners. They only check the nurses and doctors before they leave," I told her.

Élizabeth frowned for a while as she gazed at the floor. "That's good," she murmured before she looked at me. "Listen to me. Here is some medicine. Take this out tonight after work, find Mama, and give it to her. Do you think you can do that for me?" Élizabeth asked.

"Of course," I immediately replied as Élizabeth handed me medicine from her pocket. The rags I wore did not have any pockets, so I slid them into my undergarment. "How did you get your hands on these?" I asked her, and she gave me a sad smile.

"I injured myself so that I could come here," she said, but the expression on my face made her continue. "I'm a nurse, remember? Inflicting injury was easy. Getting here and making sure I was alone long enough to grab the medicine was the difficult part," she sighed," And I did not know how to smuggle it out of the hospital. But I have you now," Élizabeth whispered gratefully, and I hugged her again. Both of us froze when we heard footsteps from outside. "She is in the medical barracks," Élizabeth said quickly and hid me behind the cabinet as the door flung open. I held my hand up to my mouth to muffle my breathing as a doctor walked into the room with an x-ray sheet.

"Well, it looks like a fracture to the radius, but there is nothing to worry about. We put a cast on it, and it will be as good as new in a couple of weeks. The sling is not necessary. Otherwise, you cannot continue the work," the doctor said with little empathy. "I'll come back with the plaster in a minute," he said and left the room.

I stepped forward as the doctor left. I looked at Élizabeth, and all the questions that swarmed through my mind when I first saw her came back, flooding my mind. "What work? Élizabeth; why do you look different from us?" I asked her, and Élizabeth sighed.

"It's a long story, but I'd better be quick," she hurried, "Our life turned into a nightmare when the soldiers came knocking on our door to take us to the *Vel' d'Hiv*," Élizabeth started, and I sat there listening to her story with a big knot in my stomach. I was acutely aware that I had heard the consequences of my actions.

The soldiers had shot her father in Munich months before the rest of the family was transferred here. She told me that she was assigned to the *Kanada Kommando* on the other side of the camp as soon as she arrived. She explained that they were prisoners but treated far better than everyone else. They collected all the belongings from the wagons and took them to the sorting facility, nicknamed *Kanada*, which was a privileged job with many benefits. People who worked here had extra food and civilian clothing and slept in the warehouse rather than the main barracks. They still faced the guards' wrath if they were caught smuggling contraband or bribing Kapos, fellow prisoners promoted by the SS to supervise us. The Nazis shot them right on the spot, just like any other prisoners, but life was slightly better.

Kanada is somewhat isolated from the rest of the camp, which explains why I had not even known about Élizabeth being here or had seen Ludwig around for years. He was fired from his highly respected job at the embassy and was assigned as a low-ranking *Blockführer* in Auschwitz, but he still had enough influence to oversee the sorting facility. When Élizabeth stepped off the wagon, Ludwig immediately assigned her to the sorting facility.

Obviously, Ludwig's obsession with Élizabeth had not subsided over the years. I learned that he often invited her into his quarters for dinner. He let her take a bath, get out of her uniform, and would give her a lovely dress to change into for dinner. He cooked fine meals for her, gave her wine, and even turned the gramophone on so they could dance together after dinner.

"If it wasn't for the constant smell of death in the air, it could have almost been a dinner date," Élizabeth said sadly with a sigh before she continued. "I was extremely fearful of those dinners. But the more frequent they became, the more I started looking forward to them. It is so strange, Cécile. I have no idea what I feel anymore, and that scares me. These dinners with Ludwig became my escape from reality, and I wanted to enjoy them, even if they were for a few hours. That is how strange I have become," she whispered shamefully. I wonder if this charade were to mask the fact that he is also fond of men or if he genuinely liked Élizabeth. Maybe both.

Ludwig never laid his hands on her, nor did he ever force her to do anything. All he wanted was her company. Élizabeth talked about how much Ludwig tried to get on her good side. He almost desperately wanted her to love him. Ludwig often asked her to tell him stories of how they would live after the war, how they would move to the south of France together, have a farm, grow grapes, and tend to their children. Because of these visits, Élizabeth's health was in good condition compared to everyone else. It was evident that she was not like the other prisoners. No one ever dared to hit her or drag her around. Élizabeth was treated like an equal, and she never had to face the cruelty of the camps. Ludwig made sure she was out of harm's way.

The same could not be said for Élizabeth's mother. Like many others around her, she was sick with typhoid, and a high fever ravaged her already weak body. The doctors did not waste medicine on prisoners to cure them, only to use them as part of their experiments. Typhoid was a slow death sentence for her without treatment. Élizabeth needed to get to the hospital, so she asked another prisoner to hit her arm with an iron wrench. She hoped that she would be sent to the hospital if it broke. It was a gamble, but she was willing to pay the price for it. The guard could have easily just shot her, but she bet Ludwig would not let that happen, and she was right. Ludwig personally took her to the hospital to have it taken care of.

After hearing about Élizabeth's story, my mind became numb. I never thought that Élizabeth could be living here comfortably. I had expected her to be just as ragged and haggard as I was, but she was in better hands. I felt nothing but relief. Élizabeth was fine, and she was doing much better than the other prisoners here in the camps. It made me feel like a burden had been lifted from my shoulders.

"They're not giving you a sling," I gently muttered as I touched her arm.

"Even without the sling, my bone will heal. It would be better if I had one, but it is still the best option. At least I got what I came here for. I have the medicine I need and was lucky enough to run into you, Cécile. All this pain will be worth it as long as Mama gets better. You are a Godsend, Cécile," Élizabeth whispered.

"I promise you that I'll get these to your mother. What about Mimi? Is she here? Is she well?" I quickly fired my questions at Élizabeth as I grabbed the bucket and mop I had hidden behind the cabinet.

Élizabeth's eyes watered, and she sniffled. "If there's anything you can do for her, then please, help her get out of here," she whispered, and I nodded.

"I'll do my best," I promised her and swiftly walked out of the examination room.

I tried not to think much about the medicine hiding in my undergarment or appearing suspicious. My hands were trembling, but the guards noticed the bruise on my face and passed it off as nothing noteworthy. Élizabeth told me about the barracks where her mother was placed with Mimi, and instead of going back to mine, I decided to visit Élizabeth's mother. I walked into the barracks and noticed Mimi sitting beside her mother. The woman on the bed was hardly recognizable as she lay there shivering.

"Mimi?" I whispered, and Mimi turned around to see me. Her face went from being worried to furious. She stood up and strode across the room with her hand raised. However, before she could strike me, she noticed that my face was already swollen.

"Don't." Élizabeth's mother said in a raspy voice, and Mimi took a deep breath to calm herself.

"What are you doing here?" She asked me with hatred in her voice, which quickly changed to curiosity. "Wait, what are you doing here?

You're not a Jew, Cécile. Then why... are you here?" She asked me as realization dawned on her.

"I'm here because I wanted to explain to the officers back in Paris that they made a mistake, but it was already too late when I realized you were not in the *Vel' d'Hiv*. I pretended to be a Jew so I could get inside the camp to find you," I whispered as I pulled her aside.

"You're mad," Mimi whispered as she shook her head. "You got us in here, and now you want to get us out? How can we trust you?" She asked me furiously. "If it weren't for you, we wouldn't be here!" She shook me harshly, and I let her.

I did not have enough energy to fight back or explain myself. I quickly took the package out and handed it to Mimi. "I met Élizabeth today, and she asked me to give you these medicines." I took out a piece of paper as well. "She wrote down the doses here." I handed the paper over as I looked around nervously. We did not have enough time, and I needed to get out before a guard back at my barracks noticed me missing.

"How is she? Is she doing well?" Mimi asked me quickly.

"They don't let you meet her." It was not a question, but Mimi shook her head in response.

"No. I haven't seen Élizabeth since they took her to a different camp. Mama and I thought that maybe she was dead," Mimi whispered as she opened up the piece of paper and sniffled. "How is she?" She asked me again, fighting her tears back.

I wanted to tell her that Élizabeth was doing well. Élizabeth was doing better than any of us here. Even Mimi seemed a bit malnourished and haggard. She was so young, only thirteen, yet, fear was etched on her face. Her head was shaved, and I spotted a few bruises around her arms. Élizabeth might have been treated better than most prisoners here, but Mimi and her mother were no exceptions.

"Believe me when I say this, but Élizabeth is doing well. I cannot tell you anything, which might harm Élizabeth, but she is alive and well. She's doing better than any of us," I said, but Mimi only seemed confused.

"I'm sorry for –"

Mimi cut me off, "Don't apologize. Because no one will accept your apology here," Mimi hatefully said as she sat down on her mother's bed. "I'll never accept your apology, so don't waste it on me. Just get out of our lives and leave us alone. None of this would have happened if it were not for you. We were doing fine without you," she whispered hatefully, and I took a deep breath to calm myself.

"I promised Élizabeth to take care of your mother for her," I said and turned around to leave.

I knew I deserved this and did not expect a warm welcome, but seeing them all alive sparked hope inside me. I knew what I needed to do next and was ready to do it no matter what it took. On my way back to the barracks, I tried to think of a way to get Mimi out, and I was so wrapped in my thoughts that I did not notice a guard eyeing me from across the field.

"Where are you going?" The guard asked me, and I bit my lip.

"To the washroom," I said hastily, but it was not much of a lie. I still needed to wash the dry blood off my face. The officer grabbed me by the arm and dragged me to one of the washrooms.

I did not know what he wanted, but I quickly washed my hands and face. I knew not to question the guard, but I felt his eyes piercing my body from behind. Suddenly, an idea popped into my head as I turned around. I had a hunch about what I had to do to get Mimi out, but I needed to confirm something.

"What are you looking at?" The guard asked me, but he did not sound furious.

"Nothing." I swallowed and walked past him, but he held onto my arm and pulled me closer to him.

I shuddered in disgust when he leaned in to whisper in my ear. "If you need anything, you can just use yourself to get it," the guard said.

"I can give it to you, but not for free," he groped my back before letting me go. I gulped down my fear.

I nodded quickly, and he guided me back to the barracks. The guard had confirmed my suspicions. Most of the female prisoners were selling themselves for food and medicine. I knew what I had to do, and it killed me inside, but I reminded myself that I owed this to Élizabeth and her family. With that thought lingering in my head, I closed my eyes. I fell asleep devising my plan to save Mimi and make good by Élizabeth.

★★★

Hénri pulled his coat together as he exited the *Centre Hospitalier Sainte-Anne.* Even the razor-sharp winter air could not snap him out of what seemed to be the longest dream in his life. He wandered down the street in a semi-hazed stage, consumed by his thoughts. People were rushing by him with bags of presents; couples cuddled up for warmth as they stopped to admire the Christmas displays. It was late, nearly eight o'clock. Shops started to close for the night, and Hénri realized he had spent his entire day in the hospital.

Cécile had broken her silence; all she needed was her journal and a pencil to break her fifty-four-year silence, the stillness of time. He tucked his chin into his wool scarf as the snow started to fall and looked for the closest *Métro* station to head home.

Christmas Eve was right around the corner, and Hénri's mother planned to come to Paris for the holidays, her favorite time, and she always spent it with her only son. Besides, she claimed the hot-mulled wine was much better in Paris than in Lyon. Hénri's mind was not focused on Christmas, and he was so absorbed with Cécile that he nearly forgot that his mother was arriving in the morning.

CHAPTER 20

LOVE AND HATRED

Wednesday, 22 December 1999

After much-dreaded shopping with Frances, Hénri could not wait to return to the hospital in the afternoon. His mother's obsession with Christmas went beyond her sipping mulled wine at the Christmas market.

She was the queen of holiday dinners. There was chestnut soup, roasted duck, and *Bûche de Noël,* a sponge cake resembling a yule log, which, despite its description, is downright fabulous. *Hors d'oeuvres* and cheese are served before and after, with several bottles of fine wine meticulously paired with every meal. Hénri knew this year would not be any different.

He did not mind shopping with his mother, but he did not enjoy buying food with her. She was a connoisseur, and she paid a lot of attention to the details of the ingredients—maybe too much. Before settling on the duck, she sent the poor butcher back at least five times to find a better bird. Hénri's mind was very detached from the whirling crowd of Christmas shoppers, and he longed for some quiet that the psychiatric ward offered. He chuckled when he realized what he wished for. Serenity and a mental hospital seemed to be a divine example of an oxymoron.

Still, Hénri wanted his mother to go with him to visit Cécile, but she would rather stay behind and sip hot wine and catch up with old friends. He could not blame her and promised to join later in the day at the best Christmas market in Paris by the *Hôtel de Ville.*

Dr. Pelletier was just as shocked by Cécile's sudden behavior change as Hénri. While standard protocol would not allow a non-medical professional to partake in a patient's therapy, Dr. Pelletier made an exception with Hénri. He even allowed Cécile to keep the pencil overnight. He broke every rule, but he did not want her to regress. When the nurse came to wake her, she found Cécile sitting on her bed, hunched over her diary, rocking back and forth ever so slightly. She had stayed up all night writing in her journal.

★★★

Smuggling medicine from the hospital ward to the barracks was daunting. The guards conducted random checks, and my heart involuntarily squeezed whenever they looked in my direction as I tried to make my way back to the barracks. It was not easy to live through the fear of being shot if I were caught, but it was worth it in the end. Élizabeth's mother was slowly recovering. Color returned to her pale skin. She could finally open her eyes without much effort and even eat a few bites. I sat beside her and handed her the bread I had saved from lunch.

"You don't have to bring me food anymore," Élizabeth's mother whispered as she held my hand, and it reminded me of my recovery and Jadwiga's devotion. "I feel much better thanks to you, Cécile. I think you should stop before the guards find out and shoot us both dead," she told me, and she was right. I took a deep breath and sighed in relief.

Élizabeth's mother forgave me after she heard why I had entered the camps. I was shocked that she did not hate me for what I did. She said, "We would have ended up here, either way, darling. It was in our fate." Although her words were forgiving, the pain was evident in her voice, and she wept for the pain my mother must be going through. I was her only child, after all. My mother had lost her brother to the first war and now lost her only living child to the second war. I felt awful for putting her through this, but I would rather die here than live with regret for the rest of my life.

I handed a soldier's cap to Mimi before leaving. She looked at me strangely, "Where are you getting these from, Cécile? How are you getting these things?" She asked as she hid the hat under her bunker. Mimi's anger toward me vanished as I slowly nursed her mother back to health.

"You don't need to know that!" I told her firmly. I did not want to recall what I had done to get the cap. I needed to sneak around more with the soldiers before assembling the whole outfit for her. Selling myself was a necessity. I was a number, an enemy, and a commodity. The soldiers were rough sometimes and twisted my body around like they wanted to break it. The pain never dulled, and my abdomen always felt like it was on fire, but I had already decided to do whatever it took to get Mimi out.

I ensured I slept with soldiers from different units to decrease my chances of getting caught after stealing their clothes. They were in such a frenzy, either because they broke the rules by sleeping with prisoners or because the guards knew they would get into trouble over lost articles. My body was not in the best shape, but I learned how to use it. I realized the soldiers needed a way to vent, and the only way these animals knew how to release tension was to take it out on the prisoners by beating them to death or raping a woman. I hated every second of it; it made me sick to my stomach, but I always told myself that this would be worth it—that this would help, help all of us in some twisted way.

Mimi seemed a bit disheartened by my lack of response. She always asked me where I got the clothes, but I never told her. I had managed to steal a cap and a coat, and now I needed to steal a pair of trousers. It was not easy to steal their garments since some would hardly take them off during sex, if I could even call it that, but somehow, I always found a way.

Finding a size that more or less did not swallow her whole posed a greater challenge. Mimi was only thirteen, but I felt she was catching onto what I was doing. I decided to distract her with our plan, but unfortunately, it was not much of a plan at the moment, and it was not mine. It was Jadwiga's, and I had convinced her to take Mimi with her.

"I'll come again tomorrow if I can," I said and left for the night. I went back to my barrack to talk to Jadwiga and get more details about her escape plan. This time, I would not allow a plan to remain unfinished, and I would not fail.

"A truck is leaving in the next three days," Jadwiga whispered. "We must ensure we have all the uniforms by then."

"I just need to get a pair of trousers for Mimi," I said, and Jadwiga nodded before a look of concern covered her face.

She grabbed my hand abruptly, and I felt nauseated by the touch. My body reacted before my mind could decipher, and I snatched my hand away. Jadwiga sighed as if she understood my pain, but I clenched my hands tightly.

"Sorry," I stuttered, and she shook her head with sadness clouding her eyes.

"It's okay," she replied softly. "I still think you should come with us, Cécile. You will be killed before those soldiers can even torture you to death."

"I can't leave. Not without Élizabeth," I replied immediately.

Jadwiga pursed her lips as if she disagreed with me. I knew she cared about me, but I could not leave Élizabeth and her mother here. I looked at Jadwiga with desperation, "Please, just get Mimi out of here," I pleaded, and she sighed deeply.

"Of course, I will. I'll do everything I can even if it costs my life," Jadwiga said with much determination. "It's a pity you're not coming with us, Cécile. But I cannot force you. I hope you make it out alive one day," she said and turned around so that she could catch a few hours of sleep.

I stared at the bottom of the top bunk and wondered if that 'day' would ever come. I closed my eyes, still hoping this was a bad dream and I will wake up from an afternoon nap lying on a sunchair in a white dress, a cocktail next to me, as Ludwig was leaning against the steamboat's guard rail floating down the Nile River. We are on our honeymoon.

Élizabeth's mother had recovered, and I was excited to share the news. I did not have to wait long. Élizabeth was brought in again with a large bruise covering her face. Her cheekbone must have been broken because her face looked worse than mine when Ludwig struck me. I knew she had goaded him into hitting her so she could help me sneak medicine out. We all played our parts.

"Élizabeth!" I whispered as I passed the examination room with my mop. The door was wide open, which was highly unusual.

Élizabeth hurriedly waved me in, "How's mother doing?" She asked me immediately.

"She's doing well. She made a full recovery, thanks to you," I replied. "You don't have to come in here anymore," I said, and Élizabeth sighed in relief.

She tried to put the medicine bottle back into the cabinet when a hand caught hers. I jumped in fright as we turned around to see Ludwig standing there with blazing eyes. If I ever thought Ludwig looked horrifying before, he looked downright frightening at that moment. He tugged Élizabeth's arms harshly so that she shuddered against him.

"I see it now," he whispered into Élizabeth's ear, and I realized that he had heard our conversation. I did not understand Ludwig's bizarre behavior. He was always explosive, but right now, he was calm. Too calm. Only his eyes gave his internal fury away.

I wanted to say something, but my throat dried up, and I felt like I was choking as Ludwig ordered the soldier to grab me. He dragged Élizabeth out of the room while the officer grabbed my arm, and we followed them. I felt my heart thundering in my chest horribly as I noticed the direction Ludwig was leading us toward.

"Where are you taking us?" Élizabeth cried out, but Ludwig did not respond.

He bulldozed his way through the people. At some point, Élizabeth tripped over her feet, but Ludwig did not stop. He dragged her through the cold frozen ground, and Élizabeth quickly realized where they were going even though she had never seen this part of the camps before. She begged him to forgive her and stop, but her desperate cries were ignored. He stomped inside the barrack and pushed Élizabeth inside. The SS officer dragging me also shoved me to the floor harshly. I winced as the ground bit my knees and scraped my hands with cuts, but I stood up almost immediately.

Élizabeth looked around fearfully, and her eyes finally fell on her mother. Mimi was sitting beside her on the bed, and her eyes widened when she noticed Élizabeth still on her knees, sobbing with fear. Ludwig kicked her in the chest and walked toward Élizabeth's mother.

"This is the price you have to pay for fooling me! I knew something was wrong when you started hurting yourself, Élizabeth. I knew something was wrong when you provoked me to hit you. I thought it was all for meeting up with your shit friend, but you went behind my back and decided to nurse a fucking Jew!" Ludwig said, clenching his teeth.

"She is my mother!" Élizabeth wildly screamed as she recovered from his punch and stood up in front of Ludwig. "Please don't do this. Please. I will—I will do whatever you want. Just leave my mother out of this," she sobbed.

Ludwig grabbed Élizabeth by her hair and pushed her aside. I was petrified by the man who once loved Élizabeth and me, and I was terrified of the man I had once loved. I could not believe this was the same charming and collected Ludwig I had known. He was like a raging bull now, and everything happened quickly.

"It's too late," he said, and I watched as Ludwig pushed Élizabeth away and pointed his gun toward Élizabeth's mother, who watched everything in shock.

She did not get a chance to utter her last words as Ludwig pulled the trigger and shot her in the forehead. The sound of a gunshot was not new, but it meant something different this time. It rang in my ear, and it slowed down time. All the other prisoners turned their heads away. Élizabeth's wretched scream echoed around the barrack. My knees gave out, and I fell to the floor as Élizabeth rushed to her mother and hugged her dead body.

"No, no, no! Mama, wake up! Mama, Mama, Mama!" Élizabeth called out to her desperately like a lost child in a park, her cries breaking my heart. Ludwig turned his head and looked at Élizabeth with satisfaction in his eyes as she wept over her mother.

I crawled toward Mimi, staring at her mother's dead body with shock written over her face, her mother's blood dripping from her cheeks. She was frozen like a statue. Before I could reach Mimi, she passed out and crashed to the floor. Ludwig hardly paid attention to her as he grabbed Élizabeth by the wrist and tried to get her out of the barracks, but Élizabeth held onto her mother's lifeless body tightly and refused to let her go.

"Get away from her!" Ludwig ordered, but for the first time ever, Élizabeth defied his orders and refused to budge.

"Mama! Mama. I am so sorry. I'm so sorry for everything," she harshly cried as she gripped her mother's body in her arms.

Ludwig struggled to pull Élizabeth off her mother's body and only succeeded when she allowed herself to be jerked away. Élizabeth turned around, and without realizing where she was, she slapped Ludwig across the face sharply. Smack! The sound echoed around the room. She hit him repeatedly until he caught her wrist and slammed her into the wooden pole that supported the roof.

"Do you want to die?" He screamed at her. Ludwig's eerie calmness immediately turned into fury.

"Yes, I want to die, but I will only die after killing you. I hate you!" She screamed at him as if she had lost her mind. "I hate you so much! I wish you were dead! You are a disgrace, Ludwig. Do you hear me? A disgrace! I hate you!" She kept repeating her words until he knocked her out by hitting her in the head with his gun. The other officer pulled his weapon and was about to shoot her, but Ludwig motioned him to stop, although he knew he should have let him kill her right there.

Ludwig carried Élizabeth's limp body as the Kapo came in to take her mother's dead, bleeding body away. I did not realize I was following Ludwig until he stopped, and I bumped into his back, and he turned around to give me one last deadly look that froze me in my steps.

"Where do you think you're going?" He asked me, and I mustered up enough courage to speak.

"Where are you taking her?" I asked him faintly, and Ludwig looked at me with disgust.

"You should start worrying about yourself, Cécile. I'm coming for you after I am done with her," Ludwig warned me, and I called out after him.

"Don't. . . hurt her." I choked, but Ludwig only glared at me before leaving.

I looked back to see the chaos he had made. Blood was dripping down on the bedpost, and remnants of brain matter were splattered on the wall. I had become numb to the sight of carnage at the hospital, but this was the remains of my dearest friend's mother. It made me sick to my stomach.

I turned to Mimi, but she still lay frozen on the ground with her eyes closed.

"Mimi?" I asked softly, and she opened her eyes. She stared at me painfully but did not say a word. I did not know what to say to her, so I hugged her until she could finally start crying. "I promise I'll get you out of here. I promise," I said, but my promises hardly made a difference in this situation. I am not even sure she heard me.

That was when I realized that the lines between love and hate could become so blurry that they fade to nonexistence. We feel love just as intensely as we feel hatred. I no longer knew whether Ludwig loved Élizabeth or if he were simply obsessed with her. Did he love her? Did he hate her? What did he want from her? What did he want from me? Ludwig killed Élizabeth's mother that day, and simultaneously managed to kill my hope for Élizabeth. For the first time, I prayed that Ludwig genuinely loved Élizabeth enough to spare her. As painful as it was, I hoped he loved Élizabeth enough not to kill her.

Chapter 21
Your God

Hénri felt the love and the hatred oozing through the pages of Cécile's journal as he looked up and rested his eyes on Cécile. He wondered what he would have done. Would he have had the courage? He knew Natalie would, although she would have had a much more thought-out plan.

Still, Cécile was more resilient than they could have ever been. She was no longer a naïve young Parisian girl madly in love and awed by handsome actors. Cécile was carrying the weight of the world on her shoulders. She played her part, and what Hénri had not realized, he played his.

Dr. Pelletier put his hand on Hénri's shoulder, which startled him. He was not sure of the doctor's intent with his gentle nudge. He either wanted to go home or wanted to know how the story continued. Hénri could not tell, but they both knew how it ended. Hénri let out a sigh and continued reading the diary.

★★★

In just a matter of time, Ludwig's wrath reached all of us. His anger and hatred hit their boiling points, and they were ready to spill over. I needed to get Mimi out. I had given her the proper uniform, and the deal I made with Jadwiga a while ago was set in motion. All they had to do now was to crawl through the small hole Jadwiga had been digging for years in a janitorial storage room in the hospital.

For years, she had been dumping pockets of dirt into the bucket after we finished mopping to remove the evidence. The time has come to execute the plan.

As soon as Mimi is safe, I will no longer have to sell myself to the soldiers, and I will no longer have to make a bed with these monsters, feeding the Nazi killing machine. That thought gave me comfort but also worried me. If the routine has gone, then what is next?

My days blended, and I could no longer tell them apart, but my nights brought a little bit of variety in a twisted way. The deeper I sunk into the dark pits of prostitution, the more I told myself that this was my punishment—the only way I could atone for my sins, My judgment day. Although I was not yet ready to meet my maker, dead or alive, it no longer stung me when the soldiers called me names or became abusive.

I had stooped far too low and could no longer cling to my dignity when it no longer existed. I was merely a woman who had nothing but her body and fragmented soul to offer. It did not hurt me as much as I thought it would. After all, I had been reduced to a number before becoming a prostitute.

"Tonight's the night," Jadwiga whispered nervously. I watched her put on the uniform she had collected on her own.

"Please take care of Mimi for me," I murmured in the darkness. It was almost midnight, and everyone else was asleep, and the guards were sparsely covering the grounds while Jadwiga was getting ready to make her escape.

"Leave it up to me, darling," she whispered with a sad smile.

I stood up after she got ready, and Jadwiga rushed to hug me. Instead of stiffening up in response, I decided to hug her back. She had been a great friend to me, and I truly hoped she would be able to get out. Not because Mimi's life depended on her but also because she was my friend. More than a friend. We were family. We shared tears and some laughter, but mainly we shared hope, hope that one day this will all end, one way or another.

"We'll meet outside these walls one day," Jadwiga promised me and looked to Mimi for confirmation. But at that moment, she doubted her own words.

I was fighting back my tears. I knew I would die here on this foreign soil, but I nodded, and it was the first time I came to terms with my death.

Jadwiga squeezed me tightly in her arms before she moved back. The *Kapo* she paid off was waiting for her outside the barracks. She opened the door slightly, and I watched her and Mimi disappear into the deep darkness. I stood there in silence a little longer as I stared into the blackness. I saw silhouettes of Mimi waving at me, and I waved back, but I knew it was a mirage.

"Run, little girl, run," I whispered, and a sense of calm came over me. I prayed in my bed to whatever God was out there to help them get as far away from here as possible without getting caught. To guide and protect them, I prayed until my eyes hurt, and I eventually fell asleep, only to be awakened what seemed like an hour later by the roll call—a monotonous start to the day. Still, more tension was in the air on this frightful dawn as we lined up for a headcount. I was nervous. My body was shaking, and my stomach was in a tight knot.

I was waiting to witness something horrifying. I waited for the SS to bring forth the escapees and execute them in front of everyone. But nothing happened. My nervousness turned to confusion. Was this some twisted plot to hide escape attempts from prisoners to kill their hope? Or have the soldiers not noticed that some prisoners were missing?

I looked around for Jadwiga or Mimi, but they were not there. In my heart, I rejoiced and believed that they had escaped because I was too scared to accept anything else. Mimi was finally free. It was time to get Élizabeth out. I feared it would be nearly impossible, as I recalled my brutal beating in the stadium just for trying. It would be my death sentence here, as Ludwig probably does not let her out of his sight.

Besides, I had not seen Élizabeth in the ward since Ludwig's savage act of torturing her by shooting her mother in cold blood right in front of her.

Given the circumstances, I was in a slightly better mood when I walked into the hospital. I was singing my favorite melodies in my head as I mopped the floor, feeling triumphant until a shadowy figure stepped up to me. I looked up to see who it was and let out a surprised sigh. It was Élizabeth. She looked healthy and free from bruises. I was glad Ludwig had enough heart in his blackened soul to spare the woman he genuinely loved.

"Élizabeth," I whispered, and she looked back at me with hopelessness in her eyes.

"Mama is dead," she said, and a rare moment of happiness vanished into thin air. I felt dizzy at the accusation in her voice.

"I'm sorry!" I said suddenly, but I looked up with a bit of pride. "Mimi escaped," I said, and Élizabeth's eyes flickered with an unreadable expression. She was dazed as if she were on a high dose of morphine.

"She did?" She plainly asked like it did not matter.

"The plan worked. Mimi escaped; she must have. The guards acted like nothing had happened this morning, and there were no rumors of dead escapees. That could only mean that Mimi was free," I said with too much excitement, but I remembered lowering my tone.

Élizabeth stumbled back a little and nearly fell over. I hoped the weight on her shoulders lifted and made her weak for a second. I caught her by the arms, and she looked at me like she could not believe me. I nodded at her to let her know I was not lying, and Élizabeth's shoulder slumped.

"Why did you do this to us, Cécile? Why did you do this to yourself?" Élizabeth whispered as she cupped my face in her hands gently. "None of this would have happened if you had just kept your mouth shut," she said sharply but with no anger in her voice. There was only sorrow, but her strange behavior concerned me. I started to believe that Ludwig made her addicted to morphine, and she was here to get more.

"I'm sorry," I said again and looked away. These words were never going to fix everything that had happened, and it was never going to change what was about to happen.

"There's nothing we can do," Élizabeth whispered. "I'll always remember what you did, but I forgive you and thank you. Thank you for getting Mimi out of here," Élizabeth said, and the small morphine bottles clinked as they shuffled around in her pocket. She quickly rushed into an examination room as the sound of military boots became louder.

Élizabeth forgave me. She forgave me for what I had done. Her redemption of my sins drowned in my tears.

***

These words sent a shiver down Hénri's spine, and he struggled to hold his tears back. He sniffled and closed the journal. The large clock on the wall neared 8 o'clock. Hénri was so consumed with Cécile's story that he almost forgot he made a promise to his mother tonight at the *Hôtel de Ville*, but he had a tough time leaving Cécile alone for the night.

She had a firm hold on him, an invisible rope that tied Hénri's present to Cécile's past. He knew, however, that she was not alone at all, although it seemed that way. She was still with Élizabeth in Auschwitz, and Dr. Pelletier was here to help her navigate the present.

"It's getting rather late, and I'd better get going," Hénri said and grabbed his coat off the rack. "I'll be back tomorrow if you don't mind," he said, but it sounded more like a question.

"Oh, by all means, please do come by. *Mademoiselle* Cécile is very much fond of your visits." Dr. Pelletier assured Hénri, then continued, "I know it's hard to tell, but we notice the slightest change in our patient's behavior, and I can tell you that she is aware of you. But I beg your pardon. I need to go." The doctor adjusted his glasses and hurried out of the room as the front desk called him on the loudspeaker.

Hénri wrapped his scarf around his neck and took a step toward Cécile on an instinct, maybe to hug her, but she did not turn around. "She is aware," mumbled Hénri and headed out of the hospital.

Frances was already on her third mug of mulled wine when Hénri arrived. The crowd was cheery, drunk with the festivities, moving around the vendor's stables in waves. Everyone smelled like a warm mix of cinnamon, orange, and clove. A tall, lush Christmas tree stood in the center, with a beautiful antique carousel next to it, looking as if someone borrowed it from King Louis XIV, a dominant French king who ruled during the baroque era in the late 17th century. The extravagant carousel, with its red velvet platform, delicate horses, and painted ceiling, resembled something that should be displayed in the Louvre, not on an amusement ride that played Christmas music.

Children's laughter became louder and then faded rhythmically with each round. Hénri easily spotted Frances in the crowd as she always found a spot next to the Christmas tree vendor. She loved the smell of pine and sap. She was talking to the stall owner as she sipped her wine.

Frances was indeed the queen of small talk. She could engage anyone and have a wonderful time getting to know the person. Frances was very much into the conversation, talking with her hands, not noticing her approaching son. Hénri felt he had left his thoughts back in the hospital, and he could not switch his mind and go from Auschwitz to celebrating in a blink of an eye. He was under Cécile's spell, and he wished he were not there at all.

It did not take Frances long to see Hénri's internal struggle. After finding a quiet bench and another mug of wine, they sat down and shut out the crowd. They closed the door of reality, and Hénri told his mother everything from the last time they spoke a few months back.

"What remarkable progress Hénri! I can't even begin to imagine all the horrors this woman witnessed and put herself through to save her friend!" Frances said with excitement, but her voice was also laced with sorrow, which is also how Hénri felt.

"I don't know what to do. Everything happened too fast. I cannot explain, but I feel I need to save her ... whatever that means!" Hénri said, doubting everything he had done.

★★★

New Year's Eve. We are in Agnes's apartment, listening to the radio, laughing, and dancing. Esther is here. I say her name, and she turns around with a big smile. Locks of her hair bounce on her cheek. We are dancing, smoking our cigarettes, drinking champagne, and gushing over every handsome actor we could name. The clock hits midnight, and the radio blares, but I realize I was dreaming and hearing the alarm for roll call.

A guard grabbed me by the arm and yanked me out of the lineup.

"Come with me. You have an appointment with Dr. Clauberg," the guard said firmly and started dragging me through the camp toward the hospital, knocking me out of my vegetative mental state, and I immediately became very alert. Besides cleaning and brutal conditions, I had never suffered any further, unlike the others. I had never been a lab rat for their experiments. But I knew too well where you end up once the doctors put you on the table. I will die today, I thought to myself as the hospital door flung open.

"Wait!" I said, "*Warten bitte!*" I tried in German. "*Wohin gehen wir?* Where are we going? I have work to do." I pleaded and tried halting, but the guard's grip was tight. She did not tell me where she was taking me and owed me nothing. She was following orders, and her order was to take prisoner no. 23871 to see Dr. Clauberg.

I panicked as we approached the operating room at the end of the hallway. I started fighting and flailed my arms to resist being dragged beyond a point of no return, but I was so weak that my attempts did not even faze her. She pulled me through the door and pushed me against the table in the center of the room with two footrests facing the door.

Dr. Clauberg sat behind the examination table with a small reading lamp at a small desk. He was a short, overweight man whose hairline receded to the middle of his head. He wore thick, black round-framed glasses that called more attention to his bald, round head. His thin lips were in an eternal smile, but his eyes were expressionless. He did not even look up from his notes as he said, "Mandatory sterilization of prisoner no. 23871."

I felt like my mind had gone numb after hearing those words. What were they going to do to me?

"Get undressed," Dr. Clauberg said after he stood up and turned around. He looked at me with a menacing glare, "Lie down here with your feet up," he ordered, pointing to the table.

I wanted to cringe and cry in fear. My entire body trembled as I stood there. I thought I could disappear, but Dr. Clauberg motioned me to move.

I started taking my clothes off, revealing my skeleton-thin body. I no longer knew whether I was shaking out of fear, out of being cold, or out of hunger. I no longer knew whether I would be alive tomorrow. I knew nothing about my fate as I lay down on the table. I was certain I was going to die. I closed my eyes, but I did not know that I wished I had died that day.

Dr. Clauberg restrained both of my arms and legs with heavy leather straps. They were very tight and cut into my skin, which hurt. My wrist and ankles were so thin that it would have only taken another notch on the strap to shatter my fragile bones. He put his gloves on and rolled his stool between my open legs. I tried to close them, but the doctor kept pushing them apart and growled at me to stop moving.

I felt something cold penetrating me. I was the least prepared, and it made me jolt. A nurse later injected some warm liquid into my right arm, making me drowsy. The whole room was swirling. Dr. Clauberg's face turned to mush, and his voice was distorted, slow, and very deep.

I could not make out a word he said. I was screaming, but no sound left my lips. All the doctor could see were silent tears pouring down my face. I could not make a noise. I was not crying for myself, however. I was shedding my tears for my mama and the children who I will never be able to bear. The Nazis broke my body long ago, and now they were stealing my dreams, the last bit of hope I hung onto.

After Dr. Clauberg was finished, he went back to his desk. He took out his notebook and his pocket watch and sat down. He watched me closely as if he were waiting for something to happen. I was in a heavily drugged daze but not sedated enough before it hit me.

Suddenly, I felt a sharp pain on the right side of my abdomen, which burned like fire from the inside out. I tried to free myself, but the restraints held me down tightly, and the drugs paralyzed me enough that I just imagined I was trying to escape, but in reality, I did not even flinch. The pain intensified with every second, but I lay still, and I did not even feel the blood that started flowing down into the bin out of my body. My screams became louder and louder but only in my head, and they echoed around my mind and rang in my ears until the pain eventually overwhelmed me, and I lost consciousness. The doctor injected vesicants into my ovaries, causing an internal chemical burn, eating through my flesh.

I do not know how much time has passed. The pain returned when I opened my eyes, but it was rhythmical this time. It no longer felt like I was burning alive but as if someone were bludgeoning me with a sledgehammer. I was still restrained on the table with my limbs secured, and I could see a pale figure standing between my legs. He was forcing himself into me with one hand covering my mouth and the other gripping my ankle.

As soon as my brain processed what was happening to me, the pain increased tenfold. My body was no longer paralyzed, and my brain started to clear just enough to see that Ludwig was raping me. *"Mandatory sterilization of prisoner no. 23871,"* echoed in my ear as I lay there in shock and pain, drifting in and out of consciousness. I was gravely mistaken if I thought the pain and torture would end here; it only worsened as time passed. He had me submerged in freezing water for what seemed like an eternity, not long after they sterilized me, and Ludwig raped me. At least the chilly water slowed down the bleeding. Time became never-ending as the torture stretched on and on.

Days blurred into each other, but Ludwig did not stop there. He ordered the doctors to quickly nurse me back to a decent state so he could do it all over again. While I was recovering from these various experiments and illnesses, Ludwig raped me repeatedly daily, whether I was conscious or not. He only said between those moments, "You're mine to kill, Cécile. I am your God."

If he were truly my God, I prayed to him every day to let me die so I could finally leave everything behind me. But he was a merciless God, and I was a helpless follower of his.

CHAPTER 22

LUDWIG'S PROMISE

Ludwig kept his promise and tormented me every day. I could not sleep for days, and even when I did, I was back in the ward with my legs spread open. I always woke up screaming, but no one was there to hold me in their arms. No one was there to wipe my tears away, comfort me, and tell me it would be all right. I was always left alone and would have to hold myself together until I passed out from exhaustion.

Death was the salvation I longed for. I forgot how to daydream about my life but repeatedly replayed my demise in my head. I saw my headstone next to my parents' and Camille's-the sister I never knew. I saw fresh-cut flowers and wondered who had brought them. Was it Mimi? Or Jadwiga? Will I even have a grave? Will I ever be known as Cécile Dubonnet, or will I forever remain a number even in my death?

One foggy Sunday morning in November, I noticed a shift in the atmosphere. The guards did not conduct their roll call as they usually did. They read numbers off their paper randomly, and one of them picked a woman out of line. I kept my head down because I did not want to see who would be taken away this time.

"23871," an officer yelled, and my stomach churned. A guard stepped behind me and pushed me forward, but I stumbled and fell. The guards laughed, and their breath in the cold air looked like an evil dragon breathing fire.

"You will come with us," one yelled, and I slowly got up from the frozen ground.

This is it, I thought to myself again. This is the end. I knew that many prisoners were shot on the spot or rounded up to march toward their deaths. I kept quiet, but my mind did not stop wondering where they would take me. If they wanted to shoot me, why were they not shooting me? Why now? I would rather be executed on the spot than taken back to the hospital for their nefarious purposes. I did not think I could have lived through another day of torture, but the situation's uncertainty terrified me more than death itself.

I was not the only one picked that morning, but I was the only one left standing after the women left for work. I was left waiting for my impending doom. Two guards escorted me to the main entrance. They collected nine more women along the way, and we were all marching to nowhere. I kept looking around and tried to put the pieces together. They were not taking us toward the hospital, but they were not taking us toward the back of the camp, either to the place of no return. Are we marching toward freedom? I asked myself as we approached the gates. There was a faint glimpse of hope in my heart that we might be set free.

I glanced at the other women. I was unsure what I was trying to find. Reassurance, maybe. I noticed they were in a lot better shape than I was. I concluded that they must have arrived recently, and since they were only nine of them, they were probably not marching to their death, although I could not be too sure. I simultaneously became increasingly anxious, nervous, and hopeful as we approached the main gates. It is true. They let us free.

At last, my nervousness quickly turned to excitement. My heart was pounding so hard that it almost jumped out of my chest. Thoughts were running through my mind, imagining what I would do as soon as I arrived home. I would take a long bath and ask Mama to cook all my favorite food. Then, I would lie in my bed and drift off to sleep without worrying about waking up to terror. It would feel as if I were lying in the clouds. We passed the barbed wire fence, and the guards pointed at a truck parked by the train tracks.

"*Schnell*! Hurry," said one of the guards and poked me in the back with his baton, snapping me back to reality. "Get on that truck, and we will take you to your new job," he said and snickered.

I looked back at him briefly and quietly climbed into the truck. I sat on the bench by the gate, and the guards released the tarp. It closed as the theatre curtain would at the end of the play, indicating that my hope for freedom was now over. There was no intermission.

We only drove for ten minutes before the truck pulled into a village and approached another camp. I supposed it was another camp because it had barbed wires everywhere. But this was much smaller and had proper houses and buildings instead of the wooden make-shift barracks. We passed through a large iron gate that said, "*Arbeit Macht Frei.*" My German was good enough to know that it said, "Work Sets You Free."

I wondered if this message was meant for the Nazis or us. Everyone worked, but their work was far more sinister. The truck pulled up to the first building on the left. A black, square sign on the wall read "24 Block" with white letters, but nothing further. The guards ordered everyone to get off the truck and made us form a single line. I was still frightened of the unknown; by now, I was convinced this would not be my last day. In some unfathomable way, this felt like a relief. Ludwig will not have the opportunity to torture and rape me anymore. That made me feel somewhat at ease with my new surroundings.

I wondered what this new job was going to be about. I believed any job would be better than cleaning in the hospital. Little did I know that I was going to miss my custodial work. A female SS guard walked up and down in front of us while stomping her boots on the ground. She kept scrutinizing us as she approached the first woman in line.

"Take off your scarf and your coat," she ordered. The woman obeyed and slowly untied her scarf and took her coat off. The SS officer stepped up to her. She examined her face and hair and then turned her head from side to side.

"Open your mouth. Wider. Now smile." She kept up with the same orders as she continued down the line. She separated eight women to the right and one to the left and said, "She is no good." She pointed to the woman on the left. The guard from the truck stepped up and shot her in the head.

The sound made me jump, and my heart thundered in my chest. I tried with every ounce of strength not to look up as the guard finally came to me. I was the last one standing in the line, and I was certain he would shoot me next, but he did not.

"What's your name?" The guard asked, which took me by surprise. I did not have a name for so many years.

"Cécile," I whispered, and my name sounded foreign.

"Ah, so you are Cécile. You look worse than I thought," said the guard with disappointment. "But I promised Ludwig, and I cannot renege," she concluded.

I looked up when I heard Ludwig's name and shivered in fear. The guard smirked and turned to the remaining women without inspecting me.

"My name is Irma Grese," she shouted, "and you are assigned to work in the *Sonderbauten*, a special building we call "Puff." You are here today to clean up and get into your quarters, and you will work here every day from eight to ten o'clock after your regular shift ends and on Sunday afternoons. You may address me as *Frau* Grese."

Irma Grese was just as cruel as Ludwig, if not worse. She was a hyena with a twisted mind, and her tortures and brutality preceded her. I could have never imagined it was possible to die over and over again.

As *Frau* Grese continued, I started to understand Ludwig's intention. According to his plan, I would be transported to Block 24, the Puff, to work as a prostitute. A special one. There were strict rules in the brothel, but Ludwig wanted me to be the one to whom the rules did not apply.

The women worked here as part of an incentive program for male prisoners. If the men worked hard, they were provided a trip to the brothel. However, the race law only allowed Slavic men to visit Slavic women and German men to visit German women. The master was paired with the slave, and Jews and Russians were strictly forbidden.

The couples could only have intercourse in a missionary position, and the guards ensured through the door's peepholes that everyone obeyed these rules. The women also had been set a quota.

We had to have sex with six to eight men during our two-hour shift.

After going through the rules, we were escorted to the common washing area inside the block. We were stripped, hosed down with freezing water, and our hair washed with soap. They had a routine exam to ensure we were all sterilized, and each of us received a tub of disinfectant cream to apply after each intercourse.

Frau Grese gave us luxurious lingerie and high heels, but she told us to keep our old clothes to change back into after our shift. It felt strange to wear someone else's intimate pieces, someone who may not even be alive anymore. I knew the garments came from *Kanada*, the sorting facility, where Élizabeth, too, methodically went through hundreds and thousands of suitcases taken from the platforms. She gave us mascara and red lipstick to make ourselves more desirable, but it was a sad attempt to hide our slow demise.

Frau Grese separated us by nationality, and each of us was given a nice small room with furniture and a comfortable bed. The guards kept a check on the rooms, except for Room 2122. That was my chamber. I knew that because my door did not have a peephole. I did not know how to feel or what I felt after the door closed behind me. I had a bed and should have felt lucky, but I just stood in the middle of this small room, shivering like I saw the devil.

Most men were just in and out, obeying because they did not want to lose their privileges. But plenty of SS officers with sadistic natures wanted to play out their sick sexual fantasies, which Ludwig designated me to fulfill.

He visited me on my first day. "They cleaned you up nicely," Ludwig said as he flopped into the armchair and lit his cigarette.

I was sitting on the bed in beige lingerie that was too big for my thin, malnourished frame. My ashy skin was not much of a contrast against this dull color. The cigarette smoke slowly floated and danced around like clouds in a summer sky. The smell immediately took me back to Paris and the time we passionately shared. I was surrounded by beauty and nature. I reminisced about the day I met Ludwig. I remembered how dreamy and charming he looked in my eyes. It took me back to the best time of my life, and my eyes teared up.

I began to realize who I was and desperately wanted to be, no matter the cost. If I could go back in time, I would fix everything and would have left Ludwig alone. I could never have guessed that my love for him would lead me to this point.

I knew my life would be normal if I had never met him, and perhaps I would be married by now with my own children. Memories of the *Tabac* and freedom I once had compressed into a single tear, which rolled down my face. I did not care that Ludwig saw me like this because he had already killed me.

Ludwig stood up and stepped behind me, "You know, Cécile, everything would have been fine if you kept your mouth shut. Sooner or later, I would have found the group your friend Agnes's father led that helped the Jews, but you are just a stupid little whore that could not keep quiet. You betrayed your best friend, but you also crossed me," he said. Ludwig was eerily calm, and I could tell he was on the path to taking revenge and was in the position to do so.

"I'm done with you," he continued, "but I want to ensure that you will die here. I want you to keep regretting the day you decided to call the embassy."

He grabbed me by the jaw and made me look into his eyes. All I could see was destruction. "Oh, I know it was you! I want you to keep wishing you could turn back time, and I want you to regret it for the rest of your life."

Tears were now running down my face, and I could feel the makeup mixing with my sorrow. I stared at him quietly without saying a word, not because I did not have enough strength to say anything, but through my silence, I wanted Ludwig to relive that pain from that phone call and feel tormented for the rest of his life. That was my revenge.

He put out his cigarette, stood up, and slapped me. Even if I were weak, I looked at him and gave him a small smile—my way of showing him that I would never regret betraying him.

"Every man who comes through that door is here because I want them to be here. Don't forget that!" Ludwig said before leaving. I thought my hell would end here, but Ludwig showed me a new side of hell that day.

By that evening, I was tied up, raped, sodomized, beaten, and my skin was used as an ashtray. I was choked and tortured; I lost count after the fifth client as I passed out from the pain, exhaustion, and morphine Ludwig ordered *Frau* Grese to inject me with. I felt like a lifeless doll, and the doll I became for these men to take their frustrations out on, which turned into my evening routine, and I was looking forward to it all day in a sick way. The morphine did its job, and Ludwig became my God, just as he promised.

★★★

Hénri's stomach turned, and he felt nauseous. He had to leave the room and get some fresh air so as not to be sick. He stepped out of the building in the freezing cold and took a deep breath. The razor-cold air reached every part of his lungs, and he exhaled with a loud sigh as he looked around.

The hospital garden was covered in snow, and the street was quiet. The snow muffled everything and increased the calmness, even in a bustling city like Paris. Hénri took another deep breath and followed the vapor he exhaled. He was shivering outside in a sweater, but his mind was far away. He wondered whether he was helping Cécile or destroying her. He felt selfish for chasing this urge to find the owner of this journal, and his initial excitement turned to sorrow. As Hénri turned around to go back inside, he saw Cécile's broken frame by the window and started crying.

Chapter 23

Edge of Eternity

Hénri wiped his tears with the sleeve of his sweater and went back inside. Cécile was still sitting by the window, motionless as the nurse got her medication ready.

"You should go," a nurse who Hénri had not seen before politely said.

Hénri nodded and took his coat off the rack.

"I'll be back tomorrow," he said, and the nurse gave him a confirming smile.

Hénri realized it was Christmas Eve, but he hoped he could bring his mother to visit Cécile, even if just for a brief moment. He buttoned up his coat and walked to the window. He stood next to Cécile and looked out. In that split moment, Hénri realized she was not looking at the garden or the life outside. Cécile was staring at her reflection in the window. She was looking herself in the eye.

Hénri walked to the *Glaciére Métro* station, where he could catch the green line, taking him straight home. The outdoor platform was busy with last-minute shoppers hurrying home with their presents before the children saw them.

Hénri hoped the chilly air would help clear his mind when he saw an old woman beside the station entrance selling candles and hand-made Christmas wreaths. She only had a few items spread out on the newspaper, and gauging from the box next to her, she had not sold much. Her petite frame was hunched over as she rocked back and forth to stay warm.

He took all the cash he had and bought every item she was selling in exchange for letting him photograph her. Hénri no longer wanted to capture the soul of the dead in the cemeteries, and he no longer chased the beauty of immortality.

What Natalie killed in him; Cécile awoke. She opened his eyes to want to connect, to bond with people, not just capture their smiles and sorrows, but more importantly, to link to the forgotten generation—the ones no one hears anymore as they slowly exit this world.

Hénri caught his reflection in the *Métro* car's window and looked himself in the eye, just like Cécile did. "Thank you," he whispered.

★★★

I never thought a day like this would ever come in my life. I died every night only to be jolted back to the living the following morning. I finally lost sense of time. I did not even know it was Christmas until one of the SS officers gave me finger marks around my neck as a Christmas present.

"Merry Christmas, you Jewish fuck. This pretty necklace will look good on you," he spat out the words while loosening his grip on my throat, and I gasped for air. I no longer had any energy to correct anyone who called me a Jew. They would never listen to me in the first place, and Ludwig abhorred me to the point of keeping that truth hidden from everyone.

It was 1944, and I tried to remember my last Christmas with my family. I tried to relive my life before this nightmare started, but I only saw faceless fragments. I could not remember what Mama looked like when she smiled or what Papa did whenever he gave me advice. I could only recall the smell of her cooking and Papa's coffee. I could only picture Mama with her back to me while she cooked us breakfast at the stove. I could only see Papa hidden behind a newspaper and a steaming cup of coffee in front of him on the table. I only saw Agnes walking away from me. Why cannot I remember what they looked like? What did I look like?

In my head, I created a different reality. I was no longer being brutally attacked by shadowy men in the brothel. They came and went as if they were using the washroom and nothing more. It was mechanical. I had to be stitched together so many times from being sodomized just by about every object the Nazis found that I stopped feeling pain. My nerves, including my rectum, were damaged everywhere, and my lower body was numb. It did not feel like part of my body anymore. Once a cradle of life became a garbage bag for discarded items, as I pictured my waist detaching from my legs.

My mind refused to accept this reality, and I slept, dreaming about the life I had invented.

I was weak to the point where I stopped caring about my cruel clients. No one could help me make it through the winter. A nameless woman at the barracks tended to my wounds and gave me food. I knew Jadwiga would have risked her life to get some medicine for me if she had been here. But I hoped she was somewhere safe with Mimi. The woman tried to keep my body alive, but my soul died long ago. It was time for everything to perish now—mind, body, and soul. There was still hope for Élizabeth, even if there was no hope for me.

There was apparent angst in the razor-frigid air as December turned into January. News from the outside world slipped in from time to time from soldiers who visited me in groups. Sometimes they discussed politics with each other. They knew they did not have to fear me since I could only hear snippets of information, but one thing was clear even to me. The liberating Soviet Red Army besieged Warsaw and Budapest, and it was just a matter of time before they reached Auschwitz.

German soldiers were hauling document after document out of the buildings and setting them on fire in the open air. Some of the piles were taller than the barracks themselves. The guards started gathering stronger prisoners over a few days, making them leave camp on foot to go to other camps. Some were lucky to survive the sometimes days-long journey in the brutal Polish winter, but most marched straight to their deaths. The ones left behind were shot in vast numbers and pushed into massive graves they dug themselves.

I never thought things could worsen, but Ludwig would always prove me wrong. He visited me one day, but he remained eerily quiet. He did not say anything while I sat on the bed with my knees to my chest in a distant delirium, and I peered at him through my knees while he paced back and forth in my room. He did not yell at me and did not act hastily but had death etched into his eyes. He was fuming inside; I could tell.

"Dress up!" He instructed me and threw my old rags on the bed.

I was too weak and too gone to ask questions and obeyed quietly. That seemed to have fueled Ludwig's anger even further. He sat down and lit his cigarette.

"I know what you did, you whore," he said as he exhaled the smoke, which he kept in for a few seconds, "I beat it out of her."

I looked at him in confusion and wondered what he was talking about until it dawned on me. I felt horror creep into my body like a sharp blade of ice going down the back of my neck and my spine. He was talking about Mimi, but I stayed quiet.

I had to show no sign of emotion that would give the slightest confirmation to Ludwig that I had anything to do with their escape. I knew Jadwiga's plan of escaping in the back of a medical truck carrying specimens to Berlin worked, and everyone was safe. Otherwise, Ludwig would not be here, or he would parade their dead bodies out of spite.

Élizabeth was in Ludwig's favor and was living as best as she could under the circumstances, and she had a chance of survival. They both did, and I had felt slight relief when Mimi had escaped. It was my way of undoing all this nightmare I had put my friend and her family through. I felt good, but Ludwig killed my last hope when he laughed at me.

"Élizabeth told me all about it. You got her in here, got yourself in here, and now she betrayed you. She told on you, and it seems that you two are not on good terms anymore. I guess she owed that to you. And do not worry, we will find Mimi too," Ludwig continued, "Let's go."

He put out his cigarette and grabbed me by the arm. He dragged me to his car. As we drove back to camp, the vehicle passed groups of prisoners marching out of the gate toward the unknown. I wished them farewell in my head as they disappeared from my sight.

The camp was in mayhem. Piles of paperwork were being burned, and larger groups headed to the crematorium. My excitement quickly evaporated when Ludwig pulled up in front of it and pushed me into one of the chambers. The room was empty and cold, and the gray concrete walls screamed death. I thought I had gotten used to the smell of death, but I was reminded I was human.

My ears caught murmurs from another room separated by a large steel door with a lever and a small round glass window.

Suddenly Ludwig slammed my head against the steel door. The force cracked the skin above my eyebrow, and the noise echoed through the room. I felt the blood flowing down my cheek.

"Look what you did to your friend," he said and turned my head toward the small window. My face pressed against the window, and the word friend hit me in the stomach. I frantically looked through the round window on the door and saw hundreds of naked people crammed into the room. There was no space between them; they were standing under what appeared to be a community shower room.

I nearly fainted when my eyes finally caught Élizabeth, but Ludwig's grip was firm, which kept me pinned to the door. She was standing in the crowd, her head shaven, naked, and terrified.

"No, no, no, you can't do this! Get her out of there! Ludwig, please, please, do not do this to her. You love her, don't you? Why would you do that to her?" I begged him, but Ludwig only sneered at me.

"This is all your fault, Cécile. You never know when to sit still and shut up. I didn't put her in there. You did!" Ludwig said as he kept pressing my head against the window. The blood from my face left a smeared imprint on the glass. Élizabeth looked terrified and out of place in between all the skeleton-like bodies. Her cheeks were red, and her body was bruised from head to toe. One of her eyes was swollen and bleeding. I wanted to look away but could not escape Ludwig's grasp. I shut my eyes. My heart was thundering as I cried for her. The blood from my wound flowed into my eye and rolled down my face. I cried blood.

Élizabeth finally noticed me at the window and made her way to the door. "Cécile!" Élizabeth placed her hand on the glass; her muffled voice was filled with horror, but her eyes were filled with tears of hope. Hope for Mimi.

"She'll be fine, Cécile. I know she will be fine," she told me. "Don't worry about Mimi anymore. Ludwig will never lay his hands on her."

"I knew you were behind her escape," Ludwig said from behind as he tightened his grip and turned me around.

I did not care what he did to me anymore as I looked at him firmly. I stood tall and proud but only in my head. My weak body was barely standing. Ludwig roared in anger as he slapped me across the face. I fell to the floor, and he repeatedly kicked me in the stomach. I only laughed at him until he picked me up and dragged me back to the door.

"This is the price you have to pay," Ludwig said, holding my hand up.

I did not know what he meant until he pushed it toward a button on the wall and forced me to press it. I heard rattling through the ceiling, but nothing happened for a few seconds, then the shouting started. Ludwig forced me to hit the button, signaling the release of hydrogen cyanide, Zyklon B, into the chamber through the ceiling vents. I screamed and fought against Ludwig to make it stop, but he pushed me away from the control panel. There was no going back.

I scrambled toward the window where Élizabeth was standing on the other side. Her face was scrunched up in pain. The prisoners were fighting to get to the door and open it, but it was sealed shut. Their fate was determined long ago; the heavy door closing behind them marked their end. I watched as they slowly died in agony right in front of me.

I felt like I was dying with them as they all perished. Élizabeth writhed in pain until her body gave in and collapsed. I stood there, locking eyes with her as my sanity slipped away hand in hand with the life leaving her body.

"We're not done yet," Ludwig said as he grabbed me by the arm and tossed me aside as he prepared to open the door. I lost all sense of time and could have stood there for a minute or an hour and would not have known.

"You're going to carry out the bodies."

I shook my head vigorously, hoping Ludwig would shoot me right there, but he knew that would have been my salvation. I moved ghost-like and did not know who I was or became as I dragged the bodies out one by one. Ludwig sat there watching as I slowly descended into madness. He let out a loud smirk when he saw me trying to lift Élizabeth's lifeless body, only to fall over and over again.

After an SS officer shoved the bodies into a pile, he threw me on top and spat on me.

"It's better if you die with them," Ludwig said with panic as the sirens went off all around camp. He jumped into a car with the other officer and fled. I lay atop the pile of corpses with my arms wrapped around the bodies, protecting them from evil until my last breath. The world was a blur, and it was getting darker.

"Élizabeth," I whispered one last time, and my mind broke into million little pieces.

Chapter 24

Mission

Friday, 24 December 1999

Hénri looked around hastily as he stopped reading her entry aloud, but Dr. Pelletier signaled him to stay quiet. The doctor was unsure how Cécile would react to hearing her ordeal and living through it again, but she remained silent. Cécile was sitting on her bed motionless, and the doctor wondered whether she would start speaking now that her fragmented mind recalled her trauma. Still, he wanted to tread lightly because he did not want Cécile to collapse back into darkness now that she was showing signs of recovering memory.

Hénri felt as if he had drowned in his nightmares and could not wake up. He felt guilt, compassion, and sadness for Cécile and for chasing the story. He squeezed his mother's hand and wanted to thank her for coming, but not a single word came out of his mouth.

This cannot be it, Hénri thought to himself as he ran his hand through his hair and rested his face in his hands. Everyone makes mistakes. While Cécile's mistake was grave, it still did not justify the cruelty she had gone through in her life. She did not deserve to be tortured and raped every day. The only dreadful mistake she made in Hénri's eyes was falling for an abhorrent man like Ludwig. Her only mistake was falling in love with the wrong man. But often, that alone can be enough to be fatal.

Thoughts raced through Hénri's head with lightning speed as his memory recalled the lives of Cécile, Esther, and Agnes before they became engulfed in the flames of war. Over and over, he replayed their days in his head. What occurred should not have happened, and he was not ready to accept the end. Not like this. What was next, he wondered in his confused mind when he realized he had utterly forgotten about Mimi.

What if Mimi had survived? Did she live a good life like Cécile had hoped? Where was Mimi now? What if she was still alive? He needed to know and wanted her to be here in this moment and connect with Cécile. That thought chilled him to the bone. He found Cécile, after all, so why would he not be successful in tracking down Mimi? These thoughts stopped Hénri, and he jumped up from the spartan hospital chair. Hénri had an idea, but he knew that this idea was somewhat foolish.

"I can't believe I had been so blind all along. What if Mimi is still alive?" asked Hénri with renewed excitement, but his question was rhetorical.

"How?" Dr. Pelletier asked, raising his eyebrow as he pushed his glasses up his nose. He doubted this idea. "I will be honest with you, young man, even if you find her, prepare yourself that it may not change Cécile's state," said the doctor; then he continued, "I know we made a lot of progress, and we will continue her therapy now knowing what had happened, but ..."

"Mimi," whispered Cécile as she interrupted Dr. Pelletier, who was startled by her sudden expression.

"I will find her," Hénri assured Cécile and looked at the doctor for validation. Emotions flooded Hénri, and without thinking, he sat next to Cécile and hugged this frail woman. Tears silently ran down Cécile's scarred face as she leaned over to Hénri and quietly rested her head on his shoulders.

Hénri and Frances walked out of the hospital without saying a word. The streets were empty as families gathered around the Christmas table for dinner. Hénri pictured the children finishing their meal hurriedly to open their presents under the tree while the adults were getting tipsy.

While the three Wise Men saw a miracle, Hénri and Frances witnessed something unimaginable through the written words of a survivor. They heard her through the silence of her shattered mind. Her subconscious mind was stronger than steel, forged by the constant abuse to protect her forever, but Hénri's actions started to open the gate to her current life. Leaving Cécile alone did not feel right to Hénri, but Dr. Pelletier assured him she would be in a loving company that evening.

Back at his apartment, Hénri cracked open a bottle of Pinot Noir, and he and his mother talked about Cécile all night—her love, her friends, her desperate attempts to make things right, and her ultimate sacrifice and the price she had been paying every day for the past fifty-four years. Like other lost souls, Cécile, too, had been wandering the bank of Styx, trying to find ways to pay Charon to take her across the river.

***

Hénri spent the following day searching on the internet, but the search engine did not return credible results for Mimi Bossard. "*Déjà vu*, there is absolutely nothing on her," he said with disappointment.

"It's possible she changed her name. Think about it, Hénri. If they had successfully escaped Auschwitz, the last thing she would have wanted is to be found," Frances said while sitting on the couch, giving much-needed attention to Alice, who purred in return.

"Of course. I know Agnes had new passports arranged for them, and her real name was Ruth, but what was her last name?" Hénri asked, and he was annoyed that he could not remember.

Frances picked up the diary from the coffee table and flipped it up. "Klotz."

"Yes! Ruth Klotz slash Mimi Bossard," Hénri said triumphantly, and his hope returned as he started typing with renewed enthusiasm, but finding her seemed more arduous than he imagined. Hénri entered 'Ruth Klotz' into the search engine, which returned pages of results, but nothing immediately led him to her.

He browsed through several websites until he found one that had survivors' interviews with hundreds of clips. Even if he watched all of them, there was no guarantee Ruth had an interview for one or even survived her harrowing escape. Hénri thought he was trying to find a needle in a haystack, but it was more like finding the right hay in the haystack.

He watched hours of videos of people recalling the horrors they faced, talking about the family they lost. Some were still hopeful they would find living relatives. Hénri was about to give up and join his mother on the couch as he clicked on the last video before halting the search for the day.

"Unfortunately, I do not know what happened to my sister. ... I managed to escape when I was a young girl with ... I have been searching for her ever since ... liberated the camp," said the woman tearfully, but the video cut out here and there. She looked into the camera and continued, "Her real name was Esther, but she was imprisoned as Élizabeth. Élizabeth Bossard."

Hénri nearly fell out of his chair. He felt goosebumps all over his arms and the back of his neck. He could tell this video was at least a decade old, if not older. It was grainy and sometimes inaudible. Hénri rewatched it several times, focusing on the background for clues. Ruth looked like she was in her forties when the recording was made, and unlike others, and was not in the comfort of her home but outside where the Holocaust Memorial Museum in Washington, D.C., would eventually be built.

Hénri could not believe his luck. He hoped the museum would have a database of all the survivors, and all Hénri had to do was call. His palms started to sweat as he picked up the phone, and he did not want to be let down.

"Mom, please read the number from the screen," Hénri asked her with the receiver in his hand, forgetting to write the phone number down.

"It's Christmas Day, Hénri. I don't think you will get anyone on the line today. You'll have to wait 'til Monday," Frances said, and she changed the channel on the TV. "Come sit with me and let's watch this film. It's about to start."

"Damn it; I completely forgot!" Hénri said and realized he had spent his entire day on the computer. The machine powered down with a drowsy hum, and Hénri cozied up with his mother on the couch. He felt guilty about neglecting her, but he was so close.

"Just one more day," he thought, but soon he found himself lost in the film, and for a few hours, Hénri did not ponder about the old woman in the hospital.

***

The nurse found Cécile still in bed when she entered her room, catching her by surprise. Cécile had been an early riser since she was admitted to the hospital, and she was usually awake by 4 o'clock, just sitting in her bed waiting—waiting for the roll call that never came.

Cécile followed the same routine she had been used to in Auschwitz. She woke at dawn, washed up, dressed, made her bed, cleaned her room, and waited until she was called for breakfast. When she started using a wheelchair, she sat on her bed, patiently waiting for the nurse to help her. Cécile learned to wait quietly. Roll calls in Auschwitz often lasted hours as every prisoner was counted twice and recounted all over again if there were any discrepancies or miscounts.

Although her days were not filled with hard labor anymore, her mind was still living through the torture and abuse she suffered at the hands of the Nazis. She relived it daily, but her outside world never heard her screams and cries. Her medication controlled her tantrums, but she needed to be restrained when she became violent.

Cécile's demeanor was most unpredictable after dinner. Her nights at the brothel, where she was forced to serve officers and privileged prisoners, undeniably left her emotionally paralyzed, which the morphine temporarily numbed. Sexual torture, sodomy, aberration, and physical abuse scarred her body and killed her last bit of shame. As the evening progressed, she slowly calmed down for the night and eventually fell asleep, only to start her internal nightmare again the next day. That is how Cécile spent the last fifty-four years.

Her madness slowly blended with reality over the years, like watercolors blending, swirling, and creating a new color while the other colors ceased to exist. Psychiatrists could not properly diagnose Cécile's mother's bipolar disorder at the time, which Cécile inherited from her, although the doctors discovered that without knowing her family history.

In addition, the constant abuse and trauma she suffered caused her to dissociate from reality and create a new world with no boundaries. She could not tell where her memories ended and her other reality started as she cycled in and out of her manic-depressive state.

"*Mademoiselle* Cécile," whispered the nurse, and she gently touched her shoulder. But Cécile did not move, and the nurse pressed the call button beside her bed.

***

Hénri's fingers were shaking as he dialed the phone number for The Holocaust Museum. He was nervous and was not sure what to expect.

"Hello?" A lady answered the call, and Hénri's stomach sank.

"Yes, Hello. My name is Hénri Durand, and I am a Ph.D. student at Sorbonne University in Paris. I am researching the Holocaust, and I wonder if you could help me find someone," he said, lying about being a student.

"Of course," said the woman on the other end with an American accent, "How can I help you?"

"I am looking for a woman who was a child around eight or ten when she was a prisoner in Auschwitz, around 1943–1944. Her real name was Ruth Klotz, but if my research is right, she may have been documented under the alias of Mimi Bossard," Hénri said with more confidence since this part was true. "Perhaps, you can help me find anything about her," he continued.

"Let me see what I can do, Mr. Durand. We allow our visitors to use the microfiche, but I have to ask my supervisor since you are not here. Can you hold for a moment?" And without waiting for Hénri's response, she put him on hold.

Hénri was hopeful but incredibly nervous. It reminded him of how he felt when he was ready to take an exam at the university and was a little ill-prepared for it. It could have gone either way. He could have received an easy set of questions allowing him to pass, or the opposite. He was fortunate that he was not asked questions about things he did not study for, which would have caused him to fail his semester. The woman in Washington, D.C., did not give him any cues on how his inquiry would end.

After a few minutes that seemed like a lifetime to Hénri, the woman returned with the news.

"Mr. Durand?"

"Yes, I am here," Hénri answered. He tried to mask his excitement and fear of getting caught in his lies.

"I spoke with my supervisor, and he is willing to make an exception for you. Please give me the names and details again, and I can let you know if we have any records of her in a couple of days. A lot of our researchers are out for the holidays."

Hénri sighed with relief. He gave the woman all the information he felt she needed to track down Ruth. He did not say a word about the diary, Cécile, or that he knew Ruth escaped with a nurse named Jadwiga. She did not need to know. After they hung up, he felt uneasy, uncertain of what would be next. What if Ruth had not survived the journey? What if?

★★★

The museum called back sooner than expected, and the first few seconds of the call did not help soothe Hénri's anxiety. The researcher he spoke to found her! Or at least she thought she had found her.

"It looks like she registered with us about ten years ago in hopes of finding her relatives," said the woman, "but she has not been in touch with us since. The address we have for her is in New York, and she goes by the name of Esther Nejman."

"Esther Nejman," whispered Hénri. "She took on her sister's first name. I would never have found her."

"I beg your pardon?" the woman on the other end said.

"Oh, I am sorry, nothing," said Hénri as she pulled him back from his wandering thoughts.

"Do you have a pen close by? I can give you her address."

"Yes, give me a second," said Hénri and grabbed a newspaper lying around. He jolted down the number and address in the margin.

"She's in lower Manhattan." The address the woman at the museum gave Hénri was an art gallery in Soho. He browsed through the pages on the internet and found a picture of Esther Nejman, or Ruth Klotz and Mimi Bossard, as he knew her. An older lady with dark hair and oversized glasses smiled at him through the monitor. Her face did not reflect the horrors she saw in Auschwitz, but her eyes were filled with sadness.

Hénri saw the phone number at the bottom of the page and stared at it. "Should I call?" he thought, "But what will I say? I found the woman who put you in Auschwitz?" Hénri shook his head, telling himself it was not a good idea. Without a second thought, he opened another browser page and booked a ticket for himself from Paris to New York City. Frances did not want to join him on this quest.

225

"Oh, Hénri, you know I would love to, but I need to go back to Lyon," Frances said, "You are on this journey, and I am sure Ruth will be happy to hear that Cécile is alive, even if Élizabeth is not. It will give her closure," she encouraged Hénri. Still, he doubted Ruth would be thrilled to hear.

"Terrible idea," he said as he stood outside the airport and stared at the ticket in his hand, much like Cécile when she entered Vel' d'Hiv on a whim.

Chapter 25

Unforgiven

Wednesday, 29 December 1999

"Here goes nothing," Hénri muttered and fastened his seatbelt as the flight attendant instructed everyone over the speakers.

Hénri has always been captivated by New York every time he visited; it had a different feel from the equally vibrant but historical Paris.

The skyline and the neon lights transported Hénri back into that New World he knew. He had fallen in love with the city, where he lived for a few years as a teenager when Frances had the opportunity to work for a prestigious interior design firm. He took every chance he had to visit, so Ruth having an art gallery in the Soho spoke to his art-loving heart.

He checked himself into a hotel in lower Manhattan and looked for a place to eat. He was groggy and not in a good state of mind to do anything else but go to sleep. Flying took a toll on Hénri because he could never sleep on a plane, and he was always jealous of his fellow passengers who could sleep through a seven-hour flight sitting upright. One benefit of him not sleeping was that he was not jetlagged. He was tired, which made him a little useless that day, but his internal clock adjusted to the local time when he woke up the next day.

New York was colder than Paris, and Hénri did not prepare for the weather. As the sharp wind cut through him, he pulled his scarf up to his chin. Hénri was shivering, so he picked up the pace and walked toward the gallery. Hénri had no plan for what he would say, but he decided he would not lie to Ruth. She deserved to know the truth, even if it hurt.

Hénri was not at all surprised by how elegant the place looked. Ruth ran a high-end gallery, and he could tell she was the epitome of the American Dream for which most immigrants came here. He walked around the gallery and was as captivated by the displayed pieces as he was with the anticipation of finally meeting Ruth. Hénri carefully examined every item and read every tag.

However, he found a large painting without any tags tucked away in a hard-to-notice corner of the gallery. The sizable, ten-by-ten picture echoed so much pain that he felt his heart convulsing. The more he looked at the chaos on the canvas, the more he believed he recognized some of the events Cécile described in her journal. Or maybe Hénri just wanted to find a connection. Perhaps he wanted this to be Ruth's work. He was so immersed in this work he did not notice a petite woman walking up behind him.

"Few people find this corner," said the woman in a quiet, soft tone, but it still startled Hénri.

"Oh, I am sorry, I shouldn't be here," apologized Hénri immediately, as if he were caught stealing.

"No apology is necessary, dear. You might be at the right place," she said, almost like an oracle.

Hénri knew he was exactly where he was supposed to be and looked more closely at the woman who interrupted his thoughts. It was the woman from the video but older. It was Ruth! It had to be. He tried to calculate her age based on Cécile's diary, but his preoccupied mind was unwilling to focus on math.

He reckoned she was in her late sixties and still looked regal despite her age. She was petite, barely over five feet tall, and walked with a cane, but was exceptionally well dressed. She was elegantly minimalistic in her maroon tweed trousers and blazer. Her demeanor was calm and soft-spoken. Her naturally black hair was streaked with white and pulled back into a sophisticated bun. He wondered if Élizabeth would have looked just like Ruth if she were alive.

"You might be right," Hénri smiled as warmth replaced his nervousness. Ruth had that effect on people. She smiled back, and she had a curious look on her face.

"My name's Hénri Durand," he introduced himself, "I know this will sound strange, but I was hoping you could spare me a few minutes."

Ruth nodded, "Sure, dear, but the painting is not for sale."

"I love the painting, but that's not why I am here," Hénri paused for a few seconds before continuing, "You are Ruth Klotz, aren't you?" Hénri asked, and it caught Ruth by surprise. She had not heard this name for a long time and did not know this bohemian young man who wandered into her gallery with a French accent. It took her a moment to compose herself.

"My name is Esther Nejman," Ruth responded hesitantly, "Who are you, and why are you here?" Ruth quizzed Hénri.

Hénri took a deep breath and steeled himself. "I know you're a Holocaust survivor, and your name is Ruth Klotz. I saw your video about your sister, and I have something important to tell you," Hénri said, but he quickly realized that he may not have been as delicate as he wanted.

Ruth stiffened visibly, "I'm afraid I don't have time to spare after all," she said and turned around to leave.

"I'm sorry if I offended you in any way. I just wanted to talk to you. I know what happened to your sister," Hénri said firmly, and Ruth stopped mid-way.

She turned to glare at him, "How do you know?" she asked, and Hénri walked up to her.

He grabbed the old diary from his backpack and showed it to her.

"Is there anywhere we can sit? He asked, and Ruth stared at the journal with a dubious expression. "You will know once you read this. I am not trying to hurt you; I want you to know the truth."

"Follow me," Ruth whispered, still in doubt as she walked the hall.

Hénri sighed in relief and followed Ruth as she led him toward her office, passing the painting Hénri admired earlier. The office looked completely different from the minimalistic gallery floor. A large orange sofa took up half the space. Bookshelves, from floor to ceiling, were packed with various art books organized by the era, all in sequential order, from the early ancient times to today's contemporary masterpieces. It felt a little overwhelming, but he was awed by the collection. She pointed toward the sofa. Hénri sat down, and Ruth sat on the opposite side. They were now facing each other, making Hénri feel uncomfortable, like a suspect about to be questioned by the police.

"I need you to be very clear about why you are here," she told him firmly but quietly, and even in this state, Ruth remained calm.

Hénri nodded, "Do you remember Cécile Dubonnet?" he asked, and Ruth's expression darkened.

"I can never forget that name even if I wanted to," Ruth spat out, and Hénri was taken aback by the sudden change in her demeanor.

"I know what she did—" Hénri tried to say, but Ruth cut her off.

"If you know, why say her name in my presence?" She asked him coldly. "Just tell me about my sister. Did you find her? Is she alive? What happened to her?" Ruth fired her questions at Hénri.

Hénri did not know what to say, so he slowly handed her the diary. "This is Cécile's diary. She was the last person who saw Élizabeth alive. You need to read this part to know what happened to her," Hénri pointed to Cécile's last entry.

Ruth took the open journal from Hénri and grabbed her reading glasses from the coffee table. She read quietly, and Hénri watched as her hope that her sister was alive slowly vanished. He did not know what to do as Ruth's hand started shaking, and she slammed the diary on the table and stormed out of the room.

Hénri picked it up hesitantly. He did not know whether to leave or stay, but he decided to wait for Ruth to return. After a few minutes, Ruth returned looking more poised.

"How do I know that any of this is true?" she asked after a brief period of silence.

"Well, no one knows what happened between Cécile and Ludwig, and the only people who knew were those two. Ludwig was prosecuted with the rest of his fellow officers in Nurnberg and executed shortly after the trial."

"I hope he died in agony," Ruth murmured under her breath.

Hénri looked at Ruth. Witnessing her mother's execution and her harrowing escape in the care of a stranger must have taken a toll on Ruth in many ways. Hénri knew that her early life probably had made her bitter, but he guessed that wretchedness only came through now and then. Based on her demeanor, he thought that she was still unbreakable. She continued building her life, and her horrible early experiences arguably made Ruth immensely powerful. Hénri could not help but admire her. He thought I would have given up on life long ago if I were in her place.

"Cécile's alive," Hénri blurted, and Ruth stiffened.

"I don't want to hear about her," she responded swiftly.

"I know how you feel about Cécile after everything she has done, but she did orchestrate your escape with Jadwiga. She tried so hard to get all of you out of there. Don't you want to know what happened to her?" Hénri asked. "Did you ever. . .try to look for her?"

Ruth pursed her lips and sighed. "I only tried to look for Élizabeth. I don't care how that traitor lived or died, and I'll never forgive her for what she did to my family."

Hénri blinked in surprise, "But, Cécile helped you escape. You are alive because of her!"

Ruth looked into Hénri's eyes with a look so cold that he froze on the spot.

"Would you forgive someone even if they killed your family?" she asked him.

"Then, I guess this is it," Hénri sighed and stood up, leaving the diary on the table. "I wish you knew how much she regrets what she did, and she is still paying the price for her mistake. I left my number on the last page of her diary and wrote down Cécile's whereabouts. If you ever wanted to visit her," he said with a slight disappointment in his voice.

"You're an incredible woman, Ms. Klotz. I admire your strength, and you are one of the bravest people I know. But I hope you're also brave enough to forgive Cécile for what she has done."

Ruth went quiet for a while, and Hénri thought she might never speak up again. "Why are you doing this?" She asked him, "Are you related to her?"

"No. Not the slightest."

"Then why? Why are you doing this?"

"Because you might have moved on or tried to, Ms. Klotz, but Cécile never had the chance," Hénri replied and said his goodbyes. At that moment, he realized that this journey of forgiveness was just as much theirs as his own ability to forgive Natalie.

He turned around to look at the gallery one last time as he crossed the street. He saw Ruth standing in the middle of the floor, watching him melt into the mayhem of New York City as it prepared for New Year's Eve, just as Cécile watched her and Jadwiga disappear on that faithful night.

Ruth looked fragile and distraught. Hénri felt terrible for bringing the past back so unexpectedly and raw, but he knew she needed closure as much as Cécile did, even if she had not yet realized it.

Hénri lay on the hotel bed thinking, and while he had an early morning flight, he had too much on his mind to sleep. Questions kept creeping in about whether he had done enough, and he could not answer them. He could not force Ruth to change her mind; how could he? Ruth was not as forgiving as he hoped, even after fifty-four years, and it took the wind out of Hénri's sails.

Hénri looked at the clock on the nightstand, whose bright red number read 2:30 a.m. He rubbed his eyes, grabbed his carry-on bag, and headed downstairs. He was exhausted, but even the frigid cold air could not give him the jolt he needed.

"To the airport, Sir?" The doorman asked.

"Yes, JFK, please," said Hénri.

"I hope you had a good time in New York!"

"So, So. I couldn't finish what I came here for. I feel like I failed," Hénri sighed and surprised himself by expressing his feelings to this stranger he would never see again.

"Not to worry, Sir. Every day is a chance to begin again. Have a great journey, Sir," the doorman said in a comforting voice," and Happy New Year." He smiled and shut the taxi door. Hénri looked him in the eyes through the window and smiled back as the old man's words echoed in his ears.

CHAPTER 26
FULL CIRCLE

Monday, 31 January 2000

The nurse rushed for Dr. Pelletier. Cécile's vital signs were too low, and she feared that keeping her sedated longer might cause her to slip into a coma. She was in bed with machines constantly beeping next to her bed, signaling a faint life.

Hénri pulled up a chair next to her bed and sat down. He took her frail hand and kissed it.

"I'm sorry I couldn't bring you closure," said Hénri as he fought his tears.

Cécile had sent him on a journey he could not complete. Hénri had become part of her dreams, love, hatred, and survival. Since he found Cécile, he was now part of her life, not just fragments of it. He wished he could have done more to convince Ruth. Hénri felt he failed her on her journey to redemption, just like everyone else around her.

Cécile looked peaceful as she was lying there, and Hénri hoped she was free from her nightmares wherever she was.

"She will wake up soon, Hénri, and you can talk to her," the doctor said as he entered the room to turn off Cécile's drips. Hénri feared that he did not have much time left with her, and sadness tore through his heart.

"How is she doing, doctor?" Hénri asked, but he was terrified to hear the answer.

"She is doing better than expected. Her vitals are low, but they are improving. The best thing you can do for her is to be here," said Dr.

Pelletier and clipped the board back to the bed. Cécile suffered a mild stroke in her sleep, and the doctor decided to sedate her until they could evaluate the damage to her already broken mind. Her scans revealed that the stroke impacted part of the brain responsible for long-term memory.

"It was a hippocampal stroke," the doctor explained, "but not life-threatening. We will know more in a couple of days."

A nurse re-entered Cécile's room.

"There is a visitor here for Cécile," she announced, holding the door. Hénri looked over his shoulder with curiosity and saw Ruth walking in slowly, arm-in-arm, with a young girl, who must have been her granddaughter, a spitting image of her young self but much taller.

Ruth paused when she saw Cécile's fragile body.

"Ms. Klotz! You came," Hénri said emotionally as he jumped up to offer his seat.

"I owe it to my sister," she replied briefly but without resentment in her voice.

Ruth held a strong grudge against Cécile a few weeks ago when Hénri saw her in New York, but she must have had a change of heart, probably after reading the entire diary, so she decided to make the trip. He knew this meeting must be very difficult for Ruth as she battled her emotions. However, he realized that he had assessed her correctly as someone with great courage, and she showed it by visiting the woman who sent her entire family to their deaths but feeling grateful for owing her life to her. While Cécile provided her the opportunity not to die in Auschwitz, forgiving her for the trauma needed more strength than Hénri could ever imagine.

Ruth took the journal out of her bag and placed it gently on the bed as she sat down.

"Dr. Pelletier was just explaining that Cécile suffered a stroke, but she is getting better," Hénri said and looked over at the doctor for a quick confirmation.

Maybe the medication was wearing off, or Ruth's voice triggered something in Cécile. Whatever it was, she opened her eyes. She looked around the room in a daze but found comfort in her surroundings. She knew these white walls. Even with the bars on the window, she felt safe.

"*Mademoiselle* Cécile, someone is here to see you," said Hénri as he stepped closer, but Cécile interrupted him.

"Esther!" She whispered with a faint smile. She lifted her arm toward Ruth's granddaughter, trying to see whether she was merely a figment or really standing there.

Hénri stepped aside and joined the doctor by the window. They were both acutely alert as they watched this interaction with care, and Hénri knew the doctor was ready to intervene if he had to.

"Forgive me, please."

"Forgive me, please," Cécile begged in a raspy voice as tears rolled down her face. Tears she had been shedding inside for decades, tears that slowly etched her nightmare into her soul forever were finally set free as she repeated her words.

Hénri surmised that Cécile had shifted from one dream to another due to her stroke. Zoe walked over to Ruth and gently touched her grandmother's shoulder, encouraging her to talk, but she did not know what to say. Ruth prepared herself for this encounter in her mind and heart, but now she was at a loss for words as everything she wanted to say drowned in Cécile's tears. Zoe stepped over and held Cécile's hand for her grandmother, but Ruth stayed silent like a mute swan and let Cécile believe that she had saved Esther from her death. That Esther Klotz, her best friend, stood in front of her in all her youth.

Hénri walked out of the hospital with Ruth and her granddaughter. Ruth clutched onto Zoe more than ever. Ruth held her handkerchief tightly as she wiped her tears. She cried for herself as a little girl, her parents, and Esther. Hénri thought her memories were probably too heavy to carry, as she stopped by a bench and sat down.

"Ruth, why didn't you tell Cécile that it was your granddaughter Zoe and not Esther?" Hénri asked, and he put his arms around her for comfort. He realized how difficult this moment was for Ruth.

Ruth did not answer immediately. She looked up at Cécile's room and saw her faint silhouette by the window, but it was a mirage. Cécile was in bed smiling, resting her eyes. She was tired. The sight of Esther eased her nightmare and slowly turned into a dream.

In thinking about what Ruth said on the park bench, Hénri realized that Ruth knew that she owed her life to Cécile, but she was too late. She told him she regretted not trying to find her, "but harboring resentment and blaming Cécile for all evil was stronger than forgiveness."

They sat silently for a few minutes. Ruth knew it would be her weight to carry for the rest of her life, and she took a deep breath. Snow began to fall, and Ruth watched tiny flurries land on her coat and melt instantly. She turned to Hénri and said, "The snow no longer reminds me of the ash whirling in the air in Auschwitz. You set her free, Hénri. You set all of us free," she sighed and handed the diary back to Hénri.

"Look out for her," Ruth said, signaling to her granddaughter that it was time to leave.

"Thank you," said Hénri, and watched them disappear into the snowy evening before heading back inside.

It was well after visiting hours. The lights were dimmed in Cécile's room, and it was eerily quiet. Hénri sat next to the bed and looked at the diary. In a spur of a moment, he flipped it open and started to read Cécile's early entries aloud, gently whispering, so he did not wake the sleeping woman.

Bon Soir, my name is Cécile Dubonnet, and I live in Paris, the city of love with Mama and Papa. I wish I could say that the weather is constantly beautiful, and the air is always filled with romance, but that is not always the case. It has rained for the past few days, and the streets are wet. The autumn leaves stick to the ground or float around in the puddles like sailboats...

Hénri sat there as a mother would, reading a bedtime story and watching over her ill child. He wanted Cécile to hear her happiness, dreams, and hopes flow around the air while imagining her smiles and laughter and ignoring all the sorrows that followed.

Cécile's face brightened as she slipped further into her dream. She and Esther were heading to *Café de Luna* in *Parc des Buttes Chaumont* on a sunny autumn afternoon as the red sun set behind the trees. Angel rays danced through the foliage, coloring the air golden. Falling leaves brushed against Cécile's young skin as they hit the puddles. Esther turned around, saw something afar, and grabbed Cécile's coat for her attention. Cécile turned around and smiled. Her eyes were bright and full of hope; she was happy.

The old, frail woman in the distance smiled back at them as she took her last breath with a smile forever etched on her face. Cécile's hope was no longer haunted. She was free.

Hénri's apartment at 7 *Rue de Tlemcen* suddenly felt empty and too large. He was heartbroken but also felt at peace. Alice swirled around his leg as he dropped the mail on the coffee table. A white, laminated postcard with Doctors Without Borders's unmistakable red logo peaked through the bills and magazines. It was from Natalie. Hénri's heart pounded in his chest, and he flipped the card. Only a set of numbers were handwritten on the back. He stared at the numbers, then peaked at the clock on the wall. It was half past eight in Congo. He sighed deeply, and all his resentment, agony, and fear left his body with the air he exhaled as Hénri grabbed the receiver and dialed.

About the Author

A.P. HARPER was born in Hungary and lived in many countries before settling in Northern Virginia with her family. Cécile came into her life unexpectedly, and it is not certain if A.P. Harper created her or Cécile found her to be her voice, but now their lives are forever etched into the root of their souls in this debut.

9 798987 199275